Naked Angel

Also by Logan Belle

Blue Angel

Fallen Angel

Published by Kensington Publishing Corp.

Naked Angel

LOGAN BELLE

APHRODISIA

KENSINGTON PUBLISHING CORP.
www.kensingtonbooks.com

APHRODISIA BOOKS are published by

Kensington Publishing Corp.
119 West 40th Street
New York, NY 10018

All Kensington titles, imprints, and distributed lines are available at special quantity discounts for bulk purchases for sales promotion, premiums, fund-raising, and educational, or institutional use.

Special book excerpts or customized printings can also be created to fit specific needs. For details, write or phone the office of the Kensington Special Sales Manager: Kensington Publishing Corp., 119 West 40th Street, New York, NY 10018. Attn. Special Sales Department. Phone: 1-800-221-2647.

Aphrodisia and the A logo Reg. U.S. Pat. & TM Off.

ISBN-13: 978-0-7582-6162-5
ISBN-10: 0-7582-6162-4

First Kensington Trade Paperback Printing: April 2012

10 9 8 7 6 5 4 3 2 1

Printed in the United States of America

There is simply not a single ugly move in ballet. Not one ugly move. I like to hold burlesque to the very same standards.

—Dita Von Teese

This book series is dedicated to Bettie Page,
who continues to inspire generations of women
to be beautiful, to be sexy, and to be brave.
Her legacy lives on at www.BettiePage.com

1

"Are you nervous?" Mallory Dale's boyfriend, Alec, asked her.

"No. Should I be?" She surveyed the room, finally seeing the tangible results of nearly a year of work.

"It's a big night," Alec said.

"The first of many to come, I hope," she said, putting her arms around him. "And I'm ready."

In one hour, the club they had created would be unveiled to New York. Standing alone in the room, holding Alec's hand, she felt confident in the world they had brought to life. The Painted Lady was unlike any burlesque club in the city: After careful research and their investors' generous open checkbooks, they had managed to create a glorious throwback to the roaring twenties.

Mallory had always loved flapper style. It was fashion liberation. In that sense, flappers did for women of the 1920s what burlesque did for her: It shocked her, then irrevocably changed the way she saw herself. And now she'd helped create a space that would have made Zelda Fitzgerald proud: The Painted

Lady burlesque club was a decadent tableau of unrestrained art deco. The red walls were decorated with portraits of Josephine Baker and iconic flapper Louise Brooks, a collection of Grundworth and Yva Richard fetish photographs, and illustrated *pochoir* prints by Erté. The brass and bronze chandeliers had been designed for the 1925 Paris Exposition. And the top-notch sound system was already playing Irving Berlin's "Puttin' on the Ritz."

"You definitely look ready. You are by far the sexiest flapper ever to grace a stage. Were women allowed to be this hot in the 1920s?" Alec asked. He pulled her over so she could see her reflection in one of the mirrored picture frames.

She'd never been more excited about a costume. Her former boss—and onetime owner of the famous burlesque club the Blue Angel—had created the pink satin flapper dress and beaded headpiece for her. Then, after scouring the best vintage shops in the city, she and Alec had found the perfect accessories: ropes of pink and black beads to wear around her neck, and black patent leather heels with ankle straps. Even her face was transformed to Old World glamour: Her best friend, notorious burlesquer, model, and actress Bette Noir, had spent an hour at her apartment earlier applying her makeup to look flapper chic.

Alec kissed the back of her neck, running his hands up from her waist to her breasts. She sighed, a swell of desire rising in her chest. But she forced herself to push his hands gently away. "We don't have time. Save it for later, okay?" she said. Still, she felt a twinge between her legs. Alec could always get her going, even when she had less than one hour before the beginning of the biggest night of her New York life.

"Now that you mention it, I *am* saving something for later," he said, the tone of his voice especially devilish.

She turned to look at him. "Oh, yeah? What's going on?"

"I have a surprise for you."

"You know I don't like surprises," Mallory said.

"Hmm. The last time you told me that, things turned out okay, didn't they?"

She knew he was referring to the night he took her to her first burlesque show on her twenty-fifth birthday at the Blue Angel. Now, just two years later, it was the opening night of her own club. Well, The Painted Lady wasn't technically *her* club. But she was the creative force behind it, along with Alec. It was their baby, and after designing the look and feel of the club, hiring the staff of dancers, choreographing the début show, and writing the script for the opening night's MC, it was finally the moment of truth.

Bette Noir strutted over to them. With her signature black bob, she already looked like a modern-day Louise Brooks.

She carried a large flower arrangement wrapped in plastic. "Someone has a secret admirer," she said, handing the package to Mallory.

"Is that my surprise?" Mallory asked Alec.

"No. It's not from me." He raised an eyebrow, as if looking at her with suspicion.

"Busted—my secret lover," she teased. A year ago, it might have been true. But all of that was behind them now.

Mallory tore the plastic wrapper away to reveal a remarkable bouquet of pink flowers that happened to match the exact shade of her costume.

"Will you look at this!" she said, almost afraid to move the arrangement, it looked so delicate and perfect—more like a sculpture than a flower arrangement. A dozen or so Phalaenopsis orchids brimmed over the top of a long, rectangular vase. Underneath the flowers, circles of grass were arranged inside the glass walls, as if an artist had painted green loops with a delicate brush.

Mallory detached the card. "For Mallory: Thanks for all your hard work. Tonight, we see it bloom. Our love, Justin and Martha."

"You gotta love those guys," Bette said.

Justin Baxter and Martha Pike were the money behind The Painted Lady, and they were among Manhattan's most visible—and unusual—couples. Martha had made her millions in the vaginal rejuvenation field: She'd invented a device called the Pike Kegel Ball, and many a bold-faced name over the age of thirty, when pressed, would admit it had helped take years off her vag. Justin was a drop-dead gorgeous former playboy who'd settled down with the less-than-attractive Martha when he was in his early thirties, and the two seemed extremely happy together. They both had an appetite for beautiful young women and kinky sex, and they happily indulged their desires together. They also threw the most decadent, incredible parties on both coasts and were major patrons of the arts. When their favorite burlesque club, the Blue Angel, was bought out by a woman they knew would run it into the ground, they decided to open a club of their own. That's when Mallory and Alec had gotten their dream jobs: The club was theirs to create and run. Martha would write the checks.

"Now I'm tempted to give you my surprise," Alec said, putting his arms around Mallory. She tilted up her face so he could kiss her.

"So give it to me, baby," she said.

"Ah, my favorite thing to hear," he said, pulling her close. "But you're just going to have to get through the show."

"You're such a sadist," she said.

"And you wouldn't have it any other way."

Violet Offender paced the dressing area of the club formerly known as the Blue Angel. She ran a hand through her short-cropped, white-blond hair, her cheeks flushed with irritation.

"What do you mean it's by invitation only?" she snapped at the petite redhead busily getting into costume. For once, the sight of the woman's luscious breasts bound in a corset wasn't enough to calm Violet's nerves.

"I did what you told me to do: I went to get a ticket for the show tonight, and the woman at the door told me the opening night was by invitation. Press and friends only."

"Jesus! Why do I have to do everything myself around here? Give me a phone." The girl scrambled to hand over her iPhone. Violet punched in the number of her reluctant business partner and bankroller, the magazine publisher Billy Barton. "Billy, I need you to get off your ass and do something for this club for once: We need press passes to the opening of The Painted Lady. Apparently, I am the only one around here who seems aware of the fact that a major competitor is opening up shop tonight. I didn't buy this fucking dump to get steamrolled by Mallory Dale six months later. Call me back ASAP."

"Baby, there's nothing to worry about," said the redhead, half-dressed in her costume, a sexy equestrian ensemble complete with riding boots and crop. "We've already been open for months and months."

"Don't be an idiot," Violet snapped. "This isn't the Internet: Getting there first doesn't mean shit. It just means you're old news. Change back into regular clothes. I'm getting you into that show tonight one way or another. And I want you to report back everything: the music, the girls, the costumes. Take photos."

"They probably won't allow photos," said the redhead.

"I'm not asking you to get permission, I'm *telling* you to get photos. God, I'm tense," Violet said. She knew there was only one way to relieve her stress. Now that she was running the club, she barely had time for her former day job and favorite pastime, her work as a professional dominatrix. Fortunately, her latest fuck toy, a five foot two inch former investment banker with enormous breasts and the burlesque name Cookies 'n'

Cream, was always willing to bend over backwards—sometimes literally—to accommodate her needs.

Violet locked the dressing room door. "Take off your clothes," Violet said. "But leave on the boots."

Cookies wordlessly complied, unfastening her corset and stepping out of her lace panties. Her legs were covered in black English riding boots with zippers up the sides. The rest of her costume, including a black riding helmet and riding crop, was by her feet.

Cookies' delicate porcelain skin was red from the pressure of the corset, and it gave Violet the irresistible urge to see matching welts on her ass.

"Turn around," Violet said, picking up the crop. Cookies obeyed, letting Violet push her down so she was leaning on a vanity table, her ass in the air. "Don't move," Violet ordered. She paused for a minute to look at Cookies' pale, creamy ass, a hint of russet pubic hair visible between her legs. She resisted the urge to get on her knees and lick the girl's pussy. She knew in order to get true satisfaction she had to do things in the proper order. Violet understood the need for control, something most of her lovers did not. At least, not until she taught them.

She raised the riding crop and brought it down hard on Cookies' left ass cheek. The girl cried out, but did not move a muscle. A satisfying red mark emerged almost immediately on her flesh. Violet repeated the lashing on the other side. She dropped the crop and kneeled behind Cookies. She pressed one finger into Cookies' pussy and was satisfied to find it very wet. Violet was surprised to feel the building pressure in her own cunt. There was something about Cookies that always got her excited. She wasn't sure what it was, but it was a relief to not be bored yet.

She worked her finger in and out, reaching up to graze Cookies' clit before resuming the sharp strokes inside of her.

She slipped one hand inside her own underwear, mirroring the motions inside herself as she worked Cookies into a frenzy. She felt Cookies' pussy contract on her fingers, and the girl cried out as she came.

Violet quickly pulled off her jeans. She tugged on Cookies' hair to turn her around. Violet sat on a chair, spread her legs. Cookies knelt in front of her, hands on Violet's thighs, her tongue lapping at her wetness.

"Fuck me," Violet growled. Cookies darted her tongue in and out of Violet's pussy. Violet pulled on her head, trying to get her deeper. She felt a rush of impatience. "Use your hand."

Cookies moved her mouth to Violet's clit, her fingers pressing inside with the sharp, fast strokes she knew Violet liked. Sure enough, Violet shuddered to a silent climax. Cookies sat back on her heels, wincing when she accidentally put pressure on the freshly bruised skin on her ass.

Violet noticed her discomfort and said, "If you think your ass hurts now, you don't even want to know what it will feel like if you come back here tonight without photos of The Painted Lady show."

2

Mallory stood behind the red curtain. On the other side of it, center stage, Alec warmed up the crowd, reminding them that the more skin the performers revealed, the louder he expected the audience to get. "Foot stomping is appreciated, but not mandatory," he said to a few laughs.

"I see some familiar faces out there," he said. This was met with shouts and clapping. "As you know, this is a huge night for New York burlesque—and I don't just mean because Supersize Suzy is visiting us tonight." This brought another round of applause: Supersize Suzy was a six foot two inch, double D–breasted British transvestite who had recently been made infamous by her unbridled performance in a burlesque documentary called *Fan Dancers*. "And if that isn't enough, we are starstruck to have with us tonight—fresh off her latest movie set—the mysterious, magnificent Mistress of Delight: Bette Noir." More applause, whistles, and a few random shout-outs of her name.

From her perch behind the curtain, Mallory smiled. She remembered how, at the first show she'd gone to, the audience had gone wild when Bette's name was announced. And that was before she became world famous for dating the pop star Zebra, appearing in a national Dolce & Gabbana campaign, and getting rave reviews in an indie film directed by Jake Gyllenhaal. "But first, I have the great pleasure of introducing to you our opening performer: the sexy, sassy, incomparable Moxie!"

At the sound of her stage name, Mallory reflexively straightened her back. She tugged on her elbow-length white gloves to make sure they were easily removable, and straightened her headpiece. These were nervous, unnecessary tics. She was, as always, perfectly prepared for her performance. Maybe more so tonight than ever before.

The song "Puttin' on the Ritz"—the synth-pop 1983 cover version—filled the room. The curtain receded to one side, and Mallory felt the heat of the stage lights bathing her in a red glow. From the darkness in front of her, the full house roared. She knew she was a sight in her costume, but this wasn't a fashion show. Being a sight wasn't enough. Burlesque was all about the reveal—revealing parts of her body, yes. But in doing so, she would elicit a reaction from the audience that revealed something about them.

Mallory shimmied to the front of the stage, twirling the fluffy pink boa draped over her shoulders. She sensed the audience's collective anticipation. Although she'd practiced on the stage many times, it felt dramatically different to be in front of people. In the months since the Blue Angel had changed ownership and she'd stopped performing, she'd almost forgotten what it felt like to play off a crowd.

As the song kicked up-tempo, she swiveled her heels in opposite directions, launching into an improvised Charleston. At the same time, she tugged off one glove, throwing it into the audience to an appreciative roar. She loved the way the pink beaded fringe on her dress moved with her hips, and she exaggerated her kicks in the front and back to maximize the dramatic flair of silk.

When the song came to the lyrics "walk with sticks or umberellas," she retrieved a black walking stick from the floor and used the tip to tease off the spaghetti straps of her dress. With another shimmy, her breasts were exposed, her nipples covered in pink sequined pasties with pink tassels. The audience shouted her name, and she let the dress fall to the floor so she was clad in only the boa, pasties, a pink thong, thigh-high white fishnet stockings with garters, and her black patent heels. She used the boa to tease the crowd, covering her breasts and then revealing them in flashes. She turned her back to the audience, holding the boa in either hand, stretching it across her nearly bare ass and rubbing it back and forth. Then she bent forward and moved the boa so she was rubbing it between her thighs from the front to the back. This whipped the crowd into a frenzy, and when she turned to face them again, she dropped the boa and shimmied her shoulders so the tassels on her pasties twirled dramatically.

The red curtain closed.

"That performance would almost make Prohibition tolerable," said Bette.

Mallory was breathless and could only smile her thanks. She heard Alec retake the stage to introduce the next act.

"Another round of applause for Moxie, the sexiest flapper to grace the stage since Louise Brooks," said Alec. The audience clapped. "Moxie, come on back out here."

"What is he doing?" Mallory asked Bette. "He's interrupting the whole flow of the show."

"Better go humor him," Bette said. She handed Mallory a black silk robe.

Mallory quickly covered herself and returned to the stage. A few people stood to applaud her. This was embarrassing. What was Alec thinking?

"I don't know how many of you are aware of this, but in addition to being The Painted Lady's opening performer, Moxie is also the creative director of the club and producer of the show you are seeing tonight. And I'm hoping she might take on one more role—that of my wife!"

Alec got down on one knee. Mallory looked at him in shock.

"Oh, my God! What are you doing?"

He pulled out a small black box and opened it to reveal a beautiful art deco, antique diamond ring.

"Marry me, Mallory," he said, his voice low and husky with emotion.

Mallory wasn't sure if the low roar she heard was the sound of blood rushing to her head, or if it was the sound of the crowd, or if this was simply what it felt like to be truly shocked for the first time in her life.

"Oh, my God," she repeated.

"What do you say, Mal?" he asked with that wonderful teasing glint in his eyes.

Was this really happening? After all the years, the mind-blowing sex, the jealousy, fights, uncertainty, missteps, soul-searching, and compromise, could it really culminate in this one perfect moment?

"Yes," she managed to breathe. "I'll marry you." He stood up and hugged her. Through a blur of tears, she watched him slip the ring on her finger.

He held her tight, and all she could think was that she didn't ever want this happiness to end. She had no idea how to leave the stage. She didn't want to. She didn't trust the magic of the moment to follow her into "real life."

But on the stage, anything was possible.

Behind the red curtain backstage, Nadia Grant clapped her hands in delight. She was happy for Mallory and, to be perfectly honest, thrilled for the last-minute reprieve from having to perform immediately.

Not for the first time that night, she wondered if this was madness. Maybe her ballet friends were right: She had no business being on a burlesque stage. One of them, Anna Prince, was at the show tonight to support her, but Anna still was trying to talk her out of performing at The Painted Lady: "You're a ballet dancer. Even if you can never go *en pointe* again, you can find a place in ballet."

Easy for her to say: Anna had scored a spot in the hot new company Ballet Arts, run by one of the youngest choreographers in New York City, Max Jasper. All of her hard work was paying off, while Nadia watched hers go down the drain. How could Anna blame her for becoming intrigued when she'd learned that Mallory, the woman with whom she'd been sharing dance studio practice space for over a year, was a burlesque dancer. And of course the competitive part of her—the part that would not die no matter how bad her injury—whispered, *I can do that.* Hearing that inner voice made her feel hopeful and alive again for the first time since hearing the doctor's prognosis.

"You don't understand," Nadia told Anna. "If I can't perform in ballet, I need to do something completely different. Being near it but not a part of it just kills me."

But burlesque—now that was something to keep her mind off the tragedy of her lost ballet career. It was daring, it was glamorous, and, best of all, she had a built-in tour guide: Mallory.

It had been Mallory's idea. When Nadia had told her she wasn't going to use the practice space for a while, Mallory had been concerned enough to ask lots of questions. And when Nadia confessed that her ballet career was over, Mallory insisted that she find another outlet for performing.

"You have to get back onstage," she'd said. "It's the only way you will get through this."

Mallory was right: Studying burlesque, trying on costumes, and witnessing Mallory and Alec build the club had saved her sanity during the past few months she'd spent in physical therapy instead of in ballet rehearsals.

So she would never be reviewed by Alastair Macaulay in the *New York Times*. But she could make a name for herself in a different world—a glamorous, fascinating world that was probably more relevant to women today than ballet.

Knowing that Anna was in the audience made her nervous. Nadia had thought having a friend in the audience would make her feel better, but now she regretted it. She felt all the more pressure—that her performance must justify her choice. She imagined that somehow, if Anna saw her dance a classic striptease, she would change her mind. Anna might agree that Nadia had found the right alternative to her thwarted dance dreams. And she knew that one transcendent burlesque performance could change anyone's mind, just like watching Mallory had changed hers. Of course, she wasn't Mallory. But she had the heart of a dancer, and she had to believe that would get her through her début performance. When it came to dance, confidence was key. She couldn't waver now. "Nadia, three minutes," Bette told her.

Nadia took a deep breath. Showtime.

3

Max Jasper stretched his long legs under the table. Their seats were close to the stage. A little too close, if Max had had anything to say about it. This whole burlesque thing was making him uncomfortable. He was a man who loved women—and loved women's taking off their clothes. But he preferred it in the privacy of his bedroom, not in a crowded room surrounded by hoots, hollers, and clapping.

When Anna had told him that Nadia Grant, the promising girl who'd danced the corps de ballet with American Ballet Theatre, had become a burlesque performer, he could not believe it. Anna had urged him to come to the show.

"She needs the support of her community," Anna said.

"I don't think you should encourage her," Max told Anna.

"That's what friends do," Anna said. It was that kind of simplistic thinking that made him uninterested in sleeping with her a second time. He'd warned her about that—that he was a "one and done" kind of guy. But she hadn't believed him—they never did. And he was sure this outing to support her friend was just a ploy to get him interested in resuming their physical relationship. But if she had known him at all, she would have known that this whole scene was a huge turnoff.

So why had he gone?

"Curiosity," he told Anna. And now he regretted it.

"This is Nadia's music," Anna said with excitement as the curtain parted. The room filled with the song "The Entertainer" made famous by the 1973 Robert Redford and Paul Newman film, *The Sting.*

Max barely recognized Nadia, and if it hadn't been for her remarkably long legs and obvious ballet hands, he wouldn't have believed it was the same girl he had seen dance on some of the most prestigious stages in the city.

Nadia's slender form was sheathed in a silver, beaded sleeveless dress, with bands of silver fringe just under her breasts and at the bottom that shimmered when she moved. She wore long black gloves to her elbows. Her hair was covered with a short brunette wig, and she wore a silver sequined headband on her forehead. Her cheeks were heavily rouged, her lips outrageously red and more sensual than Max remembered.

The kicky, up-tempo song lent a playful edge to Nadia's dance, and the way she teased off her gloves suggested confidence. Her movements were a classic flapper performance, and if this were as far as the dance were to go, he could live with the idea of a once-promising ballerina carving a path for herself in this arena. But he knew that was not how these things went—and if he'd had any doubt, the first act of the night had made it very clear.

The crowd cheered when Nadia bent over suggestively as she unstrapped her shoe. That was another thing that so unsettled Max: The relationship between audience and performer in this club was so different from the respectful applause in ballet.

Now that Nadia's gloves and shoes were off, and the song was more than halfway over, it was only logical that the performance should do a rapid gearshift into nudity. She clearly had control of the crowd—the onlookers were enraptured with her every move, and Max could feel the buzz of anticipation for her to remove her dress. But just when Nadia should have been cashing in her best chips of the night, she froze: She awkwardly reverted back to earlier motions from the performance that now made no sense since she had already removed her gloves and shoes. The audience laughed, thinking her dance was taking a comedic turn—which apparently these things were known to do—but it soon became clear that Nadia was not trying to be funny.

"Oh, my God. She can't go through with it," Anna said.

"Glad to see common sense prevail," said Max.

"No, it's not good! She must be so humiliated," Anna said. Nadia wandered around the stage in a fruitless attempt to improvise an end to her performance that did not involve removing her clothes. Mercifully, the curtain closed almost before the song finished. The confused audience clapped, but with markedly less enthusiasm than before.

"This isn't a bad thing, you know," said Max. "Maybe she's got this out of her system, and now she can think of another outlet for herself."

"Do you think there's something she could do at Ballet Arts?"

"I don't know," Max said. He hated to admit it, but what he was really thinking was that he would like to do *her*. If she had taken off her clothes, he would have lost interest. But since she hadn't, he had the nagging urge to get her to finish the job. In private.

"I'm going to go talk to her," Anna said. "Meet me out front?"

"We should get going," Max said, looking at his watch.

"I need to make sure she's okay. And then I need *you* to come back to my place, and make sure *I'm* okay," she said, putting his hand on her leg.

"I have an early rehearsal tomorrow. I'm going to head home," Max said.

"No! Don't be lame. At least come with me to say hi to Nadia."

Seated at the table closest to the stage, costume designer Gemma Kole wondered what else could go wrong tonight. First, the proposal: Alec's dramatic move had completely upstaged the costumes. If there were any photos of the show that were going to make it into tomorrow's papers, it was the ones taken with Alec down on his knee in front of Mallory. And out of all the gorgeous costumes she had worked on for the past few months, The Painted Lady was going to be publicized with Mallory Dale in a silk robe that looked no more special than anything on the rack at Victoria's Secret.

Gemma hoped this wasn't a sign. She'd spent all her savings on the move from England to New York City. This was the fashion capitol of the world, after all. She didn't care what anyone said about Paris. It was New York. Of course, every aspiring designer knew this, so she was making a run on a very crowded field.

She nervously poked her tongue against the gap between her two front teeth. Growing up in Gloucester, she'd hated her teeth. Now, thanks to the Dutch model Lara Stone, her gap was super trendy, and guys told her it was hot.

"At least the audience can't complain they didn't get their money's worth tonight," Justin Baxter had said when Alec had proposed to Mallory onstage. As one of the owners of the club, he was also seated at the A-list table. Next to him, his unattractive wife, Martha, had slapped her knee and guffawed at the comment, which Gemma didn't find particularly funny.

She wondered if Martha had noticed that her husband had been stealing glances at Gemma since the moment they'd sat down. If so, it didn't seem to bother her. But then, she'd heard about the Baxters' famous "open" relationship. She doubted it was true. What woman really could live with a husband who was actively cheating on her? But now that she'd seen Martha, it was starting to make a little more sense. Justin was so handsome, and she was so . . . not. Martha Pike probably let her husband do whatever he wanted just to keep him from leaving. It didn't sound like a very satisfying relationship model to her, but then, no relationship sounded worthwhile to her. Not unless it could further her career. She supposed, in a way, Justin was doing that for her. He signed Mallory's paycheck, and Mallory had hired Agnes to design all of the costumes for The Painted Lady. And luckily for Gemma, Agnes was grooming her to take over the business. Which she would happily do—until she found a way to launch her fashion line, GemmaK.

But after tonight's setbacks, she wondered if that would ever happen.

Gemma was still reeling from the letdown of Nadia's performance. The pretty, slight brunette had been coltishly graceful as she'd emerged to the opening notes of "The Entertainer." Gemma had felt a thrill of satisfaction to see her dress with the hand-sewn silver fringe draped on Nadia's body. And she'd been eager to hear the audience's reaction to the pièce de résistance underneath—the silver-spangled pasties and matching thong.

But midway through the song, Gemma had sensed there was a problem. It was time for Nadia to unzip the easy-off dress and shimmy it to the floor. The silver material would slide off of her like mercury, and, if performed right, this was Gemma's favorite striptease of the entire show. But the song kept going, and Nadia seemed no closer to shedding her clothes. Instead, she pointlessly repeated the earliest steps of the dance. What the hell was she doing?

And that's when Gemma had realized her pride-and-joy silver pasties would never see the light of day—or, rather, light of stage. Nadia was clearly not going to get naked.

Disaster.

Gemma was grateful for the distraction when Justin leaned over to ask her, "You're coming to the after-party at my apartment, right?"

"I think so," Gemma said, in the understatement of the year. She'd spent a month working on her own costume for the party, which was continuing the evening's theme of 1920s decadence. Even only having lived in New York for a year, she'd heard about the notorious Baxter parties. Some of what she knew she'd read in Page Six or some gossip blogs—items about celebrities getting wasted on absinthe; other things she'd heard whispers of—sex shows, orgies. But the real draw for her was the access to money people—big money people, if everything she'd heard about the Baxter crowd was true.

"You won't want to miss it. Trust me," Justin said.

Gemma thought—but did not say—that once you set foot in the doorway of 40 Bond Street, trusting Justin Baxter was the last thing any sensible woman should do. And Gemma was nothing if not a sensible woman.

Nadia shoved her costume into her bag. All around her, the other girls chattered and laughed and basically went on as if the world hadn't just ended. Which, of course, it had.

How could she have failed like that? After years of dancing under pressure and through injury, turning out stellar performances that were far more challenging physically and, in some ways emotionally, than burlesquc, how could she freeze up the way she had tonight? It was ironic: All her friends were telling her that she shouldn't do burlesque, that it was beneath her, and here she was, unable to keep up with the other performers in this dressing room.

The worst part about it was that she had let Mallory down. Of course, Mallory had assured her she shouldn't worry about it—that it wasn't a big deal and that these things happened.

"You just have to get back on the bike," Mallory had told her.

Nadia didn't know about that. All she knew was that she couldn't stay and watch the rest of the show. It was painful to endure the pitying glances of the other girls. And what was the point of hanging out until eleven? She certainly wasn't going to the after-party at Justin Baxter's apartment.

She made her way out of the crowded dressing room as unobtrusively as possible. She knew she just had to slip out of the club without anyone's recognizing her—which, without her wig and in her street clothes, shouldn't be a problem. And then she was in the clear.

She hadn't counted on Anna's intercepting her at the front door.

"Nadia! Wait—are you leaving?"

For about three seconds, Nadia seriously considered just walking out the door as if she hadn't heard Anna. But she couldn't bring herself to do it, so she reluctantly turned around. It was okay, she told herself. Anna was a friend—she didn't have to be perfect in front of Anna.

Except Anna wasn't alone: She was with a tall, great-looking, dark-haired guy. And unfortunately, this wasn't just any tall, dark hottie—Nadia knew immediately it was Max Jasper.

Was Anna out of her mind bringing him there? She wanted to yell that at her, but refrained. She had embarrassed herself enough for one night.

"Thanks for coming," Nadia said, forcing herself to go on autopilot.

"Of course! I wouldn't miss it. You looked beautiful out there. You really did."

Nadia knew her friend was trying to be kind, but it just made her want to cry.

"I have to go," she said.

"I saw you dance in *Giselle*," Max Jasper said. "You are good." Reluctantly, Nadia looked up at him. Irrationally, she felt a surge of anger at this stranger for intruding on one of her worst moments and making her feel even worse just by his presence.

"I *was* good," Nadia said venomously. "I don't dance anymore."

"There are other things you can do within a company," he said.

The nerve!

"I don't recall asking you for career advice," Nadia said. Anna looked back and forth between them as if watching a tennis match.

"Maybe you should have," he said. Nadia looked at her friend, shook her head, and walked out the door of The Painted Lady. She just hoped she would have the courage to walk back in.

4

Another night, another party.

Justin Baxter observed the crowd of models, actors, film producers, magazine publishers, and artists cavorting in the infamous art deco apartment he shared with his wife. The living room was so full he couldn't see the way to the bar. Normally, such a turnout would give him a thrill so intense it was almost sexual. But after a few years of the most decadent soirées this side of Truman Capote's Black and White Ball, his excitement was waning. He didn't even feel inspired about the pinnacle of each party—picking out the woman he wanted, then seducing her into going upstairs with him so he could fuck her while Martha watched.

"Do you need a scotch, baby?" asked his wife. Martha was, as always, the least attractive person at the party. Usually, this didn't bother him; she provided companionship and love and financial security, and he still had the freedom to fuck any hot young thing that caught his eye. The only caveat was that Martha always had to be in the room. Sometimes a woman was willing to let her join in. No, he never wished his wife were more appealing to look at. So far, he'd found the perfect balance having her as his partner and other women as his excitement.

But tonight, even Martha was irritating him. It wasn't her fault—something inside of him was just . . . off.

Maybe he was more bummed out than he'd realized about the recent distance between himself and his former good friend, Billy Barton. The A-list New Yorker, man-about-town, and publisher of *Gruff* magazine used to be one of his favorite party guests and cohorts in exploring New York nightlife's seamier underbelly. But now they were owners of rival clubs. Justin would never understand what had made Billy secretly buy the Blue Angel last year, partnering with Violet Offender, a performer who had been fired from the club under its previous owner. Violet was a hot piece of ass, but there was something off about that chick. As Justin liked to put it, he wouldn't fuck her with someone else's dick.

And then Justin saw a sight that made him feel almost like his old self again.

Gemma Kole walked into the room and heads turned. Her long, dark blond hair was unkempt as usual, and unlike the other highly groomed and polished female party guests, she didn't wear makeup except for smudged black eyeliner. She wasn't the most beautiful woman in the room, but she had an unpolished sexiness that made him feel the most intense attraction he'd experienced in as long as he could remember. But because she designed costumes for Mallory—who was technically his employee, which made Gemma an employee once-removed—he'd never seriously considered getting her into bed. But tonight, with her Kardashian-esque ass poured into a tight, short dress, he didn't know if he'd be able to resist.

"She's interesting," said Martha. Billy knew what that meant. It was the green light: Go get her and call me when she's good to go.

"Yes, dear, I could use a scotch," he said. Martha shuffled off to the other room.

Justin made his way toward Gemma.

Alone, at last.

The club was empty. The last of the girls had changed, packed their costumes into their bags, and headed over to the Baxter party. The dressing room was a mess of scattered cosmetics, discarded stockings, hairpieces, and empty champagne bottles.

"This is worse than a college dorm room," Mallory said, clearing a space on the small sofa and tucking her legs under herself. She flattened her left hand on her thigh and stared at her engagement ring. It was the most perfect object she'd ever seen. She felt she would never be able to see it fully—every angle revealed a different facet of the diamonds. Even the shiny curves of the platinum band held fascination for her. "It's so beautiful. I can't stop looking at it."

"Well, you're going to have to," Alec said with a smile, sitting next to her.

"Why is that?"

"Because it's going to be really distracting for me to make love to you while you stare at your hand."

"Hmm. I don't know if I can control myself. You might have to blindfold me."

"You read my mind."

Alec pulled a silk scarf off one of the vanity tables and folded it with quick, practiced movements.

"Alec, come on. We have to at least make an appearance at the party."

"Shh," he said, straddling her and tying the scarf over her eyes.

"You're crazy," she laughed, allowing him to ease her onto

her back. She felt something under her left shoulder blade, and felt around with her hand to pull it out from under her. She guessed it was a tube of mascara. Alec took it from her hand, and she heard it hit the floor.

She felt his hands on her waist, unzipping the long black skirt she had changed into for the party. The fabric brushed the length of her legs as he slowly pulled it off her. Then she felt nothing. The room was completely silent. Had he left?

"Alec?" she said. Her hands fluttered up to move her blindfold, but before she could slip it aside to sneak a peek, Alec pulled her hands back to her sides. "So, you *are* still there," she said.

Saying nothing, he eased her panties down the same slow path as the skirt. He pushed her legs apart, and she felt air caress the folds of her pussy. She reached out for him, but he ignored her, holding her legs open and still. In the absence of his touch, her mind filled in the blank, imagining his fingers inside of her.

"Did you lock the front door?" she asked, suddenly remembering where they were. He did not answer her. On some level, she had known that he would not.

She tried to relax, to just accept the stillness and the silence. Her chest rose and fell with her quickening breath.

And then, finally, she felt the tip of his tongue graze her clit. It was so faint, she almost worried that she'd imagined it. But then, no, he gave her what she wanted: His tongue pressed deep inside, teasing her with the promise of how he would later penetrate her with his fingers and his cock. She moaned, reaching for his hands, pulling them to her. Maddeningly, he would not touch her except with his mouth. And then, not even that.

Again, the silence, the stillness, and then the air on her wet pussy. She reached for him and found his stiff cock. She ran her hand up and down it, her heart pounding. His hands toyed with her hard nipples, grazing them with his fingertips until the quivering between her legs was unbearable. She slid her hands around to his buttocks and pulled him toward her. With relief, she felt the tip of his cock pierce her needy pussy.

He pulled off her blindfold, and as he thrust inside of her, she looked right into his blue-green eyes. They were clouded with intensity. That look in his eyes, his absolute desire for her, affected her more than any touch.

They found their rhythm, and she knew she would come first. She felt the first waves of her orgasm build, and then break, in exquisite ripples that shuddered through her.

"My God, you feel so good," she whispered against his shoulder.

"I felt you come," he said. Of course he had. They knew and felt everything about one another, big and small. That was why she was so amazed he had been able to surprise her tonight. That he had been planning something so huge, and she had been clueless. . . .

"Turn over," he said.

She got on all fours. She felt his cock press against her ass as he reached around to finger her. He knew that once she came, she could reach orgasm again and again easily with his touch. Sure enough, he worked his fingers to bring her to another quick, shuddering peak. She pressed her ass against him, wanting him inside her fully. When her contractions had faded, he entered her from behind, his one hand still reaching around her so he could lightly brush her clit with his index finger.

"I want you to come, baby," she moaned. He didn't answer her, but she could tell by the urgency of his thrusting that he was close. And then she felt it—that telltale tremor, the flash of lightning before the thunder.

Alec came with a primitive yell. His hands gripped her hips so tightly it almost hurt, his thrusting so fast and rhythmic it directed her own movements with an instinctive lockstep that was as old as time. In these moments, she felt like they were one person. And then, as it sometimes did, his orgasm triggered another of her own, so quick and strong it almost made her weep.

She collapsed onto her stomach, and he fell on top of her, kissing the back of her neck. She squirmed to roll over, and he moved off so she could snuggle against him.

She lay tucked under his arm, her head on his chest where she could feel it rise and fall with his breath.

"Unbelievable," she whispered. He kissed her forehead, which was slippery with sweat. She ran her hand lightly over his chest, and he twisted her engagement ring.

"So how long were you planning this?" she asked.

"Since we woke up this morning and you said save it for later."

"No! Not the sex. The engagement." She slapped his arm playfully.

"Oh . . . that. I think ever since Beyonce told me—very wisely, I might add—if I like it, put a ring on it."

"I'm serious," Mallory said.

"So am I."

"That song is like from 2008."

"Exactly."

"You haven't been thinking about this for that many years."

"I've known I was going to marry you since our second date," he said. She propped herself up on one elbow so she could look at him. She knew he was serious, and when their eyes met, she felt hers fill with tears.

"Oh, Alec," she said.

"What? You're the one who created all the drama."

"Ugh!" she said, flopping back down. She nestled into his arms again and stretched out her hand to admire the ring. He pulled her hand over his chest so he could look at it, too.

"I'm so glad you like it," he said.

"Like it? I love it. It's so perfect. I can't even imagine how you did this." She kissed his rib cage. "Can I ask you a dumb question?"

"I don't think you're capable of a dumb question, but sure—go ahead."

Mallory took a deep breath. "Do you think our sex life will get worse after we're married?"

"Okay, I was wrong. You are capable of a dumb question," he said.

"Alec! I'm serious. You hear everyone talk about how sex dwindles after marriage. It's not like one person has said it—*everyone* says it."

"We've lived together for a long time. Why would anything change now?"

"I don't know. It just does."

"Are you really worried about that?"

She shrugged. "I guess. A little. Everything has been so great with us lately. I kind of want to just freeze this moment in time. I don't want to mess around with perfection."

"Nothing can stay the same. You have to move forward. So yes, even our sex life will change," he said.

"You really think it will?"

"Yes," he said. "It will get even better."

"I'm serious," she said.

"So am I. But there is one thing I'm wondering."

"What?"

"Do you think maybe you'll switch over to just producing shows, not performing?"

Mallory sat up. "Why would I do that?"

Alec shrugged. "I don't know. At some point, maybe you won't want to take your clothes off in front of strangers."

"Where is this coming from?" she said slowly, her voice low.

"I don't know. I guess maybe I think it will be weird for me to see my wife getting naked onstage every week. I mean, what if we have kids?"

Mallory shook her head. "See! This is what I was afraid of. We've only been engaged three hours, and already you've stopped seeing me as a sex object and are worrying about what our nonexistent children will think of me."

"First of all, I promise to always sexually objectify you. We can write it into our wedding vows." He pulled her close. "And I'm not worried about what our nonexistent children will think of you. I already know they are going to think you are the coolest mom in the world, which of course you will be, until Lady Gaga procreates."

"So then why are you asking me this stuff?"

"Mal, I'm so proud of you and everything you've accomplished the past few years. But I have to admit sometimes it's hard for me to see the woman I love getting naked and being hooted and hollered at by strange men."

"How long have you felt this way?"

"Always. I've told you this before, haven't I? I have mixed feelings about burlesque, but I know it's important for both of us to be creative and live inspired lives. I just wonder if maybe you won't segue your inspiration into producing more and, um, shaking your booty less."

Mallory let him hold her, while her heart pounded. She appreciated his honesty, but this was the last thing she wanted to hear. And in the spirit of mutual honesty, she decided she needed to tell him that.

"I don't think I can do that," she said.

Gemma knew people who called traveling from London to New York "hopping the pond." Tonight, at Justin and Martha's after-party, she felt exactly like a fish that had flopped out of its comfortable pond into much deeper waters.

Aside from the celebrities, and the chic, spare décor with its simple elegance, which was evident even through all of the

Prohibition-era props, Gemma was blown away by the costumes: Everyone who was working at the party, from the waiters circling the crowd with trays of Sidecars and Bee's Knees cocktails, to the bouncer at the door, to the live band, was dressed like he or she had stepped off the set of *The Cotton Club*. The cocktail waitresses' dresses—identical sequined shifts in gold—were more impressive than her own.

And then there was that bizarre, fishtank-like cube hanging in the entrance foyer. High above the crowd, encased in glass, two young women wearing nothing but bras, garters, fishnet stockings, and flapper-style headpieces played cards.

A gold-swathed redhead handed her a Sidecar.

"Those should come with a warning label," Justin Baxter said.

She hadn't noticed him approach, but there he was. She had to admit he was good-looking—there was no question about it. And from the way he was gazing at her, the feeling was quite mutual. But she didn't feel particularly attracted to him. This was no surprise—she never felt attracted to anyone. It was like she was missing the erogenous gene or something. She could look at a guy and know he was hot, but this didn't translate into a desire to have him touch her. On the rare occasion that she indulged someone in having sex, it was far less pleasurable than getting a decent massage.

"Thanks for the red flag," she said, taking a sip. The drink was a potent mixture of sweet and sour. She could taste the brandy. She licked some of the sugar off the rim, and she felt Justin watching her mouth.

"Is this your first time here?" he said.

"Yeah. Don't you know who's been to your home?" she asked.

"Do you know how many parties we've hosted? Sometimes I go to a big event, and people I've never seen before in my life thank me for a great night six months or even years ago."

"Hmm. Well, no. I've never been here before. It's lovely, though."

"Let me give you a tour."

Gemma cast a quick glance around the room. Justin's wife was nowhere in sight.

"Um, okay." She took another sip of the drink, then another as she followed him through the crowd to an elevator bank just off the living room.

"Is this like a townhouse or an apartment or what?"

"It's a townhouse," he said.

"I've never seen anything like it—and I've been in New York over a year!" As soon as the words were out of her mouth, she regretted them. She shouldn't admit to how little luxury she had been exposed to in her life. If he saw the shabby house she'd grown up in, the endless gray skies of the English countryside—not to mention the bland, provincial food—he would no doubt find her far less interesting. The only way she'd gotten through the bleak austerity of her adolescence and young adulthood was living for the arrival of *Vogue* and *Harper's Bazaar* at the town library every month. She'd thought maybe she'd be a model but then was surprised by her talent for making beautiful clothes, not just wearing them.

They took the elevator to the top floor, and stepped out onto a deck with—of all things—a swimming pool. Lit from below, it shimmered an almost iridescent aqua blue in the summer moonlight. "Oh, my Lord," she gasped. So much for playing it cool. "Why don't you have the party up here?"

"I prefer to keep the party up here private," Justin said.

Looking at the fourth-story view of downtown Manhattan, feeling like shc was surrounded by the wealth and privilege she had longed for all her life, feeling so close to claiming a piece of that pie for herself—the "party" Justin was offering her was one she could not refuse.

"Is the pool heated?" Gemma asked, walking to the water, careful not to totter too close to the edge in her four-inch heels.

"You tell me," Justin said with a mischievous smile. Gemma turned her back to him, gently shook off one of her shoes, and dipped the toes of one foot in the water. She was happy to discover that yes, the pool was, in fact, heated—to what seemed like a perfect temperature.

And then she felt herself nearly airborne above the water. The only thing keeping her from being submerged in six feet of water was Justin's arm circling her waist as he dangled her above the deep end.

"Oh, my God, put me down!" Gemma shrieked, her heart pounding.

"You want me to put you down?" Justin said, lowering her so her feet skimmed the water.

"No!" she yelled.

Mercifully, she felt him swing her back so she was over firm ground. When her feet touched the smooth wood planks of the deck, she whirled around and punched him in the arm. "That wasn't funny!"

"Ouch! For a little thing, you have a strong left hook. Do they raise you on boxing in England?"

"Luckily for you, no. I was raised to be a lady."

They faced each other, less than a foot apart, at the edge of the pool.

"There's nothing lucky about that. I'd much rather see you *not* acting like a lady."

"What's that supposed to mean?"

"Let me show you."

5

Nadia poured herself a glass of bourbon from the fully stocked bar in the apartment on Ninety-second and Fifth Avenue. It was her Great-Aunt Rose's apartment—she'd owned it since the 1960s, and her recent expat life in France had bestowed upon Nadia the real estate equivalent of winning the lotto jackpot. For the pricc of utilities and the care and feeding of an overweight tabby cat named Twiggy, Nadia lived far above her means. It was only her aunt's generosity that enabled her to live in Manhattan at all.

She curled up on the couch, glass in hand, Twiggy marching in place on her lap trying to get comfortable. Nadia was extremely hungry, and she knew she could order in food from any number of neighborhood restaurants willing to deliver at eleven o'clock at night, but she also knew she didn't deserve to eat. Not after her performance. After a lifetime of the discipline and rigors of ballet, such blatant failure was something she could barely process, let alone tolerate. She knew linking food to her performance was falling back into bad habits, but she didn't know any other way to deal with her disappointment.

She couldn't change what had happened onstage, but she could refrain from eating. And tomorrow she would figure out a way to make things right in her universe.

Her cell phone vibrated, and she had every intention of ignoring it. But she saw that it was Mallory, and Nadia knew she had to at least answer the call.

"Hello?" Nadia said, trying to modulate her voice so it didn't sound as if she was about to jump off the balcony.

"Hey—I just wanted to check in on you. Did you go to the after-party?" Mallory said.

"Oh, no. I wasn't really in the mood."

"Nadia, I told you—don't be so hard on yourself. The first time I went in front of a crowd, I was just a stage kitten, and I froze."

Nadia knew that story—and it was hardly the same thing.

"Yes, but it was because you saw someone from your day job in the audience. Your boss! You had a reason to lose your bearings. I didn't. I have no excuse."

"You don't need an excuse—you're doing something new. Now get yourself out of your apartment and go stop by Justin and Martha's and be with the other girls. You shouldn't be sitting home alone."

"Oh, I'm fine. I'm just tired, really. And you shouldn't be worrying about me—you have so much to celebrate tonight. Tell Alec I said congratulations again. I'll talk to you tomorrow."

Nadia turned off her phone and tossed it across the couch. She nudged the cat off her lap and got up to pour another drink.

She envied Mallory—not for her ability to perform where she herself had failed, but for having someone with whom to share her success. Maybe Nadia wouldn't feel like such a failure if she weren't alone. But then again, being with the wrong person had been worse than being alone. And right now, the thought of her ex-fiancé was only slightly less painful than the thought of what had happened tonight at The Painted Lady.

Jackson, her former fiancé, had at one time been her instructor, a masterful choreographer whose talent and ambition reminded her—perhaps too much—of what she had read about Max Jasper. She'd moved into his Upper West Side apartment. They'd set a date. And then he'd scored a huge job: He would be the choreographer on a major motion picture directed by Sofia Coppola about the Kirov Ballet. The lead actress was Emma Stone. The supporting actress was a Mila Kunis look-alike rumored to be having an affair with the film's director of photography. That rumor was false: She was having an affair with the film's choreographer.

Three months later, Nadia suffered her fourth acute facture of the fifth metatarsal in her right foot. Her doctor repeated what he had told her after the second fracture: Her foot had a structural weakness that, had it been identified in childhood, would have prohibited her from pursuing a career in ballet. She should not be dancing in *pointe* shoes. Of course, she'd chosen to ignore that information. Until the last injury, when the doctor had told her if she broke her foot again she might never recover full use of it.

Nadia carried her drink into her bedroom. Her aunt had offered her the use of the master bedroom, but Nadia felt more comfortable in the guest room, even though it had two twin beds instead of one larger one.

Nadia set the bourbon on her nightstand and shed her clothes carelessly on the floor on her way to the bathroom connected to the guest suite. She turned the shower to a temperature just shy of scalding and immersed herself in the sharp needles of water. She noticed the reflection of her body in the glass stall. It was still surprising to see the changes in her figure even after just a few months of not following the rigorous ballet schedule. She knew other dancers would be alarmed to see a hint of fullness in their breasts, or roundness at their hips, but Nadia was okay with the changes.

She soaped up her breasts, pausing for a minute to caress her nipples. She felt a slight stirring between her legs, and she continued to play with her breasts, closing her eyes, letting the hot water assault her back and shoulders.

When the stirring between her legs turned into a sharp throb, she moved her hands down to stroke her clit. She dipped her middle finger inside herself, listening to her body's cue to move it in and out, first slowly, then with sharper motions. She steadied herself with her other hand against the glass, and as she found her rhythm rubbing herself, she was startled by the mental image of Max Jasper. She was so annoyed with herself for thinking of him at that inopportune moment she almost lost the building swell of pleasure between her legs. But when she stopped fighting the direction her mind was taking her, the throbbing in her pussy grew more intense as she imagined that Max's hand was the one rubbing her engorged lips, teasing her clit, dipping in and out until, as the first wave of an orgasm broke, she turned to face the water, opening her legs to let the needles of water play on her swollen cunt. She experienced spasms of pleasure that left her spent, almost crouching against the steamed glass.

She swept the tangle of wet hair away from her face and straightened herself to stand tall under the showerhead. Her body felt light and relieved of all the tension she'd been carrying for days, if not weeks. It was unfortunate she'd let that arrogant jerk Max Jasper intrude on her fantasy, but she wrote it off as the mind's doing strange things under stress.

She decided she would order some food after all.

Justin Baxter took a step toward Gemma—that's all he needed to get his arm around her waist and pull her close to him.

She braced herself with her arms bent at the elbows, her palms pressed to his chest.

"You're not going to throw me in the pool, are you?" she said.

He could barely think to answer her, being that close to her mouth, with her obscenely pillowy lips and that incredibly sexy gap between her two front teeth. He felt his cock get hard.

He pressed his mouth against hers, and she immediately met his tongue with her own. The urgency he felt to get inside her made it impossible to think. He ran his hand down her back, to her ass, then under her short dress. He pressed his hand between her legs from behind, and she shifted her legs to give him access to her pussy.

He knew this was wrong—that he should be texting Martha to join them up here. But he was afraid that would scare Gemma away, and he wanted to fuck her more than he wanted to stay within the boundaries of his "open" marriage.

She leaned against him as his fingers reached inside her, feeling his way to the spot that would give her pleasure. Her luscious mouth was wet and parted against his neck, and all he wanted was to make her come, to hear her moan his name. Once that happened, he could fuck her and give himself release.

His hand moved in a practiced way, but he couldn't tell if she was close to a climax. He withdrew his fingers and unzipped her dress, which slid to the ground. He tugged down her panties, and she helped him get them off.

Her naked body was stunning—larger breasts than anyone would suspect seeing her in clothes, round hips, and a barely groomed thatch of blond pubic hair between her legs. Gotta love those foreigners—not yet consumed by the cult of waxing!

Justin guided her gently to one of the lounge chairs. He pressed her down on her back and parted her legs with his hands. He couldn't remember the last time he'd wanted someone so badly. He had planned on eating her pussy, making her come with his tongue, but he couldn't wait. He took his cock out of his pants and positioned it at her entrance, feeling like a teenager who had to fuck a girl before she changed her mind.

As he thrust inside, her pussy was tight, and if he hadn't known better he would have thought she wasn't turned on. But she had to be. He licked and palmed her breasts, loving her body, wanting it in every way. And yet she was so still, it was maddening. She didn't make any noise, and she did not touch him. Her hands lay at her sides. Alarmed, he looked at her face. She looked . . . bored.

"Are you okay?" he panted, making himself stop.

"Yes, fine," she said. "Go on."

She might as well have told him to just get it over with. What was with this woman?

Her apathy was thrilling. It made him want to degrade her.

He pulled his cock out and climbed up so he was on his knees, straddling her. For some reason, he had the urge to jerk off on her—anything to wake her up.

He stroked himself, his cock looming over her flat stomach. He watched her face for any hint of alarm or disdain, but her expression was as placid and unchanging as if she was watching a mildly entertaining television show. He moved his hand faster and harder, his own pleasure forgotten. All he wanted was to see his cum on her flesh.

Sure enough, with a shudder and moan, he spouted cum on her like a spigot turned on too fast. She flinched only slightly, watching him now with what seemed to be mild amusement.

Justin, breathing heavily, looked down at this odd creature, and knew with absolute certainty, he was in love.

6

Max stared out of his office window to Bryant Park five stories below. He loved that view.

When he'd been able to fully fund his passion project, the upstart Ballet Arts dance company, his first task had been finding a building that would provide a managerial office as well as practice space. He scored it in a prewar gem of a building just off Sixth Avenue.

He'd had no problem finding dancers for the company; he had money and dance space—two things that were in short supply in the ballet world. Still, he dreamed of being able to found a school some day, as Balanchine had done with the School of American Ballet. Aside from becoming a legendary school, it served as a feeder for his company. But for now, Max had to be grateful for what he had been given to work with. And he was.

With a busy afternoon ahead of him, he couldn't quite get focused. Something was nagging at him, and he hated to admit that it had to do with that woman last night. There was something wrong with the world when a talented dancer like Nadia Grant could suffer one injury and then be compelled to turn her back on everything she'd worked for. She obviously felt it was none of his business—the mere suggestion that there were other things she could do in ballet had elicited a "drop dead" glare that he was in no hurry to see directed his way again. And really, it wasn't his business.

So why was he still thinking about her? For some reason, he felt certain he knew of her for more than just her accomplishments in the city's dance scene.

He Googled her name. Sure enough, an array of articles popped up that seemed to have little to do with her work in the corps de ballet. The first headline read, "Dirty Dancing: Cheating Choreographer Gets the Boot from Live-in Love." And then he realized how he knew her name: She was the dancer who had been engaged to that Hollywood sellout, Jackson Mandel.

The receptionist buzzed his desk. His first meeting of the day.

"Thanks, April. One more thing: Is Anna Prince in the studio?"

"Yes, I think so," the receptionist told him.

Max headed down to the studio. This was going to be awkward. But he needed that phone number.

He found Anna and a group of half a dozen other dancers stretching at the barre in one of the smaller studios. He didn't want to interrupt, but as Anna dipped into a deep *plié*, he rapped on the glass window until everyone looked up. He pointed at Anna and gestured for her to come outside for a minute. She looked quizzical, but glided across the room to meet him in the corridor.

"Hey—what's up?" she said.

"I hate to interrupt you, but I need Nadia Grant's phone number."

Anna looked at him suspiciously. He thanked goodness he'd held firm and refused to take her home with him last night.

"She can't dance anymore," Anna said acidly.

"Clearly," said Max. This dig seemed to calm Anna slightly. She wiped her sweaty forehead, bent the toes of her left foot, and shuffled in place for a moment.

"What do you need it for?"

"I want to find a place for her here. There's no reason a dancer of her stature should feel she has permanently lost ballet."

"Like, doing what?"

"I don't know, Anna," Max said, getting impatient. "That's what I need to figure out. But I don't even know if she's open to the discussion until I call her."

"She's not," Anna said. "She told me it's too painful for her to be anywhere near ballet right now."

"She's got to get over it." Max held his iPhone, waiting to program the number.

Anna looked at him, and it seemed to be a standoff until she said, "Fine!" She gave him the ten digits in such rapid fire, it was as if she was daring him to get them down at all.

"Thanks, Anna. Have a good class."

She looked at him as if he were the world's biggest asshole, but he barely paused to let it register. He was, uncharacteristically, extremely excited to make this phone call.

First thing that morning, Nadia had turned on her BlackBerry to find a text from Mallory asking her to meet her at Agnes Wieczorek's costume design studio.

Nadia knew that Agnes, the former owner of the legendary burlesque club the Blue Angel, had once upon a time been a ballerina in Warsaw, Poland. Maybe Mallory wanted Agnes to give Nadia some sort of pep talk. The thought was excruciating. But after her performance last night, she felt she at least owed it to Mallory to show up. Work through the pain, she'd always been told. She believed that still applied, even though the pain was now emotional rather than physical.

The studio was an unmarked storefront on Broome Street. At eleven in the morning, the streets of Soho were filled with über-chic mommies in high heels pushing designer strollers over cobblestones, models on their way to go-sees, and European tourists. Standing in the middle of that scene, it was impossible to feel too bad about herself. Whatever her recent disappointments and failures, she was still here, living the life she'd always dreamed of. She had to find a way to stay inspired, and not retreat into an existence that was gray and safe and miserably compromised.

Nadia saw Mallory approaching from down the block. Even in the middle of a neighborhood filled with eye-catching people, she stood out. She had style, she had confidence and, at the moment, she had a giant bouquet of flowers in her arms.

"Hey!" Mallory said, kissing her on the cheek. "Grab the door for me—these are heavy."

"They're gorgeous! What are they?"

"I have no idea. But the florist said they live for weeks. I'm giving them to Agnes to thank her for doing such a great job with the costumes."

Nadia held the door and then followed Mallory into the studio. The floors were concrete; the walls were part exposed brick, part brushed steel, and were mostly obscured by racks of fabric and designs in progress. Above, the tin ceiling added an ornate finish to the otherwise industrial feel of the space. In the far corner of the room was a black desk, and next to it a winding iron staircase leading up to a second floor.

"So this is what I was thinking last night: If the performing thing doesn't work for you—and for some people it just doesn't—maybe you can learn costuming from Agnes. And then, after being around the shows, if you decide you want to be onstage again, great. If not, you still have something really integral and creative to contribute."

"I really appreciate your thinking of me, and trying to help me. But I don't think making costumes is going to fill the need I have to be onstage. I have to find a way to get over my fear," Nadia said.

Mallory looked at her with empathy and seemed about to hug her when they both heard the door open behind them.

Gemma Kole slumped in, her hair pulled into a high, messy ponytail, and big dark glasses obscuring half her face. She carried a large, green smoothie.

"I don't know why you Americans are so hell-bent on these juice concoctions," she said, dropping her hobo bag at her feet.

"So why are you drinking one?" Mallory said.

"Because the girl at the shop keeps bloody promising me they cure hangovers!"

Nadia thought, not for the first time, how carelessly sexy Gemma was. She was a cross between Sienna Miller and the Chanel model with the gap between her two front teeth. Maybe Gemma should be on the burlesque stage, and—as Mallory suggested—Nadia should be tucked away in this little shop, threading a needle. But no—she was not yet ready to concede that.

"What are you two doing here, anyway?" Gemma said. "Don't tell me I forgot a fitting."

"No, we're just visiting Agnes."

"Are those flowers for her? They're gorgeous, but slightly menacing. What are they?"

"Yes—they're for Agnes. I don't know what they are, but they live a long time," Mallory said. Nadia could tell she was second-guessing the arrangement after the word "menacing."

"Do me a favor? Go upstairs to see Agnes. I need quiet to even begin to function."

Nadia and Mallory exchanged a look and were happy to

oblige her. They climbed the narrow stairs, Nadia clutching the slim iron railing all the way.

The second floor had a shiny wood floor, and two walls were floor-to-ceiling mirrors. If it hadn't been for the bolts of fabric, containers of beads and sequins, and yards of thread and ribbon, it would have felt like a dance studio.

Agnes was seated cross-legged on the floor, wearing a pair of eyeglasses with another pair perched atop her head, and she was sewing a swatch of black fabric. She looked up when they cleared the stairs, but then went right back to sewing.

"I hear congratulations are in order," she said in her thick Polish accent before turning her attention immediately back to the work at hand.

"Yes, opening night was a huge success. And we couldn't have done it without you. I wanted you to have these," Mallory said, putting the flowers on the floor next to her.

"I'm talking about the marriage proposal," Agnes said. "And thank you. I love Sabine Pastel orchids. They live longer than most house pets."

"Oh! Yes. Alec really shocked me," Mallory said.

"I'm not surprised." Agnes turned to Nadia. "And how did you do, ballerina?"

Nadia felt her stomach sink. It was bad enough that she'd frozen in front of a hundred people last night—including Max Jasper. Now she had to admit her failure to a woman who was not only a former ballerina who'd mastered burlesque, but one who'd spent her later years at the helm of the longest-running and most successful burlesque revue in Manhattan.

"Nadia got cold feet," Mallory said, winking at her.

Agnes nodded. "It's not for everyone," she commented.

"That's true—but it also can just take time. So I was thinking maybe you could let her watch you create costumes. It's so inspiring, and if she decides she doesn't want to dance..."

"It's a lot of work," Agnes said with a heavy sigh. Nadia

wasn't sure if Agnes meant creating costumes, or showing someone else how to do it.

"I'm not ready to give up on performing," Nadia said.

"What happened to your ballet?" Agnes asked.

"I keep breaking my foot," Nadia said. Six months later, and she still felt like crying every time she said it. Agnes clucked in sympathy.

"Let me see the ring," she said to Mallory. Nadia witnessed the flush of joy on Mallory's face when she held out her hand. Agnes inspected the diamond as if it could solve the mysteries of the universe. "Very nice," she finally pronounced.

Nadia hated to think this way, but looking at Mallory's sweet satisfaction, she wondered if a good relationship was another bar she would never reach.

Her cell rang, an incoming number she didn't recognize.

"I hate cell phones," Agnes said.

"Better take that outside," advised Mallory.

"I don't even know who it is. I'm not going to answer it," said Nadia.

"Live dangerously—answer it. Just take it outside," said Agnes.

Something about the woman was so authoritative, Nadia found herself pressing the green button and saying hello. And as soon as she heard the male voice on the other end, she wished she hadn't.

Mallory decided, while Nadia dashed down the stairs to answer her phone, to use the private time with Agnes to try to end the nagging worry she'd felt since her conversation with Alec last night.

"Can I ask you a question?" Mallory said.

"Of course. Is it about the club?"

"No," Mallory said.

"Good," said Agnes.

"It's about marriage," said Mallory.

"Now that is a topic I can speak to," said Agnes. Mallory didn't know much about Agnes's personal life—it was widely assumed she had none. But Mallory had heard her mention a long-ago marriage. It had obviously ended at some point, but she didn't know when, how, or why. And considering how circumspect Agnes could be, Mallory doubted she would ever know.

"I'm afraid our relationship will change once we're married."

"Of course it will."

"For the worse."

"Of course it will," Agnes repeated.

"Really?" It might be honest, but it wasn't the answer Mallory had expected. She'd thought Agnes would tell her she was being ridiculous, as her friends surely would.

"Yes. It will get worse, and then better, and then worse, and then better, and then so bad you want to leave, and then good enough to make you stay... and there you have it. Marriage."

"Okay. I guess I know that, on some level. And everyone deals with it, right?"

Agnes, wisely knowing the question was rhetorical, said nothing. "But what if you have to change something about yourself for the marriage?"

"Marriage is all about compromise."

"Alec wants me to phase out of performing. He just admitted to me that it bothers him to see me taking off my clothes like that."

"It's good he told you."

"You think this is reasonable?"

Agnes put down her sewing and looked at Mallory. Her eyelids sagged so much Mallory wondered if the folds obscured her vision. She resisted the urge to touch her own eyelids to see if they were beginning to lose the battle with gravity.

"There is no right and wrong. How long do you think you will want to keep performing?"

Mallory shrugged. "I don't know. A few more years, maybe."

"And how much longer do you think you will want to be with Alec?"

"A lot longer than that, obviously."

"Compromise," Agnes repeated.

Mallory heard Nadia climbing back up the stairs. At least, she hoped it was Nadia, and not Gemma, who had overheard her personal conversation. The woman was clearly talented, but there was something about her Mallory didn't quite trust.

"Sorry about that." It was, in fact, Nadia, who appeared at the top of the stairs looking rather flushed, either from the flight of stairs or the phone call. Mallory hoped for Nadia it was the phone call. The woman needed to loosen up a bit. "Mallory, I have to get going."

"Everything okay?" Mallory said.

"Yes—it was just . . . a ballet choreographer who saw the show last night. He wants to talk to me. I don't know why but I agreed to meet him for coffee."

"Okay—can't hurt. I have to get going, too. I'm meeting some friends for an early lunch on the Upper East Side so I'll walk you out. Thanks again, Agnes. I'm going to come by next week to talk about the burlesque convention, okay?"

The annual Las Vegas Burlesque Festival was one of the biggest burlesque events in the country, second only to the Burlesque Hall of Fame Weekend. While the Vegas Burlesque Festival was less rooted in the rich history of burlesque, it had a more tangible effect on the world of burlesque: The festival was the brainchild of a film studio scion named Marty Bandinow. The culmination of the festival was a competition that awarded the winning troupe twenty thousand dollars, a feature in a national magazine, and, one year, a walk-on role on a primetime television show. Agnes had never wanted "her" girls to participate—she felt it was an unnecessary distraction and was philosophically against pitting dancers against one another for such high financial stakes.

"My girls do not put on a dog and pony show. This is burlesque, not the circus," she'd said.

But now that Mallory and Alec were running their own club, it was their decision to make. And they wanted to compete and make a name for themselves. Since costumes were an important criteria to be judged, they were hoping Agnes would agree to help them.

"I'm working on a theme, so maybe next Monday I can come by and we can discuss some ideas."

"I can't think about it now," Agnes said. "Check my calendar with Gemma and have her schedule a day for you to come back."

Mallory was disappointed by Agnes's lukewarm response, but not entirely surprised, given how she felt about burlesque competitions.

On the first floor, they found Gemma accepting a delivery. Mallory and Nadia both recognized the unmistakable robin's egg blue box of Tiffany's.

As soon as Gemma realized she wasn't alone, she stuffed the box in her handbag.

"Secret admirer?" Mallory joked. Gemma glared at her. Okay, not one for humor. *Note to self: Stick to business with the cranky Brit.*

"I'm going to run. I'll call you later," Nadia said, halfway out the door.

Why was everyone so uptight today?

Mallory turned back to Gemma, who was furiously texting. "Agnes told me you are handling her calendar? I need to make an appointment to come back and talk to her about costumes for the burlesque festival."

"Sure. Whatever you need. Just e-mail me sometime and we'll set it up," Gemma said, not looking up from her phone.

Great, Mallory thought. *With all of this enthusiasm, I'm sure we'll win Vegas.* She wondered if Bette had any ideas about alternate costumers. But no, Agnes would be insulted. Mallory was sure that in the end, Agnes would come through for them.

7

Violet had a problem. Lately, she could not find any sexual satisfaction without some element of voyeurism.

She felt bad about this. It made her feel weak, like the domination clients who used to pay her thousands of dollars an hour to spank them, pee on them, call them garbage, and otherwise humiliate them.

Violet paced outside the "hot sheet" motel where one such former client worked at the front desk. He'd confided in her once that the front desk "security" cameras were actually rigged to video cameras in the pay-by-the-hour rooms. He had told her this while she acted out the part of a policewoman busting him for spying on the hotel clientele.

Now, she was actually considering asking him if she could take a peek at the monitors. Maybe witnessing the sexual squalor of the place would cure her once and for all. Or maybe her desires would sink to a new low.

She wondered if this new fetish of hers had something to do with the long hours she was spending running Violet's Blue Angel. When she had been simply a burlesque performer, she would do her thing and then leave. But now she spent night after night watching the dancers at her club, and this had somehow wound its way into her psyche, and her sexual satisfaction was now tied into the need to watch, to be tantalized, to experience that moment of breathtaking anticipation.

It was a challenge to feed this visual hunger. Stumbling upon erotic encounters was more difficult than one might imagine—even in a city as crazy as New York. She hated to think she might have to pay for it, but until she got over this particular obsession she just might have to. And as long as she had Billy Barton's deep pockets to dip into, money wasn't a huge problem.

Maybe Cookies would volunteer to put on an erotic show for her. And by volunteer, she meant give in to Violet's coercion.

Speaking of Cookies, where was her report on the opening night of The Painted Lady? She was surprised it had taken her until this late in the morning to remember it. That was the problem with being sexually unsatisfied—it addled her mind.

Violet dialed her cell phone.

"Where are you?" she asked Cookies.

"I'm waiting for you at the club. I thought you said to meet here."

Sweet Jesus, she really was losing it.

"Don't move. I'm on my way."

Nadia hoped she had the right Le Pain Quotidien. In what seemed like a matter of months, the Dutch café chain had sprung up like weeds in every neighborhood in Manhattan. With its communal tables, strong coffee, and fresh bread, it had become a makeshift office for freelancers, and a preferred meeting place for both corporate executives who didn't want to spend a hundred dollars on lunch and tourists in between sights.

At 11 a.m., the place was between the breakfast rush and the lunch crowd, so she had her pick of the tables along the left side of the wide dining room. She was relieved there was a table for four available. She didn't want to talk to Max at a crowded communal table, and the two-tops seemed too intimate.

She staked her claim on the table farthest to the back. A waitress handed her a two-sided, laminated menu, and Nadia ordered a pot of coffee.

Was it a mistake for her to have agreed to meet him? She had said yes so impulsively—it was as if some part of her had completely disconnected. Now she felt unprepared and vulnerable.

Mercifully, she spotted Max before he saw her. This gave her the advantage of processing the sight of him before she had to actually deal with him. And the sight of him was, well, quite spectacular. He was tall, well over six feet, and he had wide shoulders and a tapered waist that signaled his perfectly honed athleticism. His hair was shiny and dark, with just a hint of waviness that suggested he'd had curls as a child.

Nadia ignored the stirring inside of her and pretended to be reading the menu, waiting for him to find her.

She didn't look up until he was at the table, pulling out a chair opposite her to sit.

"Thanks for meeting me," he said.

"How could I say no?" she replied. "You made it sound like you had something so urgent to discuss it couldn't be done over the phone."

"I feel it is urgent," he said. His eyes were so dark brown, the pupil was almost indistinguishable from the iris, and his long, dark lashes were dramatic against his olive skin.

"Okay, so . . . I'm here. What is it?"

The waitress appeared. He ordered coffee. Nadia was hungry and eyed the croissant at the table next to theirs. Her first impulse was to deny herself, but then she remembered she was no longer dancing ballet.

"And I'll have a croissant," she said. She couldn't help stealing a glance at Max to check if any disapproval registered in those dark eyes, but he was unreadable.

When the waitress was out of earshot, Max turned to her with a seriousness appropriate for a meeting of the National Security Council.

"I think you're making a huge mistake," he said.

"It's just one croissant," she joked.

"I'm serious, Nadia." It wasn't so much what he said, but the intensity and intimate way in which he said it that stopped her cold. "I understand that you're devastated by what the injury means for your ballet career. But ballet is your home, and if you can't perform, we will find a different kind of place for you."

"Why do you care?" she snapped, fighting the threat of tears.

"Ballet is my life, too. I live for it. And everyone knows ballet is not a solitary endeavor—it's a community. A family. We can compete fiercely amongst ourselves when it comes to the stage, but off the stage, we look out for one another. I saw you dance last year. I know what a loss this is, not just for you, but for all of us. I'm building a company that I hope can make careers, and not just for the dancers onstage. For everyone involved in dance: the choreographers, teachers, costumers, pianists. There is still a place for you in ballet if you can just stop running away, and claim it."

Nadia realized, in that moment, that Max Jasper could potentially be the biggest personality in ballet since Balanchine. She knew he had the talent, somehow he'd gotten the funding, and she was witnessing the power of his charisma. It would be so easy to let him seduce her into believing she could still find satisfaction in working around ballet in some capacity. But she had never been easily seduced—not in the bedroom, and certainly not by a brooding, dark-eyed smooth talker across a table in a crowded café.

"That's a lovely speech, Mr. Jasper. But I have a somewhat different perspective on this side of the injury."

"I'd argue that you have no perspective. That's why I had to talk to you."

"Well, thanks for the enlightenment. But despite your myopic view of the world, there are other ways to perform aside from ballet."

"Such as what? Last night? You call that performing?"

She refused to let herself be baited.

"Maybe not last night. But I'll get there."

"Why?" he demanded so loudly that other people turned to look. "Why would you expend your energy and talent on burlesque?"

"I'll tell you why: I'd rather be center stage in burlesque than sidelined in ballet."

"That's an absurd statement, because it's predicated on the idea that they are two equal options."

"Well, then I guess that makes this whole conversation absurd, because it's predicated on the notion that you have any clue about me as a person. Which, obviously, you don't."

"I think I have some idea, and not because I'm so insightful. Anna told me you can't tolerate being around the ballet—that it's too upsetting for you. You need to get over that."

"She had no right to talk to you about me."

He shrugged. "She meant well."

"I don't know about that. I can't imagine she'd think I would want her to bring you to the show last night."

"And why is that? Are you not proud of what you're doing?"

"Just stop. I don't need this, okay?" She stood up to leave. He grabbed her wrist to prevent her from walking away, and his touch stopped her in her tracks.

"Do something—if not for me, for yourself," he said. "Stop by the studio tomorrow. Around noon. I'm choreographing something new, and I'd love to hear your thoughts. I don't think anyone at BA is objective at this point."

"I'm busy tomorrow," she said.

"Please just think about it."

"You can save your misguided concern." She put a ten on the table to pay for her croissant and coffee. And then she walked out.

8

Mallory climbed the stairs out of the Seventy-seventh and Lexington Avenue subway station to emerge on Third, just a block from her destination: the Atlantic Grill. She was thrilled that her two best friends from college, Julie and Allison, had been able to be spontaneous today and meet her for lunch. She knew, from her own days working in the corporate hell of a law firm, how difficult it could be to sneak away for an hour or two. But when she'd woken up with that ring on her finger, she knew she had to try to get them to meet her.

It had been weeks since she'd seen them, and it made her think of something a TV critic once wrote about the show *Sex and the City:* She wrote that the aspect of the characters' lives she coveted most was not the expensive shoes or hot sex; it was the amount of free time they seemed to find to hang out with their girlfriends. Mallory finally understood what that writer had meant. Although, seeing one of her favorite shoe stores on the corner, Shoebox, she remembered how much she had wanted those shoes, too.

Julie and Allison were already waiting at the banquette

along the wall in the entranceway. The air inside was almost too cold, despite the heat outside. Mallory eyed a frosty martini glass being handed over the bar to a waiter with a tray.

"Explain to me why we are meeting here instead of at one of the half dozen Le Pain Quotidiens within a two-mile radius of our offices," Julie griped.

"I wanted someplace with a bar," said Mallory. "And it's the least you could do after both of you flaked on me last night." The truth was, neither had flaked. Both had told her as soon as she'd announced the date of the opening that they had set-in-stone work commitments. Julie had to work a book party in East Hampton for one of Charlie Sheen's ex-wives' memoirs. Allison had a black tie event at Michael Bloomberg's townhouse.

"Mallie, we feel terrible," said Allison, adjusting her shiny auburn ponytail. "I promise I will be at the next show—front row, making all that obnoxious noise you seem to love."

The hostess showed them to one of the large, round tables against the back wall in the main dining room.

"So are we celebrating a successful night?" Julie asked.

"You could say that," said Mallory.

She waited for them to notice her ring—the way Allison had noticed Julie's engagement ring the morning they'd had breakfast last year at City Bakery. At the time, Julie's recounting of Jonathan's proposal at the Shake Shack in Madison Square Park had sounded very romantic. Mallory could never have imagined that a year later, Alec would be proposing to her onstage in front of hundreds of people.

But Allison and Julie were apparently too absorbed in the menus to notice the diamond elephant in the room.

"I do love the chopped salad here, so I'm not going to complain anymore about the trek," said Julie.

"Do you think the salmon is wild or farmed?" said Allison.

"Can I get you ladies a drink to start?" asked the waitress.

"We'll have three margaritas. On the rocks with salt," Mallory said.

Allison and Julie exchanged a look but didn't argue.

"You do know we have to go back to work after this," Julie said.

"I thought book publishing was run on three-martini lunches," said Mallory.

"This isn't the eighties," said Julie.

"Why don't you tell us about last night," said Allison, taking a piece of bread from the basket in the center of the table.

"It was everything I hoped it would be. And more," Mallory said suggestively. No one took the bait.

Their drinks arrived. Mallory ran her finger around the salted rim and raised her glass. Julie and Allison followed.

"To The Painted Lady," said Allison. "Long may she live—and strip."

Mallory touched her short, round glass to Allison's, then to Julie's. And that's when she saw Julie hone in on the ring.

"Oh... my... God," Julie said.

"What? What's wrong?" said Allison.

Julie reached out and grabbed Mallory's hand.

"Look! Is that what I think it is?"

Her voice was so loud, people at nearby tables turned to look at them.

"Shh! Yes—Alec proposed to me last night."

"Congratulations!" Julie shrieked. "When did he do it? How did he do it?"

"In the middle of the show! He called me up onstage in between acts. I had no idea why he was doing that. I'd just finished my performance, but I threw on a robe and went back onstage. He started going on about how I wasn't just a performer but a producer of the shows, and that he hoped I would take on another role—his wife. And then he got down on one knee and gave me the ring."

Julie put her head in her hands. "I am so upset I missed it," she said.

Allison was quiet, shaking her head slowly. "Looks like smart Alec really did get smart," she said, referring to her nickname for him.

"Very funny," said Mallory.

"Seriously, bravo, Mal. A year ago this guy is begging you for a three-way with a hooker, and now he wants to tie the knot."

"She was a dominatrix, not a hooker."

"Same difference. The point is you pulled off a relationship miracle."

"Wow. Your sentimentality is getting me all choked up."

"No, I'm in awe. Congratulations. This is amazing," Allison said, reaching out and putting her hand over Mallory's.

"The ring is stunning," said Julie. "Antique?"

"Yeah. From the 1920s," said Mallory.

Allison was on her BlackBerry.

"Are we boring you?" said Julie.

"I'm Tweeting this. Seriously, Mal, Alec should have given me a heads-up. This was a great PR opportunity wasted."

"You are such a romantic," said Julie. "Maybe Mallory should charge an admission fee to her wedding."

"It was one of the best nights of my life," Mallory said. "I felt bad about one thing, though. You know Nadia, my ballet studio partner? She totally froze. She danced the first quarter of her performance beautifully, but when it came to taking off the costume, she couldn't do it."

"Well, not everyone is a superfreak like you," Allison said with a smile.

"Seriously. You just make it look deceptively easy, Mal."

Mallory smiled, but wondered if her impending marriage signaled the end of her days of superfreakdom. Maybe it was time to pass the baton to someone who needed burlesque to save her the way it had once saved Mallory.

"I'm going to help Nadia find her inner superfreak," Mallory said.

"Like Bette did for you?"

"Yes. But minus the sex."

"Oh? Are you retiring your Sapphic self?"

"We're all about monogamy these days," said Mallory.

"Hmm. I'll believe it when I see it."

"I'm serious," said Mallory. "Isn't that what marriage means?"

"Yes, for normal people," said Allison. "But we know you and Alec will never be normal. And we love you for it."

Violet found Cookies at a table in the back of the club. She wore black yoga pants and a pink hooded sweatshirt, and was smoking a cigarette while drinking a green smoothie.

"Why bother with the health drink if you're a smoker?" said Violet. She hated the hipster health vibe that had drifted across the continent from the West Coast. The East Village was littered with tiny storefronts selling atrocious, ten-dollar vegetable and fruit concoctions with names like "Hangover Helper" and "Brain Booster." Violet lived on red meat and Diet Coke, and she was healthy as a horse.

"I figure they cancel each other out and I'm on neutral ground," said Cookies.

"And I hate the whole *Girls Next Door* vibe you have going on," Violet said, pulling on the hood of Cookies' sweatshirt as she sat down.

"Someone woke up on the wrong side of the bed this morning."

"So change my mood. Tell me you've got photos of The Painted Lady show."

Cookies logged into her iPhone and slid it across the table.

"Good girl," Violet said. She slid her finger across the screen, speeding through the shots. "Who's this?" Violet paused at the picture of a willowy brunette.

"A former ballerina. She didn't do such a great job."

"Slammin' body, though." Violet was silent through the rest of the photos. When she was finished, she sat back in her seat. "The costumes are phenomenal. Who did them?"

"I think most of them were done by some British chick working with Agnes."

"What's her name?"

"Gemma Kole."

"I have to talk to her."

"I don't think Agnes will want anyone who works for her to work for you."

"Who cares what that old bag wants? Money talks, nobody walks. I'm sure the Brit could use a few under-the-table gigs. I just need Billy to cough up a little pocket change. A boost in the costume department is exactly what we need around here."

Cookies nodded. Violet reached over and unzipped her sweatshirt. Underneath, Cookies wore a black tank top and no bra. Violet brushed her fingers against Cookies' nipples, bringing them to a point. "You know what else I need around here?" Violet said. Cookies shook her head no. "I need you to do something for me."

"Okay," Cookies said. Violet slipped her hand under the T-shirt to cup Cookies' bare breast. "I need you to let me watch someone else fuck you," she said.

"What do you mean?"

"Just what I said." Violet moved her hands to tug off Cookies' pants. Cookies raised her ass to help get them off. She eyed the door nervously. "It's locked," Violet said. She pulled Cookies' thong down to her ankles, then slid her palms underneath Cookies' ass so her pelvis tilted up. "Spread your legs," Violet said, helping Cookies get in the right position so Violet had a view of—and access to—her asshole. As always, it was pink and puckered and just waiting for her. Violet licked her finger, then pressed it into Cookies' ass, an opening so ripe and available, it made Violet wish she had a cock. She moved her finger in and out, watching Cookies' breathing get more labored, and feeling her ass relax and give more with each stroke. Cookies' fingers reached for her own clit, and Violet smacked her hand away. "You have to come just from this," she commanded. She worked her finger faster, but then she couldn't resist: Cookies' clit was so engorged she had to taste it. She pressed her tongue against the tight little knob, and Cookies cried out, her ass clenching around Violet's finger, her pussy juicing against Violet's mouth.

When Cookies was still, Violet said, "Don't you want to be able to make me come the way I always do for you?" Cookies nodded, her eyes half-closed. "Well, I'm telling you how you can."

"Okay," Cookies said.

"Good girl," said Violet. "Now get dressed. I'm going to go score us a brilliant costume designer."

9

Nadia stood on the Painted Lady stage wearing only jeans and pasties with red tassels.

Nadia had promised Mallory she wouldn't shy away after the debacle of her opening night performance. And so, in a show of what she hoped was a positive attitude in the face of gross failure, she'd decided to spend the morning at The Painted Lady.

She was unpleasantly surprised to find Bette Noir at the club along with Mallory. She found the black-haired beauty to be very intimidating. Nadia was thankful that Bette was leaving in a month for her next film.

"Open up your rib cage more," Mallory said from her seat at one of the tables.

Mallory was trying to teach her how to tassel-twirl. It was one of the most distinctive burlesque moves, but Nadia had shied away from it for her first performance. It wasn't the most refined movement, but she understood the value of it. "Now bounce up and down on the balls of your feet."

"But loosen your arms away from your sides more," said Bette.

"She's right," Mallory said. "If your arm is too tight against your side, it can halt the movement of the tassel."

Nadia bounced up and down, but the tassels only swung from side to side, not around in circles.

"We're going to need to get your shoulders into the mix," said Bette.

They heard the front door open, and Justin made his way into the room.

"Hi, ladies," he said.

"Hey—what brings you by?" said Mallory, kissing him on the cheek.

Nadia pulled on her T-shirt and sat on the edge of the stage. There was no way she was going to practice making her tits bounce in front of Justin.

"I wanted to run some scheduling by you. Martha's birthday is in a few weeks. I totally flaked and didn't plan anything earlier. What I'd like to do is to close this place for a night and just have a huge bash here."

"Sounds great." Mallory pulled out a big DayMinder calendar and flipped forward a few weeks. "What night of the week?"

Nadia went to the dressing room for a bottle of water. When she returned to the stage, Mallory called her down to join them at the table.

"Justin wants to ask you something," she said.

"Okay." Nadia pulled out a chair and sat across from him. He was very handsome. It was no wonder a lot of the girls talked about him in a way that was less than professional. But that happened everywhere. She knew Max Jasper had a reputation for bedding his dancers, too.

She shook the thought from her mind. She didn't want to think about him. His invitation to watch a rehearsal was nagging at her like a hangnail. A part of her thought maybe she should just go, get it out of her system, shut him up about her choices by showing him that visiting Ballet Arts would not have some magical effect on her, and then they could both move on.

"I know you had a rough time the other night, but I've seen you at rehearsals before, and you're absolutely amazing. I hope you're going to, you know, get back on the proverbial horse," Justin said.

"Oh, I will," Nadia said.

"Great. I was just telling Mallory that I'm going to have a big birthday party here for Martha in a few weeks. I usually do it out of town somewhere, but with the opening of the club it just got away from me this year. But I still have time to pull together something fantastic. A few of the girls are going to perform that night. I hope you will, too."

Nadia looked at Mallory.

"Just . . . any act?"

"We usually have a theme. I'm working on an idea for this party. I'm going to have Gemma do the costumes—it will be fun. Very A-list. It will be in all the celebrity rags, and *Vanity Fair* will cover it for their party section. Trust me—it will be great exposure for you."

"It might be too soon," Nadia said. "Obviously, I'm not doing well under pressure."

"Think about it," Mallory said. "You know what? We can choreograph something together. That way, if you freeze up, I'll be onstage to dance around it."

"If you think it's a good idea . . ." Nadia said. God, she hated herself for being so weak. It had been one bad night—she had to get over it. If she couldn't, then she might as well admit what Max was trying to sell her—once a ballet dancer, always a ballet dancer. She would have no second act.

"I think it's a tremendous idea," said Justin. "Now maybe

you ladies can help me come up with a theme. I was thinking something to do with Hollywood. Martha's obsessed with watching old movies lately. Ever since Elizabeth Taylor died and she re-watched *BUtterfield 8*, she's been on a classic film kick."

"I love that idea," said Mallory.

"You could do 'silver screen sirens,'" said Nadia.

"Yes!" Mallory and Justin said at the same time.

"I'm going to talk to Gemma about the costumes," said Justin.

"Yeah, don't distract Agnes. I need her focused on the Vegas costumes," said Mallory.

"I was thinking Gemma could do those, too," said Justin. "She did an incredible job on the opening night costumes."

"She did," Mallory said, slowly and with an obvious effort at diplomacy. "But Agnes directed her. And Vegas is too important to trust to anyone but Agnes. Winning that would get us lots of press and legitimize us as a serious club, not just another place jumping on the burlesque bandwagon. Don't get me wrong: I'm glad you like Gemma's work—I do, too. And as Agnes's apprentice she'll be helping, I'm sure. But I think it's important that Agnes is the one to actually make the costumes. I want her to see that as *her* project."

"Okay," Justin said, "I'll talk to them about the Vegas costumes and getting on a schedule. I'm going over there anyway."

"Great. Saves me a trip."

"Tell Gemma I want to see the costumes for this weekend's show by Friday," Bette said. "I don't want to look like some extra off the set of *The Tudors.*" Bette and Mallory were performing a Boleyn sisters act.

"I'll relay the message," Justin said with a smile. "And Nadia—I'm glad you're in."

Gemma spread the synthetic fur fabric on the table and cut it into six-inch strips with pinking sheers. She was relieved to finally be onto the trim of the costume. Mallory had asked her to design two Tudor-period costumes—one for her and one for Bette Noir. The bodice of each had taken Gemma days, the fronts covered with plastic jewels, pearls, sequins, and a central crucifix design made from gold Lurex. Exhausting.

She'd taken the job as an apprentice to Agnes, but the gig was turning into a sweatshop. The old woman didn't want to do anything herself. What was she working on up there, all day, every day?

There was no way Gemma could do this job for more than a year. Now, more than ever before, she felt an urgency to get her own label off the ground. But how was she going to save enough money? The money she made working for Agnes barely covered her living expenses. She needed an investor. The notion of being able to finance anything herself was naïve at best.

"Hello?"

Gemma looked up from the cutting table. She hadn't noticed that the front door had opened until Justin Baxter was standing in front of her.

"What are you doing here?" she said.

"You're that happy to see me?" He was joking, but she could tell there was something serious underneath what he was trying to pass off as banter. She felt bad: She hadn't even acknowledged his gift. It was a delicate, chain link silver bracelet. She knew she should have just called and thanked him, but she was still trying to make sense of what had happened the night of his party. She knew his reputation: Certainly, their hot little encounter was nothing remarkable to him. He probably sent gifts to everyone. So she didn't want to seem like she thought it was something more than it was. And in truth, the only additional thing she would want out of the exchange was money. Oh, not money for sex like a prostitute. But maybe his special interest in her could translate into a sweeter deal for her costuming work. If there even *was* any special interest on his part.

"I have some items of business to discuss," he said, obviously looking around the room for some place to sit. The studio was not equipped for meetings.

"Oh? I'm all ears."

Justin found a folding chair that was propped against a clothing rack, and he placed it at the cutting table so he was seated across from her. She thought, for the umpteenth time, how handsome he was. It made it all the more frustrating that, as usual, she'd felt next to nothing when they had sex. There she was, in a fabulous setting, with a gorgeous, sexy guy—who was doubly taboo because he was married *and* sort of her boss—and she still couldn't come. What was wrong with her?

"First of all, I want you to do the costumes for the Las Vegas Burlesque Festival," he said.

"Mallory told me she wants to make an appointment to speak to Agnes about that."

"I know. But I want you to create them—not Agnes."

"You'll have to work that out with Mallory and Agnes. I don't make those kinds of decisions."

"I write the checks. I make the decisions. And I want you to do the Vegas costumes."

Gemma looked at him with new interest. "So what's the second thing?"

"The second thing?"

"Yes—you said the first thing was the Vegas costumes. What is the second?"

"I wanted to see you," he said.

"You did?" She wasn't being coy. She actually found this information surprising.

"Yes. I haven't been able to stop thinking about you since the other night."

Gemma smiled and looked down at the cutting board. "I'm

sure you say that to all the girls you lure up to your swimming pool."

He reached across the table and took her hand. "No. I don't." His steely blue eyes were serious.

"I'm not sure what to say to that. Or do about it, for that matter. You're married."

"This is true. But my relationship with Martha is complicated. She isn't a typical wife. What happened between you and me isn't even entirely out of bounds with her. I just—I should have invited her to join us."

"What? Are you out of your mind?"

"No. That's our agreement."

"I don't do things like that."

"I...gathered that. And to be honest, I didn't want her to join us."

"Oh? Why not?"

"I didn't want to share you," he said, his voice low. His eyes swept down to her breasts. She knew he wanted to put his hands on her, but the table kept him at a safe distance.

"I think we should stick to business conversation," Gemma said.

"Fine," he said with a reluctant smile. "The other thing I wanted to talk to you about is that I want you to design costumes for a party I'm throwing at The Painted Lady. A few of the girls are going to be performing dressed as different silver screen movie stars. I also want to transform the room to look like an Academy Awards ceremony. Maybe you can help with that, too."

"What's the occasion?"

"Martha's birthday."

"You can't be serious."

"Of course I am. I do something different every year. We usually go away, but we've been so distracted with the opening of the club...."

"No, I mean, are you for real asking me to work on your wife's party—me, the woman you cheated on her with? Don't you find that a tad questionable, morally speaking?"

"First of all, I told you the cheating thing isn't that black-and-white with us. Would she be thrilled about it? No, but only because I didn't follow the rules we set for stepping outside the marriage. And as for your doing the costumes and room, I think you're amazingly talented. And I always want the best."

"I'm going to be very booked up doing the Vegas costumes. As soon as Mallory decides on a theme I'll be starting straight away."

"I'll make it worth your while financially."

Now she was listening.

"What are we talking, exactly?" she said.

"I'll pay you ten grand a week while you work on the party."

"And when's the party?"

"In three weeks."

"I don't want you to tell Agnes—or even Mallory. They won't like this."

Justin smiled broadly, as if she was doing him a favor by taking a ridiculous amount of money from him. "I agree," he said.

"And what you're paying me doesn't include the budget for materials, correct?" she said.

"That's right."

She wrinkled her nose in consternation.

"What's the problem?" he asked.

"If I'm doing all this work for you, and assisting Agnes with the weekly clothes for The Painted Lady, I'll have no time to work on the fashion line I'm designing. I believe that's what they call an opportunity cost?" she said. She could tell by the expression on his face that her tough negotiating stance made him want her all the more.

"What are you saying?"

"I need you to pay me ten grand a week for as long as I'm doing the Vegas costumes, too—not just the party stuff."

"It's a deal—if *you* agree to one more thing," he said. She looked at him skeptically. "Come to dinner with me tomorrow night," he said.

"What about Martha?"

"She's at our house in LA for a few days."

"I don't know. . . ."

"We can talk business for part of the night if it makes you more comfortable," he said with a flirtatious smile.

Gemma knew she should just roll with it. Ten grand a week was money she'd never find anywhere else at this point. "Fine. But we can't make a habit of this," she said. "You know what they say about not mixing business with pleasure."

"They're wrong," he said. "No two things go better together. I'll pick you up at your place at seven thirty."

"You don't know where I live," she said.

"I'm waiting for you to tell me."

Gemma resisted the urge to roll her eyes. She knew she should find him charming, but mostly she just heard the classic refrain from the film *Jerry Maguire*: "Show me the money."

She picked up a blue Sharpie and wrote her address on the back of one of Agnes's business cards. He slipped it into his wallet and walked out the door without saying another word.

Less than a minute later, her cell phone rang. She was sure it was Justin calling to say something cheeky, but it was an unfamiliar female voice.

"Is this Gemma?" the voice said.

"Yes," Gemma said slowly. "Who is this?"

"Violet Offender. I'm a burlesque performer."

"I know who you are. You own the Blue Angel now."

"It's Violet's Blue Angel, but yeah."

"How did you get this number?" Gemma said, glancing up at the stairs to make sure Agnes wasn't on her way down.

"Burlesque is a small world."

"Yes—a little too small. I'm at work, and my boss is not a fan of yours. So maybe you should tell me why you're calling."

"First of all, Agnes shouldn't have anything against me. It's not my fault she sold the club thinking it was going to be owned and operated by Billy Barton alone."

"I don't know that much about it, to be honest. I just heard that you used to work for her, she fired you, and then you somehow ended up involved with the new incarnation of the club—and used the name she created with your own tacked on the front. I don't know what you call that here, but I think *audacity* fits the bill."

"Whatever. Now she can spend all her time sewing like any grandma should."

"Oh, come on! You really can't be serious."

"I'm always serious. You'll learn that about me. Now don't you want to know why I called?"

"I am a tad curious."

"Then meet me tomorrow night and I'll fill you in."

"I have dinner plans tomorrow night."

"So meet me after dinner. At my club. Eleven o'clock. The show will be finished; people will be heading out to the next drinking destination. We'll have the whole place to ourselves to chat."

"I don't know. . . ." Gemma said. "Why don't you at least tell me what this is about."

"If you want to know what this is about, I'll see you tomorrow night at eleven."

And she hung up.

10

Nadia couldn't control herself.

After leaving The Painted Lady, instead of taking the subway straight uptown, she got off at Forty-second Street, Grand Central. And then she walked the few blocks toward Sixth Avenue.

Max Jasper was becoming a mental distraction, and she had to put an end to it. She decided she would just make one appearance at Ballet Arts, show him that she wasn't afraid of being around ballet—that she had simply moved on—and that would be the end of it.

She found the building. Not surprisingly, it was beautiful, with a limestone façade, decorative arched doorway, and a marble-floored lobby.

She gave her name to the security guard, expecting him to call someone to grant her admittance. But he just looked on a list and said, "Mr. Jasper is expecting you."

Expecting her? *Presumptuous bastard.*

She thought about turning around and leaving, but she was

already there, and now she was curious to see exactly what the great Mr. Jasper had going on.

"Second floor," said the security guard.

As soon as she stepped out of the elevator, Nadia smelled the familiar ballet studio smell, a woodsy and stale combination of sweat, powder, and something indefinable yet universal. Every studio she had ever been in, even in other countries, smelled exactly the same.

Four rooms ran side by side, each identical with front mirrors, pianos in the back right corner, and wide windows so all classes and rehearsals could be viewed from the outside. Only one of these rooms was in use. Nadia spotted Max at the front of the room, and she took a seat on one of the benches lining the wall.

The dancers practiced a series of *fouettés en tournant*. Nadia loved that step. One of her favorite moments in ballet was the thirty-two continuous *fouettés* in the coda of "Black Swan" from *Swan Lake*.

A woman sat on the floor in the front of the room taking notes on a clipboard in her lap. Nadia knew that had to be his assistant choreographer, Pauline Penn; she'd read about her defection from the School of American Ballet for Max's company; it was big news at the time. Nadia had wondered what he'd offered Pauline to lure her away from her coveted position at SAB. Now, watching the woman gaze at Max with rapt adoration, it wasn't hard for Nadia to guess. *God, that man is a piece of work.*

As if sensing Nadia's stare, Max looked away from the dancers and directly at her. He smiled, and Nadia realized he was not smiling at her, but smiling spontaneously at the sight of her. This confused and, she hated to admit, delighted her. What was going on?

She turned her focus to the dancers. She watched them bend, arch, and leap through motions that were achingly familiar to her. As much as she wanted to be able to remain detached, each one of her senses was consumed with all that she missed about ballet. And all the confidence and bravado she'd felt while walking from the subway evaporated.

She jumped up from the bench and headed for the exit. Her heart pounded as she pressed the button for the elevator. All she could think was, *get me out of here.* When the wide elevator door opened, she wanted it to swallow her. She pressed the Close Door button, needing the fresh air of the street, anything but that ballet smell.

But just before the elevator door slid completely closed, it receded back to open again. Nadia quickly pressed the Close button repeatedly, to no avail.

And then Max stepped inside.

"Where are you running off to?" he said.

She was flabbergasted.

"You left rehearsal to ask me that?"

He shrugged. "It seems like an important question."

"I remembered that I need to be somewhere."

"Bullshit," he said. She couldn't help looking at his lips: lush, and—at the moment—quite pouty.

"What do you want from me?" Nadia said as the elevator mercifully deposited them on the ground floor. She assumed—erroneously—that reaching the front doors would put an end to this impromptu chat. But Max followed her outside.

"Did it upset you to be inside a ballet studio?" he said.

"Not at all. Did you want it to upset me?"

"No, Nadia. I did not want it to upset you. I just want you to examine what you're doing, and to admit you're not ready to walk away from ballet."

"You don't know what you're talking about," she said. But her body betrayed her yet again: To her absolute horror, her eyes teared up. Max did what anyone would do in that situation: He put his arms around her. His gesture startled her out of her crying jag, and she pulled away from him. "I'm fine," she said, wiping her eyes.

"Want to get something to eat?"

"What?" she said, not sure she'd heard him correctly.

"Eat. Food. The practice commonly known as lunch?"

"Don't you have to get back to rehearsal?"

He shrugged. "Pauline can cover for me. Come on—the least I can do is buy you lunch after I traumatized you," he said, walking toward a café on the outskirts of Bryant Park. Reluctantly, Nadia followed him.

"You didn't 'traumatize' me," she said. "I'm just feeling emotional lately."

"Understandable."

"Don't patronize me."

"I'm not patronizing you! That was empathy. Jeez, you're difficult to please," he said with a smile. Nadia supposed he thought he knew everything there was to know about "pleasing" women. But she wasn't one of his BA groupies.

There was a line at the café, and Max suggested she get a table in the park while he picked up the food.

"Okay. Can you order me a tuna salad and iced tea?" She tried to hand him a ten-dollar bill. He waved the money away, and she could tell it would be useless to fight him on it.

She walked off to find a place to sit.

It was as perfect a day as you could ask of New York in August, not scorching hot, surprisingly low humidity. The park was teeming with people on their lunch breaks, but Nadia spotted a couple just finishing their food. She hovered nearby and sat down at the table when they left.

After a few minutes, she saw Max approach in the distance. The way he moved clearly signaled the grace and strength of a dancer, though an average woman probably wouldn't know that. She would just perceive that he had something remarkably sexy going on. Nadia told herself that she did not find him attractive—that the dancer in her was simply responding to the fine form of another artist.

That fine form sat next to her, and her heart beat undeniably faster.

"Thanks," she said as he placed her salad in front of her.

He smiled and dug right into his sandwich. She decided now was as good a time as any to ask him the question she'd been wondering about since she'd first read about Ballet Arts.

"Can I ask you something?" she said.

"Yes, I'd be happy to have you work at Ballet Arts. Done."

Nadia laughed, despite herself. "That's not what I was going to ask you."

He feigned surprise and disappointment. Or maybe the disappointment wasn't feigned. "How do you manage to fund Ballet Arts? I mean, you're so young, and I didn't read about any corporate investors." Nadia assumed he had a relationship with a large benefactor, maybe a patron of the arts who supported him as Lincoln Kirstein had famously partnered with Balanchine.

"I inherited a lot of money when I was in college," he said.

"Really? *That* much money?"

He nodded. "My father ran a huge hedge fund."

"Your father died when you were in college?"

He shook his head. "He died when I was in high school."

"I'm sorry. That must have been very difficult."

"It was. But if it hadn't happened, I don't think I'd be a dancer today."

"Why not?"

"My father was completely unsupportive of my interest in ballet. It was something my mother got me into. They were divorced—honestly, I have no idea how they ever thought they could be married in the first place. Anyway, at first, when I seemed so intent on performing, he thought I was gay. And he blamed my mother, because she was a . . . performer, of sorts. And he hated that part of her life. He made her quit, and she resented it, and she encouraged me to be artistic."

"Was she a ballet dancer?"

"No," he said.

When she realized he was not going to elaborate, she asked, "So did your father ever figure out that you're straight?"

"Yeah, eventually he realized that I was actually girl-crazy. Then he felt free to tell me I was being an idiot about the dancing, and I was going to waste my life, and that if this was what I chose, I could forget about any support from him."

Nadia was surprised by this torrent of personal information. And just as she thought about how surprising it was, he said, "I'm sorry. I don't know why I'm even telling you all of this."

"No, don't apologize. It's . . . I mean, I'm happy to listen."

"So, to make a long story short, I learned when I was twenty-one that he had left me the bulk of his wealth. I'll never know what changed his mind about me, or maybe he felt confident I would come to my senses by the time I was an adult and do something else with my life."

"Maybe he realized he was wrong, and he just didn't have it in him to admit that to you face-to-face."

Max shook his head. "I doubt my father ever considered that he could be wrong. But it's a nice thought."

They fell silent. Nadia wasn't hungry. She should have been starving after the morning workout, but she felt completely off-center sitting there with Max. Why did she keep finding herself seated across from this man who did nothing but provoke her?

"Well, you made something great out of his money. So you should feel good about that," she said.

"It could be greater," he said.

"How?" she said, and instantly realized he'd baited her and she'd fallen for it.

"Come join us."

Nadia closed the plastic lid on her salad container and stood up to leave.

"Thanks for lunch. I've got to get going."

Without missing a beat, Max stood up next to her.

"You didn't even eat. And you're not dancing anymore, so there's no reason to starve yourself."

Asshole!

"I *am* dancing," she said. "Just not ballet."

They stared at each other, locked in a standoff. And then he leaned close, held her face, and before she could react, kissed her.

Mallory paced the dressing room. Eight hours until showtime, and she was missing half her show.

This was the problem with surrounding yourself with talented people: They always had other options. First, Bette's manager had called her to Vancouver for a costume fitting for the movie she was about to start shooting. Then their stage kitten—the hot young woman who picked up the discarded garments after each set—got called to LA for an audition for *Playboy*. And their newest hire, Tori Tempest, had called in sick.

"You need to relax," Alec said. "If the show is a little short tonight, that's just the way it will have to be."

"No!" Mallory said. "We haven't earned the right to have a show that's half-assed. Every show is supposed to be fantastic. I'm going to have to get up there myself tonight. But that still won't fill the show."

Alec gave her a look when she said she had to get onstage. She sighed with exasperation. "I know you want me to focus on producing, not performing. But this is no time for you to be precious about it. The best thing I can do as a producer tonight is to perform," she said.

"Who else can you call in?"

"I don't know who is around. Maybe Nadia? But she's not even comfortable with her routine yet. I was going to give her time off to practice more and then have her get back onstage with me at Justin's party."

"Just call her. You know what? Don't even ask her to perform burlesque. Let her do some ballet in a sexy costume. The audience will love it. It's an opportunity to throw something different into the show—something no one else is doing."

Mallory considered it for a minute. "I love the idea, but there's one problem: She can't go *en pointe* now. That's the whole reason she's not doing ballet."

"Couldn't she do something without wearing those crazy toe shoes? Like, when my sister did ballet, she just wore those flat little slippers. You know what I mean?"

"I do. You know what? It's worth a call. You're brilliant," she said, kissing him.

"Can I ask you something?" he said. "I know you're planning the shows for the club... and planning for the burlesque festival. But are you thinking about planning our wedding at all?"

"Um, of course," Mallory lied.

"Really? Because we've never talked about it. I mean, I don't even have an idea when you'd want to do it. This winter? Spring?"

Mallory sat down in a chair in front of one of the makeup mirrors. "Alec, there's so much going on right now. Let's just back-burner it for now, okay?"

"You want to 'back-burner' our wedding?" he said, visibly upset.

"What? No, I'm sorry—that didn't come out right. I just mean, it's a hard thing to think about right now."

He gave her a pointed look.

"Don't be angry," she pleaded.

"Fine. I'll just give you something else hard to think about," he said, pulling her hand between his legs. She felt his cock already straining against his pants. "See? Just talking about marrying you makes me excited."

"Oh, Alec!" she said, looking up at him and smiling.

"Promise me you'll start thinking about it?" he said, unzipping his pants.

"Think about it? I'm looking right at it," she said, leaning forward to run her tongue over his boxers along the length of his shaft. She slipped her hand in the flap and brought him out so she could take him in her mouth.

"You know what I mean," he said, his voice catching as she gripped his cock, her mouth working on the tip.

Pulling down his boxers, she caressed his ass, then his cock, until she slid her hand firmly from the tip to the base, her mouth following it. He moved his pelvis, pressing his cock deeper, until he reached the back of her throat and she almost gagged.

His fingertips pressed against her scalp, and she glided her mouth back to a place where she had more control. She kept a steady rhythm, her hands moving to hold his hips. He moaned, and she tasted the first bead of semen. He pressed on her head harder, and she picked up the pace of her movements, bringing one hand back to his cock to work in tandem with her mouth. His hands twisted in her hair, and she felt his body tense. Oh, God, she loved taking him in her mouth this way. He moaned as he thrust into her, and the sound turned her on. Her stomach did a little flip as it always did when she knew she had brought him such intense pleasure.

She wiped her mouth on the back of her hand and leaned back in the chair. He knelt down and kissed her, then pulled her against him in a tight embrace.

"That was incredible," he said.

"Your cock inspires me," she said. "Now, I have to go call Nadia."

"I feel so used."

"Later, I'll hope you'll use me," she said. "But first I have to salvage this show."

11

Billy Barton stretched out on the table. It was his bimonthly visit to the male grooming salon, Sugar, for the "back, crack, and sack" hair removal package. Owned and operated by his first male lover, Harvey Hixenbaugh, Sugar was more than just a part of Billy's maintenance routine: It was his refuge from the exhausting world of media, money, and celebrity.

"You need to focus on the positive," Harvey said, pulling a swath of hair from Billy's scrotum.

"Ouch! I thought you said this gets less painful after a couple of months."

"Did I say that?" Harvey said. "Now listen, you can't let that crazy bitch ruin your perspective on all the good things you have going on. Your magazine is doing great. You have a Burberry model in your bed every night. You are living the dream, my boy."

"I didn't know 'the dream' included being blackmailed into bankrolling a club for a burlesque-dancing dominatrix."

"You could put an end to that any time you want."

"And 'out' Tyler?"

"Are you protecting Tyler? Or yourself?" Harvey said, yanking off another strip with a practiced flick of his wrist.

"Ouch! That hurts."

"The truth always hurts, my love."

Billy's BlackBerry buzzed, and he reached for it next to him on the table.

"I told you to turn that thing off when you're in here."

"And I wish I listened to you. Speak of the devil: Violet says she needs to see me ASAP—urgent club business. God, I hate that woman."

"Well, she'll have to wait. Your ass crack needs my attention."

"That sentence was much more inviting in the days when you weren't wielding a hot wad of liquid sugar."

After the initial shock of Max's kiss—during which she gave in to his mouth for a few seconds, long enough to feel a surprising flip in her stomach—Nadia had come to her senses and pulled back.

"What are you doing?" she'd demanded, wondering if she could somehow be lucky enough for him not to have noticed that, for a few beats, whatever he was "doing," she was doing, too.

"*We* were kissing," he'd said, smiling. "At least, that's what they called it last time I checked. Call me old-fashioned."

His grin was an unlikely combination of sexiness and warmth, and it took everything she had not to smile back.

"I'm leaving," she'd said, realizing she should just actually walk out of the park instead of saying she was going to go. What was wrong with her?

"Good," he'd answered. And she'd felt a bubble of outrage—until he followed with, "That gives you plenty of time to think about where you want me to take you to dinner tonight."

Now, looking into his gorgeous eyes, she laughed. She couldn't help it. He was so... *obnoxious*.

"Maybe I have plans tonight," she said.

"If you do, I hope you'll break them. I don't think I could wait until tomorrow."

To her surprise and dismay, she realized she didn't want to wait until tomorrow to see him again, either.

Her phone rang. Her first impulse was to ignore it, but then she saw it was Mallory.

"Hello?"

"Am I getting you at a bad time?" Mallory said.

"Um, not really. What's up?"

"I'm in a major bind tonight. Bette, Tori, and Willow all bailed on me. Is there any way you can come in and maybe just dance or something? You don't have to do a striptease. You can do ballet, or modern—anything you want. I've seen you messing around with choreography that is better than what most people do onstage."

"I... I don't know." It was the last thing she wanted to do. But she felt she owed Mallory, Alec, and even Justin for being the low point of opening night. On the other hand, she couldn't imagine having the time to work out a performance—even one she had in part done before—and being mentally and physically prepared to appear onstage that night.

She looked over at Max, who was eyeing her like the cat that ate the canary. And she thought about his comment that she wasn't a dancer anymore. "Okay—I'll do it."

"Thank you! Oh, you are a lifesaver. Just let me know what music you need us to have for you. And seriously, Nadia—anything you choose to do tonight will be great."

Nadia placed her phone back in her bag. She could feel Max's eyes on her.

"Everything okay?" he said.

"I don't know," she said slowly. "I just agreed to dance

tonight. Not even burlesque. Mallory said I can do ballet...or anything."

"Finally—someone's come to her senses."

"Don't get me wrong—I will do burlesque on that stage. And I'll do it soon. She just didn't want to rush me tonight because it's last minute."

"I'm trying not to take this personally."

"Personally?"

"Yes. You'd do anything to have an excuse not to go to dinner with me, wouldn't you?"

She laughed. "Yes. Busted."

"Okay, rain check accepted. So what are you going to do on that stage tonight?"

"I honestly have no idea."

"Want to use one of my studios to practice? I'm sure I have free space this afternoon."

"Oh, no. Thanks, but I couldn't do that."

"Why not? You're already here. And I'd love to see what you come up with. Maybe even help you brainstorm some non-*pointe* choreography."

"Really?" Nadia hated to admit that the thought of it thrilled her.

"Absolutely. On one condition."

"What's that?" she asked guardedly.

"You bring me to the show tonight."

She smiled. "Let's see how my rehearsal goes, first."

"I'll take that as a yes," said Max.

12

Billy dutifully showed up at the meeting spot Violet had designated: the Mexican chain restaurant Chipotle on lower Park Avenue. He spotted her immediately—who wouldn't? With her platinum blond hair, tattooed arms and chest, and leather pants despite the eight-five-degree weather, she was turning heads as usual.

"I'm obsessed with this place," Violet declared, biting into a tortilla shell filled with black beans, rice, lettuce, and cheese.

Billy said nothing, trying to keep his patience as Violet kept him waiting. Finally, he said, "Do you think you could, maybe, get to the point of this little rendezvous? I do have a magazine to run."

"Here's the deal, *partner*," she said. "As you know, I'm nothing if not an amazing spotter of talent. And, as the creative force behind the club, I am responsible for bringing that talent to us. *Comprendez?*"

Billy rolled his eyes.

"There is a hot new costume designer fresh off the boat from England, and we need to enlist her services ASAP."

"What's wrong with the costumes we have?"

"Nothing's wrong with them. And nothing's right with them either. No one would talk about them either way. We need to change that. I mean, what's the difference between burlesque and stripping? The costumes. So how can we be the best burlesque club in the city if we don't have the best costume designer?"

Billy had a sinking feeling he knew where this conversation was headed.

"So go get the costumer. God knows you can be persuasive," Billy said.

"Oh, I intend to get the costumer. I just need you to write the check."

"Violet, I am hemorrhaging money for this club, with no end in sight."

"It takes money to make money, baby."

"How much do you need?"

"I'm not sure yet. I have to feel her out. My thought is we put her on retainer, and she can't work for anyone else. That's going to cost us some coin, but that's the way I roll."

Billy shook his head. "I'm not an ATM, you know. There has to be some end to this."

"End? We're just getting started. The club hasn't even been open a year. I need your support, Billy. That's the deal. Some day, when the club is successful, you can buy me out."

"Buy you out? You haven't put a dime in!"

"Sweat equity, baby."

Billy felt the words "go fuck yourself" bubbling toward his lips. Then he thought of Tyler and his fear of being outed while his modeling career was still on the rise. And then he thought of what Harvey had suggested: A part of him was still hiding, too. Was he prepared to let go of that fear? Maybe. Soon.

Violet crumpled up the gold foil that had wrapped her burrito. "I'll call you after I get the designer on board. I suggest you have your checkbook ready."

For the first time in as long as she could remember, Nadia felt comfortable in her own skin.

It barely took her half an hour before it felt like she had been dancing in Max's second-floor studio for years. The lighting, the surface of the floor, the smell—it was home. And she didn't feel wasteful that she'd bought workout pants and slippers at the Capezio store downstairs for this little impromptu rehearsal: She was proud of herself for having the good sense to run with the whole thing. She was even feeling excited about the show that night. She didn't have time to obsess over the perfect song, so she just chose something she knew well. She'd listened to the Adele song "Rolling in the Deep" endlessly after her breakup with Jackson, and she knew it backwards and forwards. After an hour of listening to it in the studio and experimenting with various moves, Nadia cobbled together a mix of modern dance and ballet that felt good for her and would look deceptively complex to the audience.

Toward the end of the song, Nadia moved her arms in *port de bras,* then, with the passionate chorus, she launched her body into a series of turns. Just the pleasure of moving in circles through the room seemed to stir her blood, and she did a *pirouette*, rising onto *demi-pointe*.

The door to the studio opened. She looked over to find Max watching her in stupefaction.

"You said you couldn't dance!" he accused.

She slowed down, putting her hands on her hips.

"I said I couldn't go *en pointe.*"

He ignored the correction and walked into the center of the room, pacing for a half a minute. "You could do a *grand jeté* just toward the end," he said.

"I don't want to jump."

"Let me lift you."

"No," she said.

"It would be beautiful just before that last turn."

"Maybe so, but what's the point? You're not going to be onstage with me tonight."

"I don't care about the show tonight. I care about what transpires in this room—I care about every step a dancer takes. Each piece of choreography should be its best. If you aren't guided by that fundamental principal, you are lost."

She admired his passion. And so she relented.

"Fine," she said. "I'll try it once just for the exercise of maximizing the choreography."

He stepped back, and she started the song from the beginning. Instead of feeling self-conscious because he was watching her, she felt exhilarated to have an audience.

She moved fluidly through the song, her anticipation building toward the moment when he would step in to do the lift. And then, it came: He placed his hands around her waist, and as he held her aloft so she could extend her legs into a "split" in the air, she felt a rush of adrenaline that had less to do with successfully executing the move than it did with the physical contact with Max.

He lowered her gently, but instead of stepping back so she could move into her next sequence of steps, he turned her to face him, and in one fluid motion, kissed her.

It took only a few seconds for Nadia to ignore the impulse to resist him. She threw her arms around his neck and pressed her body close to his, feeling a surge of desire she had not experienced in a very long time. He was a good kisser, and it was hard to stop, but the thought of any of his dancers or staff catching them made her pull away.

He held her at arm's length, smiling down at her. Looking

into his dark eyes, she felt a rush of gratitude. She was alive again. He had brought her into the ballet studio; he'd told her it was okay to want to keep some connection to ballet. And now he was reminding her that it was okay to want a man. And, as scary as it was to admit it to herself, the man she wanted was him.

13

Justin knew he was crossing a line. And yet, he felt in the grip of something he had never experienced before. In his mind, he thought of Gemma Kole as teeth-grindingly beautiful. But then, he knew she wasn't. Somehow, it was this very lack of perfection that made her the object of his fascinated lust.

For the past five years of his marriage, he'd managed to stay within the boundaries of what Martha and he defined as "just having fun." He never had sex with another woman without Martha at least watching, if not fully participating. She trusted him to scout out the women to fulfill their more outrageous sexual fantasies. And she had made it clear from the beginning that no matter what happened between them and another woman in the bedroom, he was never to see that woman alone afterward. And living up to that agreement had never been an issue. After he and Martha had their way with someone, no matter how sexy or famous she was, he lost interest.

He hadn't planned to fuck Gemma by himself the night of the party. He'd thought that once he got into it, he'd find a way to get her downstairs so he could summon Martha. But the desire he'd felt for Gemma was so strong, he'd told himself he would give in to it just that one time. Yet now here he was, sitting in his Mercedes outside of Gemma's Williamsburg apartment. In theory, he could still turn around and leave. But he had known there was no turning back from the minute he touched her.

The odd thing was, she was probably the least sexual woman he'd been with in years. Typically, once he got a woman going, even the ones who were initially reluctant to do the three-way with him and Martha—once they started, it was game on. Some of the women who were most reticent at the beginning turned into the wildest ones in bed. But not Gemma. There was something cold and unreachable about her even at the point when she should be at the height of pleasure. And that, more than anything he'd experienced in his entire sexual life, turned him on.

Gemma emerged from the run-down brownstone looking, to him, like an angel. Her unkempt blond hair fanned out behind her as she practically skipped to the car. He didn't know how to read her good mood except to assume that she was excited to see him. This not only vanquished any doubts he had about what he was doing behind Martha's back, it made him hard as a rock.

"You look stunning," he said, getting out to open the car door for her. She wore a black tulle skirt and an elaborately stitched bodice top. "Did you make that outfit?"

"Yes," she said, sitting in the front seat. "By the way, I have to be somewhere at eleven. But that shouldn't be a problem, right?"

Justin's spirits—and erection—flagged.

"You have plans after dinner?"

"Well, yeah. It's sort of business. Couldn't be avoided. Sorry," she said.

He eyed her pillowy lips, the inviting gap between her front teeth. He thought about how still and quiet she had been when he fucked her in the way that made most other girls writhe and scream.

"I forgive you," he said. "We'll just have to eat quickly."

"Our reservation is at seven thirty. That should give us plenty of time."

"We also need time to stop at my place after dinner."

"Oh, really? Isn't that a bit presumptuous of you?"

"Maybe. But your tight scheduling has forced me to be less than subtle."

"Hmm. My tight scheduling. So what's been your excuse up 'til now?"

He laughed and put a hand on her pale thigh. He had no idea how he would make it through dinner. Maybe he wouldn't have to.

"If you're so short on time, maybe we should just head over to my place and order in."

"Whatever you want," she said, looking at her BlackBerry.

He wasn't sure what to make of her lack of enthusiasm. Was that a yes? It certainly was not the kind of response he was used to getting to an invitation. But she wouldn't say okay if she wasn't somewhat interested—would she?

He supposed he would just have to take her home and find out.

Nadia felt no trepidation as she stepped out from behind the red Painted Lady stage curtain. Mallory had expertly pinned Bette's costume—a Tudor-style bodice and full skirt with an easy-off side seam—to fit her. It had only been slightly big to start, and although Mallory grumbled under her breath that she didn't know why Gemma wasn't answering her phone on the night of a show, it turned out fine in the end. And it was a gorgeous creation, with stitching so fine and detail so elaborate, Nadia couldn't help wondering if it wasn't wasted on the burlesque crowd. After all, the costume was intended to end up on the floor. Except, on her it would not. She hoped she wasn't making a mistake trying to get away with a non-striptease dance number. Mallory assured her that burlesque shows were made for variety, and that the crowd would appreciate her piece. Nadia would just have to take her word for it.

On any other night, she might have been more nervous. But her mind was occupied with an endless replay loop of the kiss with Max. She knew he was in the audience, and she knew that they would leave together when the show was over. The only question was what would happen after that.

The rich, throaty sound of Adele's voice filled the room, and Nadia moved into *arabesque penchée.* The crowd watched with rapt attention. When the lusty chorus kicked in, she went into a series of turns. Her heart raced with the thrill of motion. She used to cry to this song, thinking of Jackson. Now the song would always be attached to the memory of the first time Max had touched her.

A sense of abandon overtook her, and by the time the song swelled toward its rapturous ending, she did not hesitate to throw herself into the *grand jeté.*

The curtain came down, and she heard the crowd cheering and whistling. With a sense of confidence she hadn't felt in months, she walked into the dressing room with the pride of a dancer. Maybe she could just perform like this for the club . . . a little ballet to give the show variety, like Mallory had said. It would be so easy. . . .

"Bravo," said Poppy LaRue, zipping up her thigh-high red patent leather boot. "Now next time, give us some burlesque!"

14

Gemma waited for Justin to hold open the door to his townhouse. She stepped inside tentatively, as if expecting a crowd to jump out at her.

"It feels so different empty like this," she said. And it was true: It was difficult to connect this spare, quiet place with the raucous party where she had ended up being fucked poolside.

Justin said nothing, but followed behind her as she wandered slowly through the living room. As much as she wanted to maintain her distance from Justin and all he tried to impress her with, she couldn't help being moved by the art collection. She paused in front of a print by the street artist, Banksy.

"He's from England, too," she said. "I think he's a genius."

Justin nodded. The way he stared at her was a little unnerving, but at least she knew she had him on the line, so to speak.

"Who else do you like?" he said.

"Hmm," she said, thinking. "I like de Kooning."

Justin smiled. "We have some of his work upstairs."

"Really?" she said. "From what period?"

"His 'Woman' series. Do you want to see them?"

She nodded. She did want to see them. But, more important, she wanted to just get this part of her night over with. She would let him fuck her and would know she was locking in the money to get her through the next year without worrying about a steady job. And next, she would get him on board with helping her start her own clothing line. She knew it was just a matter of dangling the right bait. It was not a big deal, really. He was good-looking; he was nice enough. A lot of girls had to do a lot worse to get their careers off the ground.

Justin took her by the hand and led her up the stairs to the third floor master bedroom. On the right wall was the painting *Woman III*. Gemma found the series fascinating, filled with women with distorted facial features and overripe breasts. Her college professor had suggested they represented the threat all men felt from women. She wondered if this was true in Justin's case, or if his wife had been the one to invest in the de Kooning Woman.

"Do you have others?" she asked. But before she could get an answer, Justin had moved behind her, his hands untying the lacing of her top.

Gemma remained motionless, still facing the wall. Her dress fell to her ankles, giving Justin a view of her bare back and her ass in her nude-colored, lace panties. His hands reached around and cupped her breasts, and she felt his hard cock pressing against her back through his pants.

"Are you really going to get me the money you promised for the costume work?" she said to the wall. One of his hands moved from her breast and she felt it behind her, fumbling to get his own pants off.

"Yes," he said, his voice thick with desire. "Money is not an issue for me."

This statement, more than anything he was doing to her nipples, almost made her wet.

Almost.

As usual, as his hands slipped inside her panties, his bare cock now flush against her ass, she felt something close to boredom. All this frantic rubbing against another person just struck her as silly and pointless. The last boyfriend she'd had, Roberto, had broken up with her because she was a "cold fish" in bed. Although he had said it in Spanish, so it sounded almost romantic. But he had not meant it to be romantic—he was infuriated by her lack of responsiveness.

Justin, on the other hand, seemed almost excited by it. Unless she was misreading the situation, he seemed utterly undeterred by her apathy.

She braced herself with one hand on the wall while he fingered her. There had been times, with other lovers, when she had faked small noises to indicate pleasure. She no longer bothered. Instead, she looked up at the painting, pretending she was at a museum, ignoring the poking between her legs.

After a few minutes, he turned her around to face him. He seemed to consider kissing her mouth, but something about her facial expression must have changed his mind. Instead, he moved her to the bed, where he spread her out like a buffet. He bent his head to her breasts, licking and sucking like a greedy child. She wondered if he was going to masturbate on her again, or if he would just fuck her this time. At least the masturbation had offered some entertainment. But no, tonight he took the pedestrian approach of moving her knees apart with his own, then shoving his big cock inside her. She grunted with momentary discomfort, but she suspected he misinterpreted it as pleasure. The pace at which he was thrusting was so frantic she was almost afraid he would hurt himself. The entire bed shook and creaked—her teeth almost chattered.

In what had to be less than two minutes, he came with a sharp cry and a shudder. By the time he rolled off of her, she was already thinking about her meeting with Violet Offender.

He turned to look at her, but she kept staring at the ceiling.

She hoped he didn't say something like, "Was it good for you?" Anything but that.

Mercifully, he kept his mouth shut. She excused herself to use the bathroom.

And then it was on to the next item of business.

Nadia joined everyone congregating backstage after the show. Amidst the flurry of packing up costumes and makeup and changing into street clothes, ideas about where to go next were bandied around the room.

Justin Baxter stepped inside and apologized for missing the show.

"Then you at least have to come out with us," said Poppy. Mallory backed her up on this, insisting Justin join them for their usual post-show drinks, and added he could even choose the place.

Max put his arm around Nadia. She felt her stomach do a flip.

"Let's get out of here," he whispered. Nadia was thinking something along the same lines: She was uncomfortable hanging out with him backstage. Sure, Alec was there, and Poppy's girlfriend was there, too. But it wasn't like she and Max were a couple. Plus, she knew how he felt about the whole burlesque scene, so the less he saw to judge, the better as far as she was concerned.

"Where do you want to go?" she said.

"Come out with us," Poppy said. "We're going to get some drinks."

"Oh, that's okay," Nadia said. "It's been a long day. I didn't even plan on being here tonight. I'm going to head on home."

"Party pooper," said Poppy.

"No, it's true. She stepped in at the last minute to help fill in for everyone who bailed. Thanks, Nadia. You were amazing. I'm tempted to ask you to dance like that at every show, but then you'd never move on to burlesque. And I know you will be equally stunning in a burlesque performance," Mallory said.

"Thanks," Nadia said uncomfortably.

"See you tomorrow—don't forget rehearsal for Justin's party," Mallory called on her way out the door.

"So . . . you're going to go home?" Max asked.

"Yes," she said. "But you're welcome to come with me." She couldn't believe she'd said it like that. So forward! But it was the first time she had felt attracted to someone since Jackson. And after that afternoon preview of what it felt like to have Max's hands on her body, she didn't have the patience to play games. Even if this were a one-time thing, even if he lost what little respect for her he might have, she knew she wanted to join the legion of women who knew what it was like to have Max Jasper as a lover.

Gemma informed the young woman at the door that she was not late for the show and that she was not paying the twenty-dollar admittance fee. She was, in fact, there for a meeting with Violet.

The woman ran one hand over her shaved, tattooed head and left her entranceway perch in a huff. The sound of Lady Gaga's "Judas" played from deep inside the club. Gemma shifted in her heels. Her body was tired—she felt like she'd just been fucked, which she had. Hard.

It was difficult to comprehend Justin Baxter's ardor for her. But it was always like that with men: Their want, their need was so frantic and consuming, it left no room for her to feel much of anything.

It was stifling in that entrance corridor. She had the impulse to leave and told herself she would count to sixty. She'd reached fifty-five by the time the bald girl returned.

"Follow me," she said.

Gemma dutifully trailed her into the club. The room was

loud and crowded. She noticed that people were smoking cigarettes despite the citywide ban on indoor smoking. Onstage, a woman clambered up a pole like an insect, wearing what appeared to be nothing more than a wide ace bandage wrapped around her body. Her long black hair fanned out behind her, and once she reached the top, she disengaged her legs and scissored them around the pole. Gemma stopped in her tracks, riveted.

"Who is that?" Gemma said.

"That's Violet. You probably don't recognize her because of the wig."

Gemma watched Violet's body contort into positions that would seem impossible on the ground, never mind fifteen feet in the air.

"Is that... considered burlesque?"

"It is in here," said the girl. "Violet wants you to wait for her in her office. She'll be with you in a minute."

They looped around the back of the room and then down a flight of stairs to a small room. Gemma sat on a red leather couch that faced a glass desk. The desk held only a Mac laptop and a stack of magazines.

The bald girl left her alone.

Gemma realized she was hungry. Skipping dinner probably hadn't been the best idea. But she had known what Justin wanted, and her goal had been to get him more invested in her, not to have a long, drawn-out date.

She checked her BlackBerry, then reapplied her lipstick even though it was still fresh from when she'd dressed at Justin's. Nervous and increasingly uncomfortable, she wondered if she should leave.

The door opened and closed just as quickly. Violet Offender leaned against the door as if holding off a tornado.

"What a fucking night," she said, walking to the chair behind the glass desk. Her body was slick with sweat and shiny with glitter. She wore a long, white T-shirt so thin it was sheer. Her bare breasts and black lace panties were clearly visible through it. On her feet she wore four-inch heels with wide straps and lots of buckles. Gemma recognized them from Jimmy Choo's latest collection. She'd wanted a pair herself, but of course could not afford them. *Burlesque must pay from the other side of the desk.*

"Did you get to see any of the show?" Violet asked, putting her feet up on the desk. The T-shirt hiked up to her waist, and Gemma couldn't help admiring her long, tanned legs with toned thighs, and her obviously taut stomach. And then, her glance sweeping upward, Gemma took in the swell of Violet's high, pert but round breasts.

From across the desk, Violet's wide green eyes appraised Gemma right back. Gemma felt terribly pale and terribly British. An hour ago it had seemed obvious why Justin Baxter should lust for her with such intensity. Now, she wondered how a man could want anyone but Violet Offender. She seemed, at that moment, to be the epitome of feminine allure.

"Yes," Gemma said. "I . . . saw you."

"What'd ya think?"

"I've never seen anything quite like it," Gemma said.

Violent nodded as if hearing something profound. "Exactly," she said. "That's where you come in."

"I don't follow," Gemma said.

"Did you see what I was wearing?"

"Yes."

"What was it?"

"A . . . dress? A dress that looked like a bandage wrapped around your body."

"Close: It *was* a bandage wrapped around my body. Now, don't you think a performance of that caliber deserves a more sophisticated costume?"

"Um, yeah?"

"So that's why I called you here. I saw photos of costumes you've done for The Painted Lady. I want you to stop working for them and work for me. Exclusively."

"Well, I'm afraid that's not possible. I don't work for The Painted Lady. I work for Agnes, and she gives me the assignments."

"Oh, well then this should be easier than I thought. I know that old bat is cheap as hell. I'll pay you more."

"It's not that simple. I'm also doing some side work for Justin Baxter. And he might be putting me on retainer."

"How convenient. Are you fucking him?"

Gemma blanched. "Of course not," she said.

"Yeah, right," said Violet. "So what's the guy you're *not* fucking offering to pay to keep you on retainer? 'Cause let me tell you, I don't care how great you're blowing him, it's his wife who holds the purse strings."

"Justin made the offer, not his wife."

"I'm sure he did. I'm just saying, no matter how pussy-whipped you've got him, he can only pay you what Martha lets him pay you."

"I don't know anything about that."

"Fine. See for yourself. Let me know what he offers you. In the meantime, at the very least, I need you to do our costumes for the Las Vegas Burlesque Festival."

"I'm already working on that for Justin."

"I'm sure. What's The Painted Lady doing for their theme?"

"I don't think I should discuss that with you."

"You'll just have to make sure ours is better."

"I'm not working with you, Violet. Working exclusively for The Painted Lady means no outside work—not even for the Vegas Burlesque Fest."

Violet leaned back in her chair, stretching. Gemma watched Violet's hard nipples strain against the sheer fabric.

"Are you from London?" Violet asked.

"No," said Gemma.

"But you are from England, right?"

"Yes."

"I'm going to call you London," said Violet. "That okay with you?"

"Certainly not," Gemma said.

"So tell me, London: Have you ever been dominated?" Violet said.

"Excuse me?"

"Have you ever been tied up? Blindfolded?"

Gemma said nothing. She simply stared at Violet blankly.

"Is that a yes?" said Violet.

"No. It's . . . no."

"You've never been whipped?"

"Lord, no!" said Gemma.

Violet straightened up in her chair, then leaned forward, elbows on the desk. She tapped her fingertips on her jaw. Gemma noticed her nails were painted a purple so dark it was nearly black. She wondered if she could get away with that color on her own hands.

Violet focused her eyes on her with an intensity that made Gemma squirm.

"I think you'd like it," Violet said finally.

"Like what?"

"Being dominated."

Gemma exhaled a nervous laugh. Violet rose from her seat and walked around to the front of the desk. She was so close Gemma could smell her. Gemma felt Violet appraising her like a piece of cattle, her eyes moving from Gemma's feet, sweeping over her body, trying to make eye contact, which Gemma resisted. "And I'm never wrong about these things."

Gemma found herself holding her breath. She didn't dare look at Violet until Violet moved from her perch in front of the desk to walk past her to the front of the small office. She opened the door and held it.

"When—and not if, *when*—Justin flakes on paying you, give me a call. I'll be waiting."

15

Nadia led Max through the lobby of her building, as self-conscious as if she was sneaking a boy into her dorm. The doorman, Francisco, eyed Max warily even as he greeted Nadia with his usual, "Good evening, Ms. Grant." Francisco had been a big fan of Jackson. They always used to talk about basketball. Nadia had never followed a professional sports team—she couldn't name a professional athlete if her life depended on it. Not even the ones married to Kardashians.

"Do you like basketball?" she asked Max, searching for conversation as they were enveloped in the intimate space of the elevator. She tried to ignore the pain in her back, a sharp twinge on the lower right side just above her buttocks. Ever since her last injury, she felt this pain every time she exerted herself on her feet. She accepted it as part of the new reality of her life and resolved not to let it ruin her night.

"No," he said. She took this as a positive sign. "But I do occasionally watch ice hockey."

"Really? Why ice hockey?"

"My mother was Canadian," he said. And something about his face looked strained when he mentioned her. She remembered him saying that his parents had been an unlikely couple, and that they never should have married. She wanted to ask him about that. "The sport is so ingrained in Canadians that I couldn't help but inherit some of her enthusiasm for it." He reached for Nadia's hand.

She felt a flutter in her stomach. He was the most irresistible guy she had met in as long as she could remember. Maybe ever. Luckily, she had already made peace with the notion that she had no intention of resisting. It was time for her to get back in the game, and he was the perfect player to bring her onto the court again. Or, the ice, as the case might be.

She opened the door to the apartment, Max following closely behind her. Whenever she brought a guest to the apartment for the first time, she saw the grandness through her guest's eyes, and was instantly compelled to explain, "It's my great aunt's. She's in Paris now, and I'm taking care of it for her."

"It's beautiful. Really classic."

She felt proud of the apartment and more comfortable on her own turf than she ever had felt before in Max's presence. If it weren't for the pain in her back, prodding her to get off her feet, she could almost have forgotten the turmoil of the past nine months.

She offered him a drink, but he said he just wanted water. He sat on the couch, prompting Twiggy to jump off in a huff.

Nadia made her way to the kitchen, and the twinge shot through her right side more deeply. She inadvertently cried out.

"What's wrong?" Max asked, jumping up.

"Oh, nothing," she said, hiding behind the kitchen counter as she rubbed her lower back.

"That didn't sound like nothing," Max said, appearing in the entranceway to the kitchen.

She forced herself to straighten up and retrieved the filtered water from the refrigerator.

"It's not a big deal. Sometimes my back hurts after I've been on my feet a while."

"You do physical therapy since the injury, right?"

"Of course."

"Have you told them about the back pain?"

"Yes. They said it's normal to compensate for loss of balance or strength in one area by overextending yourself in another area—usually your back. They said in time, when my leg muscles have returned to full strength, the pain will go away."

She handed him a glass of water. He set it on the black marble countertop and put his arm around her shoulders, steering her back to the living room, where he took her by the hand and seated her on the couch.

"Lie down," he said.

"Excuse me?"

"Lie down on your stomach. I'll massage your back."

She thought she'd gone into this evening ready to roll, but now, in the moment of truth, she froze.

"No, no—I'm fine. Really. That's not necessary."

"Nadia, don't be ridiculous."

He sat on the couch and looked at her with his big, dark eyes.

She knew that she *was* probably being ridiculous. Also overriding her reserve was the fact that she wanted him to touch her, and that compelled her to follow his direction; she stretched out on the couch in front of him, taking care that her long sundress stayed down over her legs, not hiking up, as she moved into the prone position.

She turned her face to the side, fanning her hair over her cheek so she felt less on display.

The sundress left her back bare to the middle, with thin straps. Max eased the straps over her shoulders and pulled the swath of fabric in the middle of her back down even farther so he had room to work.

He pressed both hands into her upper back, spreading his palms over her shoulder blades. She exhaled deeply, experiencing an instant release of muscle tension.

"Do you have any lotion?" he said.

"Um, yeah. I'll get it."

"No—stay relaxed. Just tell me where to find it."

She directed him to the linen closet in the hallway outside the master bedroom. She was fairly certain there was an unopened container of Lubriderm from her last shopping trip to CVS. Of course, there was definitely an open moisturizer in her own bathroom, but she couldn't recall what condition she'd left the bathroom in that morning, so she wouldn't risk sending him in there.

He left her on the couch, and she immediately missed the warmth and gentle pressure of his hands. When he returned to smooth the moisturizer along her back, she sighed with pleasure.

"You're good at this," she said.

"I think you just really needed it."

He hit a knot at the base of her neck, and she tensed as his fingers worked at it.

"Breathe through it," he told her. His hands worked down her spine, until he pressed the base of each hand against her upper buttocks, kneading them gently, which elicited a tingling, rolling sensation of pleasure that made her squirm.

He lifted her dress to her upper thighs and moved his hands down her legs. Even her muscled legs, crafted by the toughest taskmaster—ballet—were no match for the strength of his hands. He kneaded her thighs, then her calves, and she felt her muscles yield to his firm but gentle touch, melting away months of pressure. And when his hands continued moving up, she did not object as he pulled her dress above her waist, his thumbs grazing the inside of her thighs.

This is it, she thought, as his fingers skimmed the edge of her panties.

"Turn over," he said, so quietly she was not sure he'd actually said it. But when he stopped touching her, she realized he had. He was waiting for her to move.

She complied, moving onto her back. The skirt of her dress twisted around her waist. When she tried to adjust it, he held her hands at her sides.

"Relax," he said. She felt her heart beating fast.

"Okay," she said. And then she let him lift her dress up, over her shoulders, her arms reaching above her head to let him remove it entirely.

His eyes swept over her. She wished that, for once, she'd worn a bra. It would have at least bought her a few more minutes of modesty. But with her tiny build, she never bothered with what was ultimately a useless undergarment. And so she was there on display for him, nude except for her petal pink lace underwear.

The expression in his eyes as he looked down at her was one of such intensity, she almost couldn't endure looking at him. He did not say she was beautiful, but his gaze told her so.

He dipped his head, his dark hair brushing across her chest softly as he took one nipple into his mouth. The gesture seemed audacious to her, just as everything he said and did was audacious.

She moved one hand to stroke his hair, and she felt a warm throbbing between her legs from the mere flicker of his tongue against her breast. When his teeth grazed her nipple, she surprised herself by moaning.

Max moved one hand down her body as his mouth kissed and sucked her breasts. She found herself spreading her legs for him even before his fingers reached her, and when his finger was inside her, she had to resist the urge to use her own hands to press him even deeper.

"That feels so good," she said. He moved his body almost on top of hers, now kissing her neck and then her mouth. She used both hands to hold his face to hers, kissing him until she was breathless.

"Do you want to move to the bedroom?" he asked.

She didn't—the logistics of getting to the other room, naked and highly aroused, were not appealing to her. But on a practical level, it would be more comfortable. Plus, she had condoms in her nightstand—from the early days with Jackson, before they were engaged, before she had gone on the pill. Before he was cheating on her.

Ugh. She pushed away all thoughts of Jackson. "Sure." He moved off of her and helped her stand. She pulled a chenille blanket from the far end of the couch and wrapped it around herself.

"Why are you bashful?" he said. "You have the most beautiful body I've ever seen."

She didn't know what to say to this, so she simply walked to her room and let him follow.

Nadia sat on the edge of the twin bed. "I decided when I moved in not to use the master bedroom," she explained. "This just felt more comfortable to me."

"It's cute," he said, pulling her to him and kissing her. "Kind of like a dorm room."

This made her smile since she had thought of a dorm, too, when she'd brought him through the lobby. And it was possible she had not been this nervous with a man since college.

He gently pulled the blanket from her and pressed her down on her bed. She lay back and watched him remove his shirt and pants. She knew she was spoiled with these dancers as lovers:

Their bodies were so magnificent. His thighs were long and lean with visible muscles—how could she not want them wrapped around her?

She reached one arm back and pulled open the drawer of her nightstand, feeling around for the plastic of the condom wrapper. She found it and handed it to Max.

He took it wordlessly as she set her eyes on his cock for the first time. The sight of it, big and hard for her, stilled all of her anxious thoughts. She was free to act on instinct and drive, and so she leaned forward and licked the length of his cock, down to his balls, then brushed her lips over the tip before taking him in her mouth. While she sucked his cock, his hands played over her breasts.

"Nadia," he moaned, and the sound of him saying her name like that, thick with desire, set her off.

"Fuck me," she said, shocking herself. Where had that come from? That was not part of her typical verbal repertoire. Nonetheless, it seemed to do the trick: Max had the condom on before she could blink twice.

He knelt over her, and she lay back, looked up at his cock. She ran her hand over it lightly, and their eyes locked. His desire for her, so evident in his eyes, removed any last ounce of reserve. She spread her legs and guided him inside her.

She gasped. His cock filled her completely—any more, and it would have been too much.

"Is this okay?" he said.

"Yes," she breathed, kissing his neck. She felt the strength of his body as he fucked her. She didn't want him to worry about her—she was small, but not delicate.

"I've wanted you so much," he said, his hands underneath her, cupping her ass, helping her body move more seamlessly with his own.

She knew she was going to come and was embarrassed that it

took so little. She felt herself contract around him, the wave of pleasure through her body, and then a sense of calm. Her head cleared for a moment, as if she were coming out of a daydream.

And then Max's movements quickened, the thrusting of his pelvis so fast and hard it carried her own body along with its rhythm. She felt he was literally riding her, and along with the thrusting, she felt his cock almost vibrating inside of her. The sensations were so extreme and exciting that, to her shock, she shuddered with another orgasm, more powerful than the first. Seconds later, he cried out, his mouth open against her cheek, his hands clutching her ass.

After a moment of stillness, he rolled off her. They were both slick with sweat.

He reached for her hand.

"You were worth the wait," he said.

"What wait? I've known you for just a few days!"

"Exactly," he said, and they laughed.

Nadia curled her body against his. She felt a sense of calm that she recognized as relief. Between the months of celibacy following her breakup with Jackson, and the limits on her dancing after the accident, she had felt completely out of touch with her body. Working with Mallory had helped a little. But the way she had felt while Max made love to her was like surfacing after being underwater for too long.

The magnitude of how miserable she had been finally hit her, and she started to cry. She rolled over, hoping to hide her tears from him, but he wouldn't let her.

"What's wrong?" he said, pulling her back to him.

"Nothing's wrong. Just the opposite—I'm so relieved. I feel like you gave me my body back."

He held her face in his hands and kissed her forehead, her nose.

"If I've given it back to you, then I should have a say in how you treat it," he smiled. "Don't throw it away on that club, Nadia. Spend time with me at the studio. You have a place there."

She sat up, pulling her sheet over her breasts.

"You're too hard on the burlesque thing," she said. "As much as you've given me something tonight, burlesque got me out of this apartment when I just wanted to hide under the covers forever. It's so important for me to feel like I'm moving on with my life, not trying to go back to something that doesn't exist anymore."

Max sighed. "I'm not saying burlesque didn't serve a purpose. I'm saying it's not right for you long-term."

"I haven't even successfully performed yet."

"Yes, you did. You were magnificent tonight."

She sighed. "I didn't take my clothes off."

"You shouldn't have to. It's beneath you."

"No—it's not. You have to stop thinking like that. That is the art form. I believe in art forms as they are defined—for ballet, it's dancing *en pointe*, which I can no longer do. For burlesque, it's a striptease. I'm not going to dance ballet half-assed, and I'm not doing burlesque half-assed, either. And I want you to stop asking me to."

"Why are you so hell-bent on this? It's not like you have a full schedule of club dates set. When's your next performance?"

"A few weeks. I'm performing at Martha Pike's birthday party."

"Her birthday party," Max repeated.

"Yes. Justin and Martha throw big, elaborate parties. Mallory told me the guest list is always the most interesting mix of celebrities, artists, socialites. . . ."

"Yes. I've heard."

"It will be good exposure for me."

"*Exposure* being the operative word."

"Please just back off on this, Max. It's not your business."

He sighed. "I care about you. I can't just sit back and let you make a huge mistake."

"It's not a mistake. And even if it is, it's my mistake to make."

"If we're going to be together, then we have to be able to discuss this."

"Are we going to . . . be together?" Nadia said.

"I'm starting to suspect we might," he said, pulling her against him. It felt so good to be in his arms, it was tempting to just give in, to let him hold her and love her and tell her their relationship was the most important thing. But she'd believed in that sort of thing once before, and where had it gotten her?

"Then you're going to have to learn to accept the fact that I'm done with ballet, and I've moved on to burlesque."

He kissed the top of her head. "I don't know if I can do that," he said.

"Then we're going to have a problem."

16

Mallory and Justin Baxter were among the last few left at Nolita House, a bar and restaurant around the corner from The Painted Lady. Alec was deep in conversation with one of his old cronies from his days as a staff writer at the magazine *Gruff*, leaving Mallory to make a run to the bar for one last round. Justin joined her to pay the tab.

"You don't have to do that," she said.

"I want to," he said. "Martha and I are so happy with everything you and Alec have accomplished so far with the club. If things continue at this rate, we might actually make a profit by the end of our second year."

"Well, I appreciate that, but remember we're riding on the buzz of being new," Mallory said. "We need to make sure we continue the momentum. That's why I'm putting so much energy into the LVBF, and I'm trying to make sure the girls feel that passion to win. Plus, the prize money could go back into your pockets and maybe help you feel even better about keeping the train rolling."

"Don't worry about that, Mallory. What I'm trying to tell you is that we do feel good about it. And I know you're focused on the LVBF, but when that's done, you should think about your wedding. I know that's where Alec wants to invest *his* time."

She looked at him suspiciously. Was he being reproachful? Had Alec said something to him about her not exactly being Martha Stewart–esque about the wedding planning?

"Jeez, I just got engaged a few days ago, and I have a flurry of events on deck—not least of which is your party for Martha."

"Oh, I know," he said with a smile, and she realized he was just making conversation, not judging her. "And speaking of Martha—she wanted me to make sure you knew that if you had any trouble booking the venue for the wedding, she'd be happy to call in some favors. You know how places get booked so far in advance."

"Oh, that's really sweet. But I'm not in a rush.... I'm sure we'll find something for next year. But I really appreciate it. Martha's the best."

A pained look crossed Justin's face.

"What is it?" Mallory asked. "Is something wrong with Martha?"

He shook his head. "No," he said. "It's me. Can I tell you something that's strictly between us?" he asked. Mallory glanced at Alec across the room. He caught her eye and smiled at her, holding up his index finger to indicate one more minute. She nodded to let him know she was fine.

"Um, sure," she said, not at all certain she wanted to hear whatever it was Justin was going to share with her. But she wanted to be supportive. He'd been a good friend to her and Alec. He and Martha both had.

"I met a woman. And I crossed a line I shouldn't have crossed," he said.

Mallory nodded, not sure what she was supposed to say. So she said the first thing that came to mind.

"But don't you and Martha have an... open relationship?" she asked. She'd heard the stories—from very reliable sources—about the Baxters' sexcapades. She couldn't imagine what constituted "crossing a line" in their world. But then again, there had been a time when people had assumed she and Alec had an open relationship, but in the end the only thing "open" about their extracurricular activities were the wounds they created.

"Compared to most couples, yes. But we have what you'd call our own rules. And I'm violating them and I can't seem to stop."

He was so visibly upset, Mallory put her hand over his to calm him down.

"I know from my own relationship how hard and confusing it is to have a relationship in which, with the best of intentions, you give each other some 'freedom.' Alec and I tried to make it work for a while, and then we realized that we had to close ranks in order to protect what we had—that our intimacy was more valuable than freedom. Maybe it's time for you and Martha to do the same. You guys are a great couple, Justin. I'm guessing that she makes you happy in ways that have nothing to do with sex. I know you both have been really adventurous, but maybe it's opening you up to temptations that just aren't fair—to yourself or to her."

"It isn't the freedom that's the problem. It's that I've genuinely fallen for someone else."

"Oh, Justin!" Mallory put her head in her hands. She hated to see this happen to the Baxters. They were quirky, yes—perhaps even a bit subversive. But also one of the most lively, creative, inspiring couples she'd ever known. She had believed that their shared love of art and pussy made them bulletproof.

"I don't know what to do."

"Try taking some time away from the other woman," Mallory said. "Go away with Martha. Or, bring someone else home for the two of you. Find some way to connect with her."

"Okay," Justin said. But Mallory could tell his response was rote. He was already halfway out the door, and he wanted permission to close it behind him. She could not give him that.

She looked across the bar at Alec and thought of how close they had come to losing each other. She thought of something Agnes had once told her about what sustains a marriage: A marriage lasts when there is never a time that both people want to end it at the same moment. "Because everyone thinks of leaving at one time or another," she said.

"Everyone thinks of leaving sometimes," Mallory said to Justin, wanting to impart some bit of Agnes's wisdom and let him know the feelings were normal so he wouldn't do anything impulsive.

"I feel like I should tell her," he said.

"No!" Mallory said, so loudly and vehemently she surprised even herself. "Don't. Trust me. It will only hurt her. You need to try to get past this on your own. And if you do, she never has to know. Martha loves you. I think this is what she would want. Don't you?"

He nodded. "I just don't know what I want," he said.

Alec made his way over to them and put his arm around Mallory. She leaned into him, breathing in his smell and resolving to be more proactive about their wedding plans. She would take Martha up on her offer to find a venue.

"Ready to go?" Alec asked, kissing the top of her head.

"Ready when you are," she said.

"You're a lucky man," Justin said to Alec, doing his best to smile. If Alec noticed that their boss's usual bravado was absent, he didn't let on. Mallory twisted her engagement ring, thankful the days of doubt and drama between Alec and her were long behind them.

She planned to keep it that way.

* * *

Justin opened the door to his apartment, thinking that just five hours earlier he'd walked in with Gemma by his side. He hoped his bed still smelled like her.

"Hey, baby—surprise!" Martha roused her bulky frame from the couch and greeted him at the door.

"Jesus! You startled me. What are you doing back so soon?"

"Business is booming, but I missed my hubby. Is that so wrong?"

He let her embrace him, and as he put his arms around her thick frame, he felt conflicted. He wished he could confide in her how he felt about Gemma. In most ways Martha was his best friend, and she would probably understand how he felt. She was a woman of huge appetites herself. She'd noticed Gemma at their party the opening night of The Painted Lady and had given him the go-ahead to bring her upstairs for the two of them. If he confessed now and promised to stop, she would forgive him. There would be damage, sure—but not irreparable.

The problem was, he knew he wasn't ready to stop.

His thoughts turned immediately to the state of the bedroom. What condition had he left it in? And had she been upstairs already?

"Why didn't you text me that you were coming home early?" he said.

"I wanted to surprise you!" she said, clearly without guile. Justin thought that if his evening had gone as originally planned, she would have been the one surprised. "Did you go to the club tonight?"

"Yes," he said, hiding the lie he was about to tell by walking to the bar and pouring himself a scotch. "It was a packed house. Mallory had Nadia dance some sort of modern ballet hybrid that was a hit even though she didn't take off her costume. And then afterward we all went to Nolita House for drinks. I wish you'd told me you were back. You could have met us there." He sat next to her on the couch.

"I'm too exhausted for any of that," she said, smiling. "I'm just happy to be here and see your gorgeous face."

"I'm happy to see you, too," he lied. Actually, it was half-true. He was happy to see her. He just wished he'd had the good sense to keep their relationship on a freelance basis.

Justin had been twenty-six years old when he'd met the then thirty-two-year-old Martha, a self-made millionairess who ran her own sex toy empire. He had just been fired from his job at a Wall Street firm on an ethics violation. He'd never work on Wall Street again, and after a few months of living off his savings, had few options other than returning to his hometown of Roslyn, Long Island, with his tail between his legs to work at his father's car dealership. That's when he'd met his old girlfriend from NYU, Lexy Kleiner, for drinks one night. Lexy was one of the few people around whom he could relax his male ego and confide his dire financial situation. Lexy was as much of a scrappy, streetwise gambler as himself. And sure enough, when he'd told her he was broke and virtually unemployable, she had said she had the perfect gig for him: She and a friend were running a male escort service.

And it was a perfect job: He was handsome, sexually insatiable, and genuinely loved women. Not just beautiful women, but women of every shape and type. For Justin, variety really was the spice of life—a quality that made for troubled relationships, but excellent performance in his new gig as Manhattan's most in-demand gigolo. Three months into his tenure, when he was taking home enough unreported income to not only be able to pay off his debt but also to save for a down payment on an apartment in Tribeca, he started working with his most steady client: Martha Pike. She provided not only a reliable flow of cash, but insight into what it meant to be truly wealthy: the private planes, the A-list parties, the VIP treatment at the best restaurants and stores in the city. Suddenly, his pocket money was looking like chump change.

Before long, she had him booked every weekend. Sometimes she had a female escort along for the ride. Justin couldn't believe he was getting paid for the nights of fine dining, exclusive clubbing, and three-way sex. Then the day came when she asked him to not see any other clients. Justin was fine with that arrangement—he made more than enough money with Martha alone. One day, she suggested a new business arrangement: They could get married. He would have access to all of her homes, cars, and entrée to the places he had come to know and love through his association with her. She would set him up in the business of his choosing. And they would still endeavor to have adventurous sex—sometimes with other people. The only stipulation was that he had to sign her ironclad prenup, and he was not allowed to have sex with other women without Martha's being present. He had eagerly signed on the dotted line.

For five years, it had been the perfect partnership. They traveled the world. They hosted parties that were the talk of both coasts. They were patrons of the arts and sexual connoisseurs. Martha called him her inspiration, and even named a line of dildos after him. Their relationship deepened, their notoriety spread, and her fortune grew. Justin knew most people assumed he was just with her for her money. But their friends knew it was more than that—knew that he loved her in his own way. And he truly did. Never, in all this time, had his head been turned by someone else for more than a few hours. Until now.

"The show was excellent tonight," he fabricated. "Mallory and Alec are really giving it everything they've got. But I've been thinking we could do something more to shore up the buzz on The Painted Lady."

"Oh? What?"

"We need to lock in the costume designer. Make sure she doesn't work for the competition. I think the look and feel of the club is what sets it apart, and if someone else can get that look for the right price, we're going to lose our edge."

"Don't be silly. Agnes said she barely has time to fulfill all of our work. She's not helping the competition."

"Agnes isn't doing all the work—it's her assistant making the costumes. She's young and trying to make a name for herself. She's bound to get her name out there to other clubs. I think she's the real brains and talent behind Agnes's operation, and I don't want her working for someone like Violet or anyone else who is just waiting for the novelty of The Painted Lady to wear off."

"So what are you suggesting?" Martha asked, squinting at him. He knew she was switching out of doting wife mode and into shrewd business mind mode.

"I say we put her on retainer. Give her a contract. She does all of our work and no one else's. We pay her a flat monthly rate for all the costumes, no matter how many."

"Or how few," she countered.

"It will be a lot of work."

Martha stood and walked to the bar. She eased the strain on her hip by leaning heavily on her cane. The trip had clearly taken a toll on her.

"Let me do that for you," he said, stepping in to pour her vodka.

"How much are you thinking?" she said.

He told her the amount, and she laughed.

"That's absurd. For that blond girl? Honey, if you're paying her that much money, she'd better be giving us something more than costumes. And since I haven't seen her pussy yet, I'll give you the benefit of the doubt that she's not. The answer is no. We pay her and Agnes per show. I don't mind putting money into this club, but I'm not that little chippie's benefactor." She took her glass from him, and her eyes were hard and unusually cold to him. "And you'd better not be either."

17

The monstrous, illogical event that was Martha Baxter's birthday bash incurred a major glitch one week before the party. Justin happened to mention to Mallory how many people were invited, prompting Mallory to check the fire ordinance legal occupancy limit of the club. Of course, Justin's guest list exceeded it.

"You have to move the party," she told him.

"I'll just pay the fine," he told her.

"It's a safety hazard!" Mallory insisted. And so he agreed to move it to the only possible alternative venue on such short notice: his apartment.

Fortunately, 40 Bond Street was dramatic enough to make the transition from club to apartment relatively painless. Gemma worked her magic and transformed the living room into an Oscar night venue in Old Hollywood style. In keeping with the theme of Hollywood's Golden Age, guests were instructed to come dressed in their finest mid-twentieth century ensembles. As for the dancers of the The Painted Lady, Poppy, Mallory, Nadia, and Bette had spent weeks preparing to perform as their silver-screen alter egos: Poppy would be Grace Kelly circa *To Catch a Thief*. Bette would perform dressed as Marlene Dietrich in her role as Lola Lola in, of course, *The Blue Angel*. And Mallory and Nadia were dressed as the Angelina Jolie and Jennifer Aniston of the 1950s: Elizabeth Taylor and Debbie Reynolds.

It had been Mallory's idea. Nadia didn't know the story of what was the biggest entertainment industry scandal of its day.

"Elizabeth Taylor was this stunningly beautiful diva, and Debbie Reynolds was America's sweetheart, married to Eddie Fisher. He left her for Elizabeth."

"Really?" said Nadia.

"Yes. Haven't you ever wondered why Carrie Fisher is so screwed up?" said Mallory.

"I thought it was from not being able to escape the Princess Leia association."

As promised, Mallory choreographed a dance for the two of them to share the stage. She hoped Nadia would be able to go through with stripping, but if not, the audience would never know that she was supposed to. She could play right into the good girl / bad girl fantasy.

"I don't know why you coddle her so much," Bette said, already dressed in her cabaret costume of frilly knickers, gartered stockings, and top hat. They were using the guest bedroom as a dressing room. Justin was keeping Martha out until eight, by which time all of the guests should have arrived. Gemma was busy with last-minute stage settings, and Nadia and Poppy were scouting out another few bottles of champagne.

"I'm not coddling her. I'm encouraging her. She's a great dancer who's trying something new. You're too judgmental."

"Agnes would never waste time on someone who couldn't go through with a performance. She'd be so out on her ass."

"Yeah, I know. And maybe Nadia will never come through.

But I think I see some of myself in her—the way I was when you showed me your wicked ways," she said with a smile.

"The difference is, it only took me about three minutes to get your clothes off."

"Okay, let's not go there. I'm almost a married woman," Mallory said, waving her ring finger.

"Yeah. So when's the big day? Shouldn't you be getting all bridezilla about now?"

Mallory sighed and gestured for Bette to help her get into her Liz Taylor as Cleopatra costume. "I should," Mallory said. "But I'm too busy thinking about Vegas."

"Is that all there is to it?" Bette said.

"Yes. Of course. What else would it be?"

"I don't know. Just checking."

"Well, thanks for your concern, but I'm fine. I will set a date and think about actually getting married when things slow down."

"And Alec is fine with that?"

"Sure. Why wouldn't he be? Besides—I need to coordinate with your schedule."

"Why with my schedule?"

"How can I get married without my maid of honor? Or, in your case, maid of dishonor."

"Are you serious?"

"Sure. Why do you look so surprised?"

"I thought you would ask one of your happy housewife friends—Julie or Allison."

"I've known them for a lot longer, it's true. But I really don't believe Alec and I would be together today if it weren't for you. You forced both of us to change in ways that saved our relationship."

Despite her efforts to maintain nonchalance, Bette beamed.

"Glad to be of service. And for the record, I'd be happy to

be your maid of dishonor. You just might have to get married at whatever film set I'm on. Now step into this bodice. I don't know how that British chick creates these things."

Justin turned his key in the apartment door, making sure Martha was close behind him. He had encouraged her not to drink too much at her birthday dinner at Per Se, and as a result she was now sober enough to appreciate the spectacle that awaited her.

"Surprise!" A chorus of costumed well-wishers greeted them with shrieks, popping corks, and clapping.

Martha turned to him with gratitude shining in her eyes.

"I can't believe you did this," she said with a smile as broad and genuine as any he'd ever seen from her. He was relieved. Ever since their conversation about paying Gemma Kole a retainer, things had been frosty between them. Or maybe the coolness was just a figment of his guilty conscience. And in the meantime, as much as his cock was aching for Gemma, he had avoided her so he could stall for time to get the money he'd promised her.

But she was there tonight, the party as much her brainchild as it had been his own. She was dressed as Brigitte Bardot—or maybe it wasn't a costume and she just looked like the French actress. Regardless, she was the embodiment of every erotic fantasy he'd ever had. With her hair in a messy loose ponytail, her big eyes smudged with dark liner, and her gap-toothed smile, it took all of his control not to break through the crowd and grab her.

The living room had been transformed into an Academy Awards theater, with rows of seating and a stage. Alec would be acting as host. Justin had worked with Alec and Mallory to write joke "awards" for their friends—Best Hamptons House, Best Divorce—and Mallory had found a Web site to order fake Oscar statuettes online. And for entertainment, they had The

Painted Lady women to perform as Hollywood legends. He knew he should focus on the party agenda, but all he could think about was the possibility of getting Gemma upstairs.

He checked to make sure Martha was occupied, and sure enough she was already enveloped in a crowd of friends. Justin broke free to head to the bar, where he found Alec drinking a beer and talking to an editor from *Vanity Fair*. Justin felt a slight pang, once again missing Billy Barton and the days when *Gruff* magazine always had the scoop on the Baxter parties.

"What time do you want to start the show?" Alec asked.

"Eight thirty. Give everyone a chance to mingle." Justin ordered a scotch. "I'll go check and see how the girls are doing upstairs."

Justin took his drink, the ice clinking reassuringly against the crystal glass. In the narrow foyer between the living room and the bar, he saw Gemma. He wanted to believe she had been looking for him, but knew that was probably wishful thinking.

"You did a great job," he said. "This place is absolutely transformed."

"Your staff was quite helpful," she said in that clipped, British way of hers.

"I'm going upstairs to check on the performers. Want to help make sure the costumes are all set?"

"Sure," she said.

But once up the stairs, he veered in the opposite direction from the girls' dressing room, pulling Gemma into his bedroom instead.

"How did I know we would end up in here?" she said.

He closed and locked the door, then turned her back to him so he could unzip her dress. The silver lamé fell to the floor.

He cupped her breasts from behind, then pushed her gently onto the bed. She tried to turn over on her back, but he held her on her stomach and spread her legs. He pressed his face between the curve of her ass and the edge of her pussy, and inhaled deeply. He saw her hand clutch a pillow, and he hoped it was because she wanted him as much as he wanted her. He licked the folds of her pussy lips, then stuck his tongue inside, his hands holding her ass. She squirmed under his grip, and he let her turn over. At the sight of her full cunt spread before him, already glistening wet, he lost any sense of pacing and hurriedly pulled off his pants. With his cock unleashed, he knelt before her at the edge of the bed. He wished she would take him in her mouth, but he knew by now that she would do nothing to him—that the most he could hope for was that she would allow him to touch and lick and fuck her until his feverish need was quieted.

He moved on top of her, his mouth tugging on her nipples while he inserted his cock inside her. As usual, she was still as a doll while he thrust and grunted like a clumsy schoolboy. He felt he could come already, and he tried to calm himself down. Who knew how many weeks he would have to wait to get her alone again—he needed to make this last. And yet the throbbing pulse in his cock told him there was no mental trick that would delay what was sure to be a monstrous orgasm.

"Wait," she said.

"What?" he managed to gasp.

"Stop."

It took every ounce of will to pull out of her, but he did. He held his red, angry penis in his hand, stroking it gently.

"What's wrong?" he said.

"I came up here to talk to you."

"To talk," he repeated, rolling onto his back and trying to ignore the urge to finish.

"Yes. You've been scarce these past few weeks. I've been working on the costumes. You owe me some money."

"Okay," he said.

"What does that mean?"

"I'm... I'll have it soon."

"You don't have the money, do you? It's all Martha's."

"She'll support what I need for the club."

"Oh, really? I hope so—for your sake. I'm not doing another stitch until you live up to your end of the bargain. So you can explain to Mallory why her girls won't have their precious costumes. And you won't be laying a finger on me ever again, that's for damn sure." She jumped up and pulled on her dress.

Justin was helpless to do anything but watch her unlock the door and walk out, slamming it behind her. Incredibly, his cock was still hard, and in an act of absolute defeat, he rubbed himself until the hands that had moments ago been touching her were left with nothing but his own mess.

18

Gemma pushed open the gates of Justin's apartment building and hurried down Bond Street. Her heart pounded as she dialed her phone. She couldn't believe Violet had been right after all. Thank goodness she'd only put her off, not blown her off.

"It's Gemma, the costume designer," Gemma said when Violet answered on the second ring.

"Oh, hello, London. Are you calling to invite me to the Baxter party? I was just reading about it on Twitter. Sounds lame. I'd be happy to get some action going."

"I just left the party," Gemma said.

"Bravo. So what can I do for you?"

"I want to take you up on your offer."

"Hmm. Hate to say I told you so. Let's get started, then." Violet gave her an address on West Fifty-seventh Street. "Take the elevator to the fifth floor. When you get there, give my name at the front desk."

"What is this place?"

"It's a private club. Don't be late."

* * *

Max took a canapé off a tray held by a Judy Garland look-alike dressed in full Dorothy regalia.

"I guess I'm not in Kansas anymore," he muttered to himself.

As a prominent member of the New York City fine arts community, he had been invited to a variety of Baxter parties over the past few years. Despite the parties' reputation for beautiful women and debauchery, Max had never been particularly interested in attending, and his initial impulse had been to ignore the latest evite, too. But when he overhead Nadia mentioning the party on the phone with Mallory, he gave it more consideration.

Then he received a follow-up evite with a listing of performers. Sure enough, "Naughty Natasha" was on the bill. And so he had RSVP'd yes.

Max had not told Nadia that he would be going to the party. He knew she would ask him not to go. He could already tell that her strategy for dealing with their disagreement on this issue was to just polarize their relationship: She would have her time with him, and her nights at The Painted Lady, and the two would never intersect. He knew—and was sure she knew on some level—that would never work.

Tonight was a chance to see if the woman he was falling in love with was really determined to do this, or if she was, as he believed, simply distracting herself from the difficult work of finding a new kind of place for herself in ballet. He supposed the real question he needed to answer was about himself: Would he be able to deal with her choice if it was to be a burlesque performer after all?

The seats in the theater room were filling up. Max was surprised not only to see the number of A-list celebrities in the room, but to see that they had played along with the dress-up theme. It truly felt like a bizarro world Oscar night. The only thing missing was Joan Rivers on the red carpet.

He found a seat near the back next to one of the actors from *Mad Men*.

The pop music that had been pulsing through the room receded, and in the sudden quiet the buzz of conversation dulled to a subtle hum just below the surface. The overhead lights dimmed, and Mallory's boyfriend took center stage in front of the red curtain.

Max looked around the room, but didn't see any of the girls from The Painted Lady. He knew Nadia was probably tucked away in another part of the townhouse, getting into her costume. Still, he continued to hope that he might catch a glimpse of her.

Alec Martin's monologue—lots of in-jokes about Justin Baxter and Martha Pike—was getting laughs from the crowd. Max supposed he would have had a better chance of appreciating the humor if he had known a thing or two about the couple hosting the party, which he absolutely did not.

"And now, ladies and gentleman, our first performer of the night is a woman who needs no introduction and whom you will next see in Ben Affleck's upcoming film *White Picket Fences*, the gorgeous, the glamorous, the *dangerous*... Bette Noir."

The song "Lola" by the Kinks filled the room, and the curtain parted to reveal Bette Noir perched on an old-fashioned barrel, smoking a cigarette and dressed in a retro cabaret outfit: a top hat, bloomers, garters, and stockings. Her hair was styled in a 1930s waved bob, and her eyebrows were penciled into a dramatically thin, high arch. Max couldn't help appreciating the way she brought Marlene Dietrich's most famous character, Lola Lola, to life.

Above her, a sign read "Blaue Engel."

The audience clapped and shouted her name. Most of them appreciated the tribute to the place where Bette Noir had first made a name for herself.

Bette tossed her cigarette to the stage floor and ground it

with the toe of her shoe. She sauntered to the front of the stage, then stood near the edge, gazing off into the distance while she gyrated her hips and slowly unhooked the first few catches of her corset top. She bent forward, pressing her breasts together as she leaned toward the audience to show her cleavage. After receiving a round of shouts and applause, she continued undoing the small front hooks. When the corset was fully unbuttoned, Bette held it closed with both hands, then flashed it open, revealing her completely bare breasts. This surprised Max for a few seconds before he realized that because they were in a private home and not a club, the performers didn't need to cover their nipples with pasties. He wondered if the dancers were going to take advantage of this freedom to get completely naked, and the thought of Nadia's doing that made his gut clench.

He watched Bette climb onto the barrel, standing on top of it and dramatically stretching out her leg as she unhooked one garter. She peeled off one stocking with painstaking slowness, then tossed it into the audience. She removed the other stocking, then slipped back into her high-heeled shoes.

She jumped off the barrel, now clad in only her top hat, heels, and bloomers. She moved fluidly into a few twirls that positioned her at center stage with her bare, alabaster back to the audience. She turned her head to the side to peek at the crowd, then she removed her hat, turned around, and used the hat to cover her breasts. She did a few showgirl kicks and walked to the front of the stage. With one hand, she slid the hat slowly down from her breasts to her belly to the front of her bloomers, her other hand obscured behind the hat as she worked to remove her pants. The audience clapped in anticipation. Sure enough, with the top hat still in place, Bette swiveled her hips until her bloomers fell to the floor. She kicked them aside.

A few guests in the front rows whistled. Max squirmed in

his seat. As the song neared its end, Bette flashed her soon-to-be movie star smile, and put the top hat back on her head—revealing her bare pussy. The curtain slid closed.

Max was the only one in the audience not cheering in appreciation. It was unthinkable that Nadia would put on this kind of display. He wasn't a prude—he loved sex as much as the next person—but the thought of the woman he cared about objectifying herself in such a way was more than he could endure. The burlesque audience was not filling seats to see choreography. They were not there for the costumes. They were interested in seeing as much naked flesh as they were allowed to see because they didn't have the balls to be honest about it and just go to a strip club.

"And that, ladies and gentleman, is why Humbert Humbert didn't stand a chance," Alec said, again taking the microphone. "Another round of applause for Bette Noir—who, incidentally, made her New York début at a Baxter party just a few short years ago." The applause grew louder. "Was anyone in this room at that party?"

A few hands shot up. "Yes, we all know *you* were there, Justin," said Alec. People laughed. "Somehow, when a hot woman gets naked, you always end up in the room."

Everyone laughed.

"Now, our next act features not one, but two stunning performers who pay homage to a Hollywood golden girl and a silver screen vixen who fought over one lucky man decades before Jennifer Aniston and Angelina Jolie were born.... Ladies and gentleman, please give it up for Moxie and Naughty Natasha."

The curtain parted to the song "Singin' in the Rain." Nadia sashayed out wearing a butter-colored raincoat that fell just below her waist, her long legs bare except for a pair of black, rubber, knee-high Hunter rain boots. She wore a matching yellow rain hat and carried an open umbrella. She posed for a moment with the umbrella open and over one shoulder, smiling with an innocent exuberance that mirrored the famous Debbie Reynolds pose in the film posters that featured the actress alongside costar Gene Kelley.

Nadia skipped to the front of the stage, twirling the umbrella. Suddenly, the music switched to the Bangles' 1980s hit "Walk Like an Egyptian." And then Mallory emerged from backstage in full Cleopatra regalia. The audience went crazy, yelling, "We love you, Liz." With her exaggerated black, arched eyebrows, blue eye shadow from lid to brow, and tumble of dark hair held in a gold beaded headdress, she did embody a young Elizabeth Taylor.

Nadia, as Debbie, paused to watch her rival. Mallory moved to the front of the stage and untied her silky white robe, letting it fall to the floor to reveal the gold tunic underneath. Debbie, not to be outdone by the flashy Liz, began unbuttoning her raincoat.

Max knew where this was going. And he couldn't let it happen.

He jumped up from his chair, almost knocking it over, and hurried up the aisle toward the stage. It was low enough that it was easy for him to jump on it, and he did, to exuberant cheers from the audience. It was clear they thought he was part of the act, perhaps anticipating him in the "Eddie Fisher" role.

"What are you doing here?" Nadia hissed, while Mallory, a consummate professional, kept performing.

"I need to talk to you," he said, pulling her toward the curtain.

"You're going for the wrong one, Eddie!" someone yelled from the audience.

"Seriously, Max—stop it. You're ruining everything!" Despite her protest, Nadia followed him off the stage, behind the curtain. He didn't harbor any illusions that she was happy to talk to him—she just wanted to end the spectacle.

"I can't let you do this," he said.

"Are you out of your mind?"

Two security guards came up the side stairs. After Nadia assured them she was fine, they turned to Max and said, "Sir, you're going to have to leave." They didn't wait for his compliance but took him by the arms. Max didn't resist or protest. He didn't try to explain himself to Nadia.

As far as he was concerned, it was mission accomplished.

19

Gemma paid the cabbie, although she wasn't at all confident he had brought her to the right location. The address did not look like it could possibly be a private club. The building looked more like it housed cheap office space or low-income apartments.

She dialed Violet's cell phone, but it went straight to voice mail. Not knowing what else to do, she walked inside the building and followed Violet's instruction to go to the fifth floor.

The doors slid open to another set of doors. These were locked. Gemma located an intercom to the right of the doors and pushed the button.

"Yes?" said a voice from somewhere on the other side of the doors.

"Um, it's Gemma. I'm here to see Violet."

There was no reply, but after a few seconds the doors buzzed and Gemma pushed them open.

The room was narrow, and directly in front of her was a dark, shiny wooden desk that looked like a Victorian antique.

Above it, in jarring contrast, was a colorful, art deco chandelier. And under the chandelier sat a remarkably pale young woman with red hair piled in a bun. She was dressed in a ruffled floral blouse and wore granny glasses. The overall effect would have been librarian-ish if the woman hadn't had lips pumped full of silicone.

"Can I help you?" said the woman.

"I'm here to see Violet."

The woman consulted the thin laptop on her desk. "You have an appointment with Mistress Violet?"

"No—I'm meeting a... business associate. Violet Offender? The burlesque dancer."

"Have a seat."

Gemma took a spot on the red velour sofa directly across from the desk. She ignored the twinge of nerves at the base of her spine. Her palms were sweaty, and she wiped them on her dress.

"Are you expecting a guest named Gemma?" the woman said into her phone. The reply on the other end must have been affirmative, because the redhead stood and gestured for Gemma to follow her.

They walked through a black curtain to a narrow hallway lined with closed black doors. The doors were numbered.

When they reached the tenth door, the woman knocked twice, then inserted a key that hung from a chain around her neck. She opened the door just a few inches until Violet was visible on the other side.

"Thanks, Petra," said Violet.

Gemma was startled. Violet was unrecognizable, covered in leather from head to toe in a formfitting catsuit with openings only for her eyes, nose, and mouth.

Gemma turned back to find the receptionist, as if she were her last contact with civilization. But the woman was already gone.

"What are you waiting for? A formal invitation? Get in," Violet said, opening the door wider.

The room was dim, and Gemma couldn't see what was inside. She hesitated only a few seconds before crossing the threshold and letting Violet close and lock the door behind her.

Violet wore knee-high black patent leather boots with at least a six-inch heel, and the catsuit exaggerated her breasts in both size and shape. The overall effect was of something not quite human, but with a feral sexuality.

"What is this place?" Gemma whispered. And then she noticed the woman on the other side of the room.

She was petite, with large breasts and vibrant red hair both on her head and on her pussy. And she was blindfolded, flat on her back, and strapped to a table, spread-eagled.

"Okay, I have no idea what's going on here...." Gemma said.

"Don't worry. I'll get you up to speed."

"I don't want to...get up to speed. I just came to talk to you about taking the costuming job you offered."

"Why didn't you say so?"

"I did! On the phone! I said I wanted to take you up on your offer."

"Oh. I thought you meant my offer to dominate you."

"What?"

"Okay, my bad. No big deal. Why don't you just help me out with this little dom session I'm doing, and we can talk business after."

"This is crazy. I'm leaving."

"See? That's why you never come."

"Excuse me?"

"That's why you never come—get off. Orgasm. Whatever you call it."

"You don't know what you're talking about."

"Don't I? I do my research, sweetheart. Plus, I can 'read the room.' Like every dominatrix worth her salt. And what I would say about you is that you don't get off because you don't give. I was wrong at first, I'll admit: I thought you were a classic dom case. But I'm revising my assessment."

"That's ridiculous," Gemma said, nervously.

"Want to bet on that?"

"What do you mean?"

"I bet that if you follow my direction, you will have the best orgasm of your life before you leave this room."

"What are we betting?" Gemma said. A part of her wanted to tell this lunatic to fuck off, but the other part—a stronger and inexplicable part of herself—kept her rooted in place.

"If you win, I'll pay you for the costume job and you don't even have to do the work. If you lose, you have to design the costumes for the money."

"But you already offered me the job!"

"And you said no. You said you were working for Justin Baxter."

"What if I refuse?"

"I'll find someone else to do the costumes. I have a large budget. I'm sure that won't be a problem."

Gemma looked at her, blinking but unable to come up with a retort. She locked eyes with Violet, and when she finally could no longer take the other woman's unnerving gaze, she said, "Fine. What do you want me to do?"

"Follow me."

Violet rolled a set of steel drawers on wheels over to the table. If the redhead sensed their approach, she gave no sign of it.

From the top drawer, Violet retrieved a riding crop, a tube of something, and a large dildo. Gemma's face must have registered horror, because Violet said, "Don't worry—I'll manage this stuff. You're going to go old-school."

She turned to the redhead and walked slowly around the

table. Suddenly, she smacked the riding crop loudly against the wall. The redhead jumped, though her movements were limited by the restraints. "I have an assistant helping me today, slave. You're so needy that it's too much work for one person, you selfish cunt," Violet shouted. "What do you have to say to that?"

"Thank you, Mistress Violet," the woman said.

Gemma could scarcely believe what she was witnessing. And yet it was oddly exciting.

"This is Mistress London," said Violet. "You are not allowed to look at her, because you are not worthy. So you must keep your blindfold on for the rest of the session."

"Yes, Mistress Violet. Mistress London."

Gemma looked at Violet in amazement. Violet smiled. She then began unbuckling the table restraints. Still, the woman remained motionless. Gemma noticed the red impressions in the woman's fair skin from the tightness of the restraints.

When every strap was loose, Violet told the woman to roll onto her stomach. She complied, and Violet then rebound her.

Violet waved for Gemma to move closer to the table. She did, and when she was next to the woman, Violet handed her the riding crop and gestured to the woman's ass. Gemma looked at her incredulously and shook her head. Violet grabbed the crop and brought it down on the woman's right ass cheek with a loud smack.

"Ahh!" the woman yelled loudly. Gemma could not tell if it was a cry of pleasure or pain. Violet handed the crop back to Gemma.

"If you want another, you are going to have to ask Mistress London. And if you are lucky, she will give it to you," said Violet.

"Mistress London, can you please smack my ass?" said the woman.

Gemma hesitated for a second and then brought the crop

down on the other cheek. To her shock, the woman moaned with what was clearly pleasure. Gemma looked at Violet, and she nodded. Again, Gemma brought the stiff crop down with a crack.

Violet reached over and stuck her hand between the woman's legs.

"I can't believe you're already wet. Now, slave, I have a dildo that you have to take. Do you want it in your ass or your pussy?"

"My ass," said the woman, to Gemma's surprise.

"Too bad—you're getting it up your pussy. I don't think Mistress London should have to deal with your filthy ass, do you?"

"No, Mistress Violet."

Violet was already squeezing lube onto the monstrously thick rubber penis. She handed it to Gemma, but Gemma shook her head no.

"Mistress London," said Violet, "you and I have a little wager going, do we not?"

Gemma nodded.

"So let's get down to business."

The woman's legs were spread and strapped down. Gemma took the dildo and stepped closer to the table. Slowly, she inserted the dildo into the woman's vagina. She was surprised by how easily it slid in, but she pressed forward slowly. Unsure what to do, she withdrew it, and then pressed it in again, more quickly this time. The woman moaned.

More confident, Gemma maneuvered it deeper, then out, then back inside. The woman yelled out unintelligible things. To her shock, Gemma felt her own pussy grow wet.

And then she felt Violet unzipping her dress.

Her silver Brigitte Bardot dress fell to the floor, but Gemma did not break stride with the dildo. By now, the woman on the table was bucking against the restraints and begging Gemma to do it harder. Gemma complied, trying not to lose focus just because she was now wearing only her thong and heels.

From behind her, Violet cupped her breasts. A ripple of pleasure shot through Gemma unlike anything she'd ever experienced. She pressed herself back against Violet and felt the leather against her bare skin. Violet pulled down her thong and pressed two fingers into her pussy. Gemma bit her lower lip to keep from crying out. The vibrations of pleasure in her pelvis were shocking and caused her to lose control. She tried to focus on keeping the dildo moving in the redhead, because the woman was crying out now in the throes of her own orgasm. Finally, Gemma couldn't hold off any longer. She withdrew the dildo, then grabbed onto the edge of the table with both hands, grinding her pussy against Violet's hand. It was impossible to stay silent, and she hardly recognized the animalistic sounds emanating from her throat as she was overtaken by the most powerful orgasm she'd ever had.

With one last shudder, the sensation eased. Violet withdrew her fingers. Gemma felt wobbly on her feet and was breathless.

"Congratulations, Mistress London. You've got yourself a job."

20

By one in the morning, Martha's birthday party had broken up into small groups and couples. The revelry had spread from the first floor up to the rooftop pool, which was now filled with half-naked and drunken partiers.

Nadia sat with her legs in the pool, her high-heeled shoes in her lap. Beside her, an actor she recognized from a popular sitcom was arduously trying to get into her pants. She'd always thought he was attractive on TV—but in person, not so much.

"So who was that dude who ran up onstage?" the actor said. She would have to look him up on the Internet when she got home to learn his name. He'd never introduced himself, operating under the assumption that she already knew who he was.

"Oh, just this guy I've been seeing," Natalie said, uncomfortably.

"What a dick," said the actor.

"It's not.... He just has issues with, you know, the idea of my taking my clothes off for a living."

"Personally, I think more women should take their clothes

off in public," he said. "Speaking of that—isn't it time for us to take a swim?"

"I have to get going," Nadia said, standing up. She felt wobbly and thought, for a terrifying second, that she was going to lose her balance and end up in the pool after all. The actor reached and grabbed her arm.

"Where are you running off to? The party's just getting started."

"Not for me," she said. In fact, the party had ended for her the minute Max got thrown out by security.

What had he been thinking? And why hadn't he told her he was going to be at the party? She was dying to ask him these things, but had ignored his texts and calls since his involuntary exit.

Nadia knew she should say good-bye to Justin or Martha on her way out, but she didn't want to spend a half hour wandering around trying to find them. She hadn't even seen Mallory, Alec, Poppy, or Bette in at least an hour. She told herself she should just go home. And yet she knew she wouldn't.

Outside, drunken tourists were taking photos of the dramatic front gate of Justin's building.

"Hey, gorgeous, get in the picture," one of them called to her. She ignored him and walked down the street, her feet hurting in her heels, looking for a cab.

She didn't know which made her more furious—the fact that Max had ruined her performance or that he'd deprived her of the chance to see if she had the nerve to go through with the striptease. But she did know that she'd never be able to sleep that night until she found out what had possessed him to do it. She also wanted to tell him how pissed off she was.

She dialed his cell phone, and he answered on the first ring.

"Where are you?" she said.

"Took you long enough to call me back."

"Long enough? You're lucky I'm calling you back at all after that little stunt you pulled. What the hell was that?"

"I think we should discuss this in person," he said calmly.

"Where are you?"

"At the studio," he said.

"It's one in the morning. What are you doing there?"

"I knew I wouldn't be able to sleep until I spoke to you so I'm working. Meet me here."

"I'm not meeting you there at this hour."

"It's on your way uptown. Just stop here so we can talk. Then I'll put you in a cab home."

She wanted to have the satisfaction of saying no, of saying "go to hell, I don't want to see you anymore." But the desire to see him and understand what he'd done was too strong.

In the distance, she saw a cab with its light on. She held out her hand.

"I'll be there in fifteen minutes."

Max met her out front. He paid for her cab and held the door for her. He wore jeans and a Ballet Arts T-shirt, and she could tell from the flush in his cheeks that he had been dancing rigorously. It was the way she used to deal with stress, too.

"Thanks for meeting me," he said. She said nothing, trying to ignore the immediate and almost overwhelming attraction she felt for him. She told herself it was just his post-workout pheromones playing on her senses. She attempted to put some physical distance between them as they walked past the twenty-four-hour security guard and made their way to the dark and quiet elevator banks.

The architectural elements of the building made it charming during the day but eerie at night. Max pushed the button for the second floor.

"I'm exhausted," she said. "This needs to be a quick conversation." The doors slid open, and she followed him to the one brightly lit studio. Inside, Ravel's "Boléro" played over the sound system. The French composer was one of her favorites, but she said nothing. For one thing, she might have told Max already. There was already a breadth to their relationship that made her lose track of things they had or had not discussed. She felt as if she'd known him far longer than she actually had.

Max turned down the music and sat on a wooden bench in the back of the room next to the piano. She sat on the bench, as far from him as she could without falling off.

"I'm sorry about tonight," he said, surprising her.

"You are?"

"Of course. I didn't plan to do that. But I care about you, and seeing you put yourself in that situation had a very intense effect on me."

"Max, I enjoy what I'm doing. At least, I'm trying to. And your attitude toward it is just so... judgmental, and reactive, and frankly, not something I can live with."

He looked at her with a smoldering intensity in his dark eyes that made it impossible for her to maintain eye contact. She glanced at their mirror image across the room. With their dark hair and long limbs and height, they looked like they belonged together. And when they made love, it certainly felt like they did. But with Jackson, she had learned the hard way that if you compromise in the beginning of a relationship on things that are fundamentally wrong, those differences will come back to hurt you in the end. Badly.

"I'm really sorry to hear that," he said. "Because I'm starting to care about you too much to ignore my feelings on this issue."

"So what are you saying?"

"I guess we should stop seeing each other."

His words almost knocked the wind out of her, and she was surprised by the intensity of her reaction. It was Jackson all over again, water in her lungs, the ground shifting beneath her feet.

"That's bullshit," Nadia said. "Don't use what I do as an excuse. I know all about you and your track record with women. You should have just told me you wanted a one-night stand in the beginning. I would have been fine with it. But to pretend like you care, and then blame me for our not being able to continue seeing each other..."

"If you care about me, then why can't you at least consider doing something other than burlesque? You haven't been doing it that long—Jesus, you haven't even completed a performance...."

"Thanks to you! I felt good up there tonight. The only thing stopping me was you."

"It was an impulse to jump up onstage. I told you I'm sorry about it. But that's how strongly I feel about not seeing you make such a mistake. And the reason I went to the party without telling you was that I was curious to see if you were going to go through with it. I *thought* I didn't want your decision tainted by me. I *thought* I wanted to see the truth of who you were in that moment. And then, I was the one who couldn't stand the truth."

"Why are you so against this? It has nothing to do with you. Why can't you just be more open-minded? You barely know me. There's more to my life than burlesque, but burlesque is the thing that has helped me the most since my injury."

"I understand that it has served a purpose up to this point. Now I'm asking you to find the strength to let go of that crutch and get back to your real life."

"You have no right to ask me to make those kinds of decisions. We barely know each other."

He reached out for her hand, holding it for a moment before letting her go.

"And I guess we never will."

21

At 7 a.m., Billy Barton had already completed his hour workout and was dressed in a Paul Smith shirt and pair of slacks. As he did at the start of every workday, he flipped through the *New York Post*, scanning Page Six. Though the gossip column had lost some luster since the days when editor Richard Johnson was at the helm, it was still part of Billy's breakfast ritual, along with his Green Mountain coffee and an Acai smoothie.

"Listen to this headline," he said to Tyler, who sat across the glass table picking at his egg white omelet. " 'Ballet Lothario Steals the Show at Burlesque Birthday Bash.' It's all about how a guest at Justin Baxter's party jumped onstage during a burlesque show and dragged his girlfriend off. And the guy is the head of Ballet Arts! I would have had a photographer there covering the party for *Gruff* if I wasn't on the outs with the Baxters over the Blue Angel. Of all the things that infuriate me about this situation, it's not the money that bothers me most—it's losing my connections."

"It's just one party," said Tyler.

Billy was about to debate this, but stopped mid-sentence

when he took a good look at the man across the table. His boyfriend's beauty never ceased to move him. He took a deep breath and said, "If you weren't so gorgeous, I'd be annoyed with you for trivializing this."

"Look, babe—we go to parties most people don't even know to dream about going to. We're out every night."

"True. Maybe it's not this particular party so much as the fact that I really miss Justin. He's a genuine character, and there aren't many of those left in New York. And Alec Martin was a damn good writer for me. He has a better understanding of subcultures than anyone since . . . well, me. I know we have tons of A-list friends. And celebrities are great. I'm the biggest starfucker. But when you lose friends who really speak your language—that's a tough hit to take."

"I don't understand why they can't be friends with you just because you own a rival club. It's so high school."

Billy shrugged. "It's the secretive way the whole thing went down—which I never would have done if Violet hadn't forced my hand. And she e-mailed me this morning that I have to meet her at the club tonight with a check for some costume designer we don't need. . . . I'm telling you, Tyler—I'm this close to telling her I'm done."

"So what's stopping you?"

Billy sighed. "I thought I was protecting you. But then I had a talk with Harvey, and he said I was going along with Violet's blackmail to prevent myself from being outed."

"Is that true?"

"It's a little of both," Billy said. This honest conversation stuff was really difficult. It was so much easier just to have sex. But he supposed if he wanted Tyler, he had to try to be in a relationship. He would just have to get used to what his shrink called "emotional honesty."

"Well, don't do it for me. I'll talk to my manager. Whatever happens, we'll deal with the fallout. I love you, and I don't want you to be under this crazy woman's thumb anymore."

Billy looked at him with amazement. "You would do that for me?"

"Yes," Tyler said without hesitation.

Feeling stupid for privately lamenting the emotional demands of the relationship, Billy stood and walked to the other side of the table and wrapped his arms around Tyler.

"Are you sure?"

"Yes. So how are you going to handle it?"

Billy straightened his back, thinking for a minute. "Right now, our private life is giving Violet a loaded gun. She holds our relationship over my head and threatens to shoot. If I put the information out there myself—and control when and how it gets out—she has nothing."

"She has the photos she took during the dom sessions."

"If she releases those photos, she will go to prison for blackmail. She's been cashing my checks for almost a year."

"So why didn't we just go to the police in the first place?"

"I had no proof she was blackmailing me. Did you want me to pull a Letterman? Then everything would have been public. I paid for the club; I bought us some time to come to terms with this. And now we have."

"How are you going to do it?"

"Darling, I'm a magazine publisher. And the online version of that magazine gets more hits than the *Daily Beast* and *Huffington Post* combined." He handed Tyler his phone. "Call your manager and your publicist. By the end of the day, we will be out."

Justin rolled over in bed. His first thought was that the party had been a huge success. Max Jasper's interruption of the show had created the type of drama they couldn't have *paid* someone to create. It further cemented the Baxter party reputation of being the place to expect the unexpected.

The only disappointment of the night had occurred right here, in his bedroom. He couldn't believe how Gemma had freaked out on him. Okay, so he owed her some money. But that shouldn't get in the way of the physical chemistry they shared.

Then again, he had to see things from her perspective. He hadn't paid her for the costume work, and he was married to another woman. What was he able to give her?

He would just have to clear up this money issue with Martha. It was time for her to loosen the purse strings. He had never pushed her on a financial issue before, but he had to hold firm on this one. What was the point of being in the marriage if he didn't have any financial freedom?

Martha was already in her second floor office. Justin knew she was consumed with her latest product idea: It was some sort of spray-on anal sanitizer that would enable couples to engage in rimming without the health risks.

He knocked on the open door.

"Come in," she said, looking up from her laptop. She was still in her robe, but had changed from her bedroom slippers to the orthopedic shoes she wore.

"I'm surprised you're up so early," he said.

"I know. Creative juices are flowing. The party was great last night, baby. You did it again!"

"I'm glad you enjoyed it."

"The show was fantastic. I love those girls. I wish Mallory would take me up on the offer to plan something for her wedding."

Justin nodded, wondering how best to segue the conversation. Then he got it: "I think the next thing Mallory's focused on is the Las Vegas Burlesque Festival," he said. "Which brings me back to the conversation we had a few weeks ago: I need to pay that costume designer to keep her on board."

Martha swiveled her chair, enabling her to face him without craning her neck.

"We already discussed this."

"Not to my satisfaction," Justin said.

"Yes," Martha purred. "I suspect this *is* all about your satisfaction. And the answer is no: I'm not giving you money for that woman."

Justin couldn't believe he had put himself in the position of having to ask his wife for money. What had possessed him to think this arrangement was a good idea? Sure, it worked as long as they both wanted the same thing. But now he was bumping up against the limitations of the deal, which brought to mind something Dr. Phil had once said: "When you marry for money, you pay for it every day."

"You said you fully supported the investment in The Painted Lady."

"And I do. But this isn't about The Painted Lady, is it?"

Here it was: the moment of truth. He could lie and try to save his marriage, or he could set himself free.

"No," he said.

"You're fucking that blonde?"

"Yes," he said, each word full of reckless abandon. He hadn't felt this good since he had trashed his bedroom in eleventh grade.

"You realize what this means, don't you?" she said, her tone distressingly businesslike. "You won't get a penny in the divorce."

"I understand," he said, his mind already flipping through a mental address book of rich friends he could ask for a loan—just enough to get Gemma her money. Just enough to get another taste of that pussy.

"You have one day to pack your things and get out," Martha said.

It was madness, he knew. But then, he'd known on some level that this day would come. Could a marriage like theirs really have lasted forever? Besides, the world was full of rich, horny women.

For now, he needed to focus on one poor, fantastically hot one.

22

The woman onstage ground against the stripper pole to the Nine Inch Nails song, "Closer," wearing only a G-string and a pig mask. Violet wished the act had come later in the night, so Gemma could have seen her.

Violet felt a tapping on her shoulder.

"Gemma Kole is here to see you," her assistant said. Violet squinted in the dim light, and there she was—her dirty blonde.

Violet pulled out a chair for Gemma to sit.

"Just in time," said Violet.

"Is your investor here already?"

"Any minute," Violet said. "But I wanted you to catch Spider's act. She's my ace in the hole for the Las Vegas Burlesque Fest. She's a burlesque dancer *and* a contortionist." The woman had her left leg around her neck while ascending the pole.

"Wow. Yeah, I see that. And I can see where she gets her name. We have to decide on a theme for the costumes, and I have to get the girls' measurements ASAP. There is no time."

"What was the theme you were working on for Mallory Dale?"

"Ballet Russes," said Gemma.

"That sounds retarded—I don't even know what that means. We'll have to come up with something else to use. I'm thinking something cool—like a comic book. Any ideas?"

"I... don't read comic books," said Gemma.

"Violet, let's make this quick. We have somewhere else to be," said Billy Barton, appearing at the side of their table.

"Nice to see you, too, Billy. Billy, this is Gemma Kole, the genius costume designer we're bringing on staff."

Billy nodded vaguely in Gemma's direction, then turned to take in the action on the stage. "You call that burlesque?" he asked.

"For your information, this wave of neo-burlesque is all about incorporating other elements of erotic entertainment," said Violet.

"Like stripping?"

Violet rolled her eyes. "You're supposed to be the 'silent' partner." She noticed Tyler hovering behind him. "Oh, you brought your butt buddy. Good to see you again, Tyler. Both of you, follow me to my office. Gemma, excuse me for a few minutes. Enjoy the show while I take care of some business."

Violet felt a surge of pride as she led Billy and his hot little sidekick through the club. She noticed that a few of her patrons recognized Tyler. Of course they would: He was on half the buses and billboards in the city. If they only knew that the hottest male model in town was on a steady diet of tube steak.

"Down these stairs," Violet directed.

"I know where the office is, Violet. And there's no need to make a big production out of this. It's going to be a very quick conversation," Billy said.

"Oh? Do you want to just hand me the check? If so, I won't belabor the point."

She opened the door to her office and closed it behind them.

Billy and Tyler exchanged a look. "There isn't going to be a check," said Billy.

"Cash is fine," said Violet.

"I'm done," said Billy.

Violet looked at the two men standing in front of her office sofa. They looked calm and vaguely amused.

"Don't fuck with me, Billy."

"Oh, I couldn't be fucking with you less. Why don't you go onto Gruffmag.com and see for yourself."

Violet shot him a dirty look before opening her razor-thin laptop. She uploaded the magazine site and gasped when she saw the color photo below the masthead: It was Billy embracing Tyler, both of them shirtless, tanned, and distressingly beautiful, on a beach somewhere obviously tropical. The headline read, "Letter from the Editor: My Summer of Love." She skimmed the first paragraph, in which Billy wasted no time in declaring to his readership that—to paraphrase—*he's here, he's queer, get used to it.*

Heart pounding, she closed the laptop.

"Nice photo," she said, spitting out each word like chips of ice. "But I have a few pics I think your readership would be more interested in."

"How many checks of mine have you cashed in the past nine months, Violet? You know, the prison term for blackmail can be pretty steep in New York State," Billy said.

Violet considered this, calculating her options. She realized that Billy Barton's bank account was no longer among them. She would, of course, have to avenge herself. But for now, her priority was damage control.

"You can see yourselves out."

She turned her back to them, her mind already racing through the financial puzzle she would have to solve. How much money did she have in the account to run the club?

Enough for another month or two, tops. She would have to find another influx of cash. What was the most immediate and likely source of funds? Winning the Vegas Burlesque Fest. And what did she need to do that? Great costumes. And so she needed Gemma Kole now more than before. But what had happened when Justin Baxter promised money and then failed to deliver? Gemma had walked. Violet had to figure out a way to keep her on board until after the competition. She knew from her career as a dominatrix that there were only two things that motivated people: money and sex. She couldn't offer money just yet, but if Gemma's little display at The Cellar last night was any indication, Violet might be the only person who could offer her what she wanted sexually—things Gemma herself didn't even know she wanted. Certainly, Violet had enough tricks up her sleeve to keep Gemma on the line until next month.

Long enough to win Las Vegas.

23

Mallory paced the Painted Lady stage.

In the middle of the afternoon, the club was empty, except for Alec and Bette sitting at a front table.

"If we're using costumes inspired by the Ballet Russes, I think everyone has to incorporate some element of ballet into her performance or it's not going to make sense," Mallory said.

"The Ballet Russes is *not* sexy," said Bette. "Burlesque is about art, but it's about sexuality, too. You're getting too cerebral about this."

"Where was this insight when we agreed on the concept?" said Mallory.

Bette narrowed her blue eyes at her. "I tried telling you it was a lame idea, but you're so infatuated with your little ballet pet, Nadia, that you lost sight of the big picture."

Mallory sat on the edge of the stage, her legs hanging off. She realized she had not sat in that position since her eighth grade play, a production of *Willy Wonka and the Chocolate Factory.*

"That's ridiculous."

"No, it's true. I've never seen that woman even successfully perform, and you let her routine dictate the whole theme. She's not even dancing at the festival, is she?"

"No, she's not," Mallory conceded. "It's just you, Poppy, and me. Only three girls are allowed per club."

"Yeah, and why isn't she one of the three? Because you can't risk her freezing on *that* night, can you?"

"Okay, ladies, let's just dial it down a notch," said Alec. "It's just a fun little competition. It's not that big a deal."

Mallory heard the front door open. "Alec, did you forget to lock the door when you came in?" she said.

"No, I locked it. Wait here."

Alec jumped up from the table and hurried to the front of the club.

"I'm sorry," Bette said. "I shouldn't be so harsh about it. I guess I'm just pissed that she's replaced me as your muse."

"Oh, Bette! No one could ever replace you—in any way. I just need to focus on other performers because you're barely around anymore. I feel like this place is just a pit stop between film sets for you."

Bette cocked her head. "Hmm. That's true," she said with a smile.

Mallory laughed and stretched out her leg to kick Bette's chair. "You're supposed to deny it!"

Alec walked in with Justin in tow.

"Bette, Justin needs to talk to Mallory and me alone for a minute," Alec said. Mallory looked at Alec questioningly but he just shrugged. Bette was busy reading something on her phone.

"Well, what do you know," she said. "Billy Barton finally came out of the closet."

"What do you mean?" said Alec.

"It's all over the Internet. Apparently he wrote something

on *Gruff* online about his relationship with that super hot Burberry model dude, Tyler."

"I had no idea he was gay," said Alec.

"I suspected," said Bette. "What about you, Justin? You guys used to party a lot. Ever see him let his freak flag fly?"

Justin, clearly not in the mood to revel in the latest Gotham gossip, merely shook his head.

"All right, well I'll leave you suits to your *business*. Mal, call me later."

Justin sat in the seat she vacated. Mallory climbed down from the stage and sat next to Alec.

"What's going on?" she asked, a tingle of concern running down her spine.

"I have some . . . bad news," he said.

"Are you okay?" Mallory reached out and put her hand over his.

"Yes. I'm fine. But my marriage isn't."

"Don't even tell me. . . ." Mallory said.

"Martha and I are getting divorced. Martha is angry, and she's cutting me off financially. The reason I'm telling you guys is . . . this club is going to be a casualty of the divorce."

Mallory gasped. Now it was Alec's turn to put his hand over hers.

"I'm really sorry about your marriage, Justin. I'm just not sure I see the connection to The Painted Lady. I thought Martha wanted the club as much as you did," said Alec.

"She did—at the time. And I know she appreciates everything you guys have done, and she loves you, Mallory. But she's really freaking out and wants nothing to do with me or, as she put it, any of our 'mutual endeavors.' "

Mallory put her head in her hands. "I can't believe this."

The three sat in silence for a minute, until Justin said,

"Maybe you can try to talk to her. See if she'll reconsider if I'm not the one doing the asking."

"I'll try," Mallory said.

"But if Martha doesn't reconsider? What's the worse case scenario?"

"She'll pay your salaries through the end of the year. She doesn't want to punish you guys; she made that clear. But the rent for the club and the operational expenses will only be covered for another month or two."

Mallory looked at Alec. She knew it wasn't right to just be thinking of the club or what she and Alec were going to lose. Justin was losing something far more significant. But she knew this had to be a result of his feelings for the woman he'd told her about the night they were out drinking. And she couldn't believe he would throw everything away for that woman.

"This isn't because of what you told me about. . . ." she said.

He nodded slowly.

"Oh, Justin," she said, shaking her head.

"What? What did I miss?" said Alec.

"I don't want to get into it right now," said Justin. "I just wanted to tell you guys as soon as possible so you could either talk to Martha or start thinking about your exit strategy."

"I don't want an exit strategy!" said Mallory. "I love this place. We haven't financed it, but we've put everything we have into it—all of our time, all of our creative energy, and a lot of emotional investment, too."

"I'm sorry I let you down," said Justin. He pushed his chair back, stood, and walked slowly out to the club exit.

"I cannot believe this," said Mallory. "If we had six months or a year, we could maybe build a strong enough reputation to find another investor. But we just opened."

"You're right. We need to buy time."

"We can't buy anything!"

"Mal, don't freak out. I just need to correct my earlier statement about the Vegas Burlesque Fest."

"What do you mean?"

"It's no longer just a fun little competition. It's going to be how we finance the club for the next six months."

24

Gemma climbed the narrow, winding stairs to the second floor of Agnes's studio. It was dark and quiet. Where was the old bat?

She couldn't wait to quit. Five months of indentured servitude was quite enough, thank you. It was onward and upward.

Way up.

It still made her wet just thinking about the other night at the crazy fetish club. Finally, she had felt that thing that had eluded her all her life: sexual gratification. She'd thought she was forever doomed to wonder what on earth all these people were so worked up over when it came to sex. She had been so tired of feeling nothing. But how could she have imagined what it would take for her to get off? And even if she had imagined it, she never would have had the nerve to seek it out. But thanks to Violet, the riddle of her own pussy had been solved.

She descended the stairs and looked around the cutting room. The costumes she'd started working on for Justin's dancers were in various stages of completion. She wished she could use parts of them for Violet's "Tank Girl" costumes, but there was nothing in the "Ballet Russes" collection that was even remotely salvageable. There was absolutely no sartorial overlap between ballet and steampunk. She would have to just abandon them. Perhaps Agnes would be able to complete them in time for Mallory to use the costumes. Gemma couldn't care less—it wasn't her problem anymore.

It was exciting to imagine the new costumes. Gemma wasn't a comic book fan, but she'd already starting researching images of Tank Girl online, and the character kicked ass—literally and visually. She would barely consider it work to create the costumes if it weren't for the ridiculously tight deadline.

The front door opened, startling her out of her thoughts.

"What are *you* doing here?" she said as Justin Baxter walked in with an armful of white roses.

"I wanted to apologize," he said, handing her the flowers with a smile. She took the bundle and dropped them on her desk as if they were on fire.

"Look, this really isn't a good time for me," she said, walking back to the front door and opening it for him.

"Can you just hear me out?"

She saw that he had no intention of leaving until she did, so she sighed and closed the door. She hadn't planned on telling him that she was quitting—she'd thought she would leave that little bit of news to Agnes to break. As far as she was concerned, she and Justin Baxter had nothing left to talk about. Ever.

"Fine. Speak. You have two minutes. Agnes will be here soon, and I need to talk to her."

"I'm sorry about the money I promised you for the Vegas costumes. I didn't think Martha would give me a hard time about it. She never has before. I think she realized you and I have been seeing each other."

Gemma looked at him like he was out of his mind.

"We are not seeing each other," said Gemma.

"Did I make you feel that way? It was more than just sex to me, Gemma. I can't stop thinking about you—I haven't been able to stop thinking about you since opening night of The Painted Lady. And now I don't have to sneak around anymore. Martha and I are getting divorced."

"Are you out of your mind?" said Gemma. "How are you going to pay for the club? And the costumes?"

"I don't know. But what does that matter to you?"

"That's the *only* thing that ever mattered to me! It was business, Justin."

The expression on his face could not have been more shocked if she had slapped him.

"So now that we can't do business together, we really have nothing left to talk about."

"You don't want to see me anymore?"

"Um... no."

"What about the Vegas costumes?"

She shrugged. "Not my problem. I'm not working at Agnes's sweatshop any more."

"I don't understand. What are you going to do?"

"I'm the new costume designer for Violet's Blue Angel."

Nadia couldn't stop thinking about Max. She knew that she had, in theory, done the right thing by not letting him dissuade her from working at The Painted Lady. But now, sitting in the empty club, she felt she had traded a real relationship for the idea of burlesque. And she had to wonder if she had just used burlesque as an excuse to avoid getting hurt again. After all, it was easier to let the argument over burlesque become a deal breaker than to actually have a relationship and see it end six months or a year down the line.

"Hello—Earth to Nadia," Mallory said.

Nadia looked across the table. "Sorry."

They were working on choreography for Vegas. For some

reason, Mallory's confidence in the Ballet Russes idea was shaken.

"I'm just afraid it's not specific enough," she had said.

"So let's focus on one particular production from that time period," Nadia had said. And then Mallory had asked her to suggest one, and Nadia had started thinking about Balanchine's staging of *Apollo* in 1928, and then she thought of his School of American Ballet, which led her to think about Ballet Arts and Max... and then she zoned out.

"Where did I lose you?" Mallory said.

"I was just thinking about Max."

"Have you spoken to him since the party?"

"I saw him later that night. He said he was sorry for what he did, but he still wants me to quit burlesque and find some way to work in ballet."

"He'll come around," Mallory said.

Nadia shook her head. "No. It's over."

"That's ridiculous, Nadia. You two will just have to agree to disagree on whatever he's being so stubborn about, and move on."

"I don't want to talk about it anymore. I'm done thinking about him; he's out of my life—it's fine. Let's just focus on Vegas. If you want a specific ballet from the Ballet Russes period, my favorite is *Apollo.* And thematically, it's perfect for this moment in burlesque because *Apollo* was very much about the reinvention of tradition. Its artistic execution was post-baroque."

She remembered the time her mother took her to see *Apollo* when she was in seventh grade. It was the first ballet she'd seen in New York.

"What's the story?" Mallory said.

"It's about the Greek god Apollo and three Muses, which is perfect for the Vegas show because you need three dancers. Okay, so most people think of Apollo as the god of the sun, but actually he represents the arts and music, in particular. In the story, Apollo helps the Muses in their arts and ultimately ascends as a god to the home of the Muses, Parnassus."

"I don't know. The idea of ancient Greek costumes sounds very high school musical."

"Coco Chanel didn't think so."

"What do you mean?"

"She did the costumes in 1929. You don't even know—the most brilliant artists have worked on this production. Baryshnikov did a revival in the 1970s. Suzanne Farrell did it in 2001. It's significant, Mallory."

"I'd have to talk to Agnes and Gemma about tailoring the costumes for this. What are the Muses?"

"They're the Muses of dance, mime, and poetry."

"I have to talk to Poppy and Bette and see who they want to be." She wrote on her notepad, then looked up at Nadia. "I really want you to come to Vegas with us just to experience the festival."

"Of course I'm going with you." Nadia was looking forward to it.

Justin walked in, and Nadia's first thought was that he looked as if someone had died.

"What's wrong?" Mallory asked, clearly sharing Nadia's assessment that Justin did not look happy.

"I need to talk to you and Alec."

"Alec's not here. He's working on a piece for *New York* magazine. What's going on?"

Justin sat down, his face pale.

"It's about the costumes."

25

Max watched the rehearsal from outside the glass.

His assistant choreographer, Pauline, was leading the group through their paces. He knew the dancers were aware of his observation. Anna, in particular, was showboating for him.

He had not slept with Anna since before the night he'd brought her to The Painted Lady. And since becoming involved with Nadia, he had not been with anyone else.

Was he wrong to put an end to things before he repeated the mistakes of the past? True, they were not his mistakes. But he had suffered because of them all the same.

Pauline glanced over at him, and he gave her the thumbs up. Satisfied that she had things under control, he left the studio for his office.

The paperwork for his budget was spread over his desk. As precise and ordered as he was in the studio, his desk and office tended toward chaos. What was that called? Entropy. He could stand the inclination toward disorder in his business, but not in his emotional life.

He logged onto his computer. The payroll program was still

on the screen from early that morning. He minimized it and, though he knew he shouldn't, he logged onto the Internet. He brought up Google Images and typed her name, "Janine Jasper."

Always, he hoped the images were gone. But of course, nothing disappeared from the Internet. And sure enough, the blocks of photographs filled the screen, some grainy, some as clear as if they'd been taken yesterday. He didn't click on any to enlarge, of course. He'd never looked at any of them closely. And yet, collectively, they were more disturbing than any single one alone.

They were what had driven his father to leave.

Max understood, in theory, that opposites attracted. But why had his father, the golden boy from Greenwich, Connecticut, a Yalie, and a superstar banker, thought he could make a life with a fetish model turned soft-core porn actress? Max certainly wasn't going to make the same mistake.

Devla, his costume designer, knocked lightly on the door frame.

"Are we still meeting at ten thirty?" she asked, her voice soft. Her long, thick black hair was pleated in a single braid that fell over her left shoulder. Devla had been a twenty-year-old undergrad at Parsons when one of his girlfriends took him to a fashion show and he spotted her work. Immediately, he'd known she was a mega talent. He had invited her to intern with his costume designer, a guy named Brad Mead. When Brad defected to a rival company, Max asked Devla to replace him. He considered the hire one of his best decisions since founding Ballet Arts.

"I'll be there. Just give me five minutes," he said, shutting down his browser.

He couldn't undo the sins of the father. But he could avoid repeating them.

"Is something wrong with the costumes? You're freaking me out," Mallory said.

Justin turned to Nadia. "Can you excuse us for a minute?"

Nadia shot Mallory a questioning look and left them alone.

"Okay, what the hell is going on?"

Justin took a deep breath.

"Remember I told you that I was in love with someone else—that I was cheating on Martha?"

"Of course," Mallory said. "And that's why you guys split."

He nodded. "There's more to it, though. The woman was Gemma Kole."

Mallory gasped. "When did that start?"

"Opening night of the club. At my party."

"Okay," she said slowly. "Why are you telling me this now?"

"She ended things. And now she won't do the costumes for Vegas."

"She's not doing the costumes for Vegas. Agnes is doing them."

He shook his head. "No. I asked Gemma to do them. Haven't you noticed she's been doing the fittings?"

"Yes—because she's Agnes's assistant. I told you I was talking to Agnes about doing the costumes, remember?"

"I know. But I wanted Gemma to do them. And Gemma said she was too busy—Agnes had her working on everything. Gemma didn't want more work. I said I would pay her on the side. And I intended to. She's so talented, Mallory. I wanted her to be our exclusive costumer."

"No," Mallory said. "You wanted her to be your mistress. How could you put us in this position? Vegas is less than a month away."

"I'm sorry. I really fucked up."

This was a disaster. "I've got to talk to Agnes. I don't understand—she's been so busy these past few weeks. What the hell is she working on if not the Vegas costumes?"

Mallory grabbed her bag and headed for the door.

* * *

Gemma followed Violet into a luxurious apartment building on Park Avenue. A white-gloved attendant held the door for them, and Violet breezed past the front desk to gold elevator banks. Gemma's favorite shoes, pink Celine heels, made a loud clacking noise on the marble floor.

"This is where I'm going to work on the costumes?"

"Yes. It's a pied-à-terre owned by one of my customers. He's in Amsterdam until Thanksgiving."

"Does he know you're using it?"

"I have a key. He's a busy man: No need to bother him with petty details."

They rode the elevator with an older woman leading a very tiny dog on a leash. The leash was covered with what Gemma guessed were hundreds of Swarovski crystals. Even in that building, it was hard to imagine an actual diamond leash.

The woman got off on the nineteenth floor. The doors opened for them on twenty-two.

Gemma followed Violet wordlessly down the carpeted hallway. The lighting was austere, the lives behind each of the doors quiet. No dogs barking, no sounds of children playing.

Violet slipped a key into the door of apartment 22B. The door opened to darkness. Heavy drapes were drawn against the afternoon sun.

"This place has northern and southern exposure, and the guy never opens the drapes," Violet said, immediately pulling them open. Sure enough, light poured into the room, revealing gorgeous moldings on the ceiling, a spare and eclectic collection of antique furniture, and a large zebra-skin rug that covered the living room floor. "The guest bedroom is virtually empty. I figure you can set up shop in there." Gemma followed her down a short, cream-colored hallway lined with black-and-white prints in identical black frames. All of the photos were of a blond child actress Gemma recognized from a spate of recent blockbuster films.

"His niece," Violet said, by way of explanation. She opened a door to a room that was surprisingly large. And it was, as Violet had predicted, empty. "You can keep all the fabric, sewing machines, cutting boards—whatever you need—here. I'll make you a key. And then as soon as I have money we'll get a real studio for you."

"What do you mean, when you have money? You told me your investor bankrolls whatever you need. Those were your exact words." Gemma tried to ignore the rise of panic in her chest. She'd already quit her job with Agnes. She'd actually been nervous to tell the old lady she was leaving, but the woman had barely blinked twice before simply wishing her luck and turning back to the white corset she was working on.

"Yes, well, there's been a slight change in my funding arrangement," said Violet. "But it's just temporary. I have a lot of wealthy former clients. It's just a matter of finding one to bring on board."

"So you can't...pay me anything?" Gemma felt faint. She sat down on the hardwood floor. Violet sat directly in front of her. Gemma looked into her eyes, which truly were cat-like, so very green with pupils narrowed into slits.

"Keep it together, London. I told you, this is temporary. And to make up for the inconvenience of this little bump in the road, I'm prepared to sweeten your deal: When I find someone to pump some cash into the club, I'll get them to set you up so you can start your clothing line."

"Is that possible?"

"Of course it is. People either have a ton of money, or they don't. Now, I can't guarantee that they won't ask for a partnership in the clothing line—you're going to have to negotiate your own deal with them. But I'll get you the money, for sure."

"How long do you think this will take?"

"I don't know! Jesus, you're such a nervous Nellie."

"What will I do for money until then? And how are you going to pay for the material for the costumes? You still want me to do the costumes for Vegas, right?"

"Of course. It's even more important now than before. I need to win that prize money, and I need to win to make the club attractive to investors. That competition gets tons of press. Hell, the guy who sponsors it might be interested in buying into us, for all I know. I have the money for the costumes if you don't go too crazy with expenses. It will be fine."

"Fine for the club, maybe—but I don't have any income. I quit my job with Agnes for you! You don't understand how fucked I am."

"Pull it together! This is America. You don't have to work in a factory or live on the dole. It's the land of free enterprise. Isn't that why you came here?"

"I came here because New York is the fashion capitol of the world."

"Well, I'll let you in on a little secret. It's also the sex capitol of the world. And I suspect your talent in design is surpassed by your talent in domination."

"What are you talking about?"

"That was an impressive little display the other night."

Gemma felt herself blush.

"Seriously. You're a natural," said Violet. "You can make a lot of money with your talent. I suggest you and I take the show on the road—book a few gigs at The Cellar, find a few private clients. You won't be worrying about paying your rent for long, I can promise you that."

"You're not serious."

"Of course I am. I wear Vuitton, McQueen, and Louboutin.

What do you think pays for it all? The cover charge at Violet's Blue Angel?"

Gemma's eyes widened. "Think about it," said Violet. "And in the meantime, get working on the Tank Girl costumes. The stakes just got higher, Mistress London."

26

Mallory rang the buzzer to Agnes's studio. She was surprised to find the door locked and the first floor dark. Gemma must be gone already.

She buzzed again. After a few minutes, she saw Agnes slowly making her way down the winding iron stairs in the center of the room.

"What are you doing here?" Agnes said, opening the door. The belt around her waist was filled with pins, needles, and thread.

"That's your greeting?" Mallory said. "May I come in?"

Agnes stepped aside with an exaggerated wave.

"I'm very busy," Agnes said.

"Yes, I know you're busy. You're always busy. I'm just wondering what you're so busy with," Mallory snapped.

"What's wrong with you?"

"What's wrong is that while you are so busy, you let that British bitch take over the Vegas costumes, and now she's AWOL and we're screwed."

"I thought you wanted her to do the costumes. That's what she told me."

"Why would I want *her* to do the costumes?"

Agnes shrugged. "She's young. She's beautiful. Fashion is for the young. I am past my time."

"That's ridiculous. This whole thing was a big misunderstanding, and now the Vegas show is three weeks away and we have no costumes. Can you step in and finish what Gemma started?"

Agnes shook her head. "I am working on something that I must finish. Then, I retire."

"What? Why?"

"I've found love," Agnes said. "After all of this time, love, again."

Mallory sat down on the bottom step. "You're in love? With whom? I didn't think you ever left this studio. I mean, you're out there dating?"

"No. Of course not. Dating is for young people. I found him on Facebook."

"Facebook," Mallory repeated.

"He was my lover in Krakow many years ago. And now we've found each other again. I'm going to meet him in Berlin."

Mallory looked up at the ceiling, trying to process this turn of events.

"I'm happy for you, Agnes. I really am. And I don't mean to sound callous or selfish when I say this, but I really need these costumes. Justin won't be able to pay for the club after a month or so—we need to win the prize money in Vegas just to get us through the year. I know we have the best performers—I have no doubt. But Vegas is really showy, you know? We need costumes."

Agnes nodded. "I wish I could help you."

Mallory ran her hand through her hair. "You can, Agnes.

You're the best costumer around. Just give me two weeks of your time. I'll find a way to pay you. Even if I could settle for someone less talented, who can I find on such short notice?"

"Ask the ballerina," said Agnes.

"Who? Nadia? She doesn't make costumes."

"I know. But she is tied into dance. And where there are dancers, there are costumers."

Mallory thought about that for a moment. "You're right. I'll ask her."

Agnes headed back toward the stairs. "Good. Then it's settled."

"Wait!" Mallory called after her. "Can you at least tell me what you've been working on all this time?"

A small smile played on Agnes's lips. "You want to see now? I was going to show you later. When finished."

"I want to see it now," said Mallory. Agnes beckoned for Mallory to follow her up the stairs.

Agnes pulled a garment bag off the wardrobe rack at the back of the room. Mallory sat on a chair, and Agnes unzipped the cream-colored plastic bag with a flourish. She removed what appeared to be a swathe of tulle, which Mallory realized was attached to a white, finely boned corset that was so narrow and delicate it almost looked like a period piece.

"Inspired by Galliano's 2009 collection in Paris. Dita Von Teese walked that show—not in a wedding gown, but in a bondage-inspired dress. Did you see photos of that show?"

Mallory shook her head, circling the dress. The more she looked at it, the more she realized the genius behind the delicate crafting of the corset: The fabric was sturdy enough to support the structure, yet obviously sheer enough to showcase the wearer's flesh underneath. And the tulle had a fullness to its draping that was almost bridal.

"This is magnificent," she said. "What is it for?"

"Your wedding," said Agnes, with an unrepentant smile.

"I haven't planned a wedding!" said Mallory. "Agnes, you shouldn't have. . . ."

"Try it on."

Mallory didn't have to try it on. She knew it would fit her perfectly. Agnes had been designing costumes for her for almost two years now. She knew Mallory's figure better than Mallory herself.

Agnes was already undoing the corset lacing. Mallory pulled off her T-shirt and jeans and stepped into the dress that Agnes held for her. She walked to the full-length mirror that Agnes still kept from the dressing room at the Blue Angel. Behind her, Agnes pulled the corset laces tight.

"You will wear with thigh-high white stockings and white Louboutins. I'm working on the veil—it will be very long to add an extra sheer layer to the dress."

The perfection of the dress rendered Mallory speechless. "This is the last thing I will create. Save the best for last," said Agnes.

Mallory started to cry. "I can't believe you did this for me," she said.

"Just promise me you will make use of it."

"I will," Mallory said, meeting Agnes's eyes in the mirror's reflection.

"Don't tell me 'I will.' Tell your boyfriend 'I do.' He loves you. Don't let fear get in the way. Life is too short."

Mallory nodded. She knew what she had to do. But first, she had to find her dancers some costumes.

Nadia wasn't sure how to classify the feelings she'd experienced since Max had walked away from her. After Jackson, she'd felt sick—unable to sleep, unable to eat. That was probably why she got injured—she'd stopped taking care of herself.

But this . . . It was more like she was numb. She tried to share in the girls' excitement about the upcoming Vegas trip, but she couldn't. She thought maybe watching Bette and Poppy rehearse would inspire her, but it did not. Alec was giving them notes on their choreography, and he wanted her input, but she kept drifting off into an almost daydream-like state, caught in the endless loop in her head: Was she being unreasonable about this, or was Max? Really, what did he care what she did with her life? Surely, not every woman he dated was a ballerina.

She kept thinking about the night they'd made love, the way he'd touched and the way he'd looked at her. . . .

"Mallory's on her way," Alec said. "She just texted me. You don't have any notes for Bette? This is probably her last rehearsal before she leaves for Toronto."

"It looks great," Nadia said. "I just hope Mallory straightened out the costume situation."

"I'm sure she's got Agnes on it. I'm not worried."

Nadia's thoughts drifted back to Max. Maybe she was on the right track thinking about his former girlfriends. Looking into his past might help her decipher this craziness.

"Hey," Mallory said, pulling out a chair and dropping into it with a dramatic show of exhaustion. Her beautiful skin was shiny with perspiration, and she didn't look happy.

"Hi, babe. What's the good word? Are we back on track with the costumes?" said Alec, rubbing her back.

"Not exactly. Justin was right—Agnes never worked on them at all. Agnes thought we wanted Gemma to do them because that's what Gemma told her. Ugh! I could strangle that little operator. And now Agnes doesn't have time to do them. She's retiring!"

"She won't retire. She can't spend five minutes without working," said Alec.

"What's going on down there?" Bette called from the stage.

"Nothing—ignore us. Keep working," Mallory said. She turned back to Alec and Nadia. "She's reconnected with an old lover and she's running off to Berlin."

"That's so romantic!" said Nadia.

"Yeah, it's romantic," Mallory conceded. "But it leaves us in bad shape."

"We'll find someone else," Nadia said. She couldn't—and didn't—believe that things could all fall apart at the last minute like this. Mallory put a hand on her arm.

"I need your help," Mallory said.

"Sure. Anything," said Nadia.

"I need you to ask Max if his costumer can do us a favor."

"Anything but that," Nadia said.

"Listen, I know what I'm asking of you. It was actually Agnes's idea, and she is right. Ballet costumers are fast, they are creative, and they have the best craftsmanship. They understand how movement affects a costume.... Agnes comes from that world. Please, Nadia. I wouldn't ask you if it wasn't our best option. Maybe our only option."

Nadia thought of her despair after the injury. The way she'd felt that she had no options, and the way Mallory had given her a new goal, a place to direct her energy. Mallory had believed in her, had brought her into this world. And now they needed her.

"I don't even know if he'll take my call," Nadia said, finally.

"Don't call. It's too easy to say no over the phone," said Alec.

"He's right. You have to go in person."

"Absolutely not," said Nadia.

Mallory and Alec looked at one another. It pained Nadia to see the intimacy and solidarity in their exchange. She ached for it.

"I'll go with you," Mallory said.

Nadia felt cornered, as if she was on the stage, lights glaring, clothes about to come off.

This was one time she had to expose herself.

"Okay," she said.

27

Max thought the receptionist was mistaken when she told him Nadia Grant was in the lobby. It surprised him enough that he had to tell the receptionist to hold.

Max stood from the desk and paced his office. He prided himself on understanding human nature and gauging character. He had been certain Nadia would not contact him, and, sadly, he knew she would not give in on the issue of performing burlesque. And yet, she was in the building.

"Please send her up," he told the receptionist.

He sat on the couch. Then he returned to the seat behind his desk. He considered going back to the couch, but by that time there was a gentle rap on his door.

"Come in," he called.

His assistant opened the door, and behind her stood Nadia and Mallory. He was confused to see Mallory, but his most immediate feeling was discomfort at how radiantly beautiful Nadia looked. Her pale brown hair was pulled back in a high ponytail, showing off her graceful neck. Her face was bare of makeup except for a berry-colored stain on her lips. He had the urge to take her lower lip gently between his teeth, to put his hands on her breasts, which pressed tight against her gray crew-neck T-shirt.

"How are you?" she said. She sounded nervous.

"I'm surprised to hear from you," he said. It was the truth, and it was the only thing he could think to say.

"I'm surprised to be here," she said with a nervous laugh. She looked at Mallory.

"We're sorry to bother you, Max. And really, this is my fault. I asked Nadia to come here."

"Why don't you ladies have a seat," he said, coming out from behind the desk and showing them to the couch. Nadia and Mallory sat side-by-side, and he half stood, half sat on the edge of his desk. "Forgive my lack of imagination, but I have no idea why you would want Nadia to come see me."

"We have a slight problem," Nadia said. "A big problem, actually. Remember I told you about that Vegas competition?"

He nodded. He'd been relieved to hear Nadia wasn't performing. Not that it mattered anymore.

"Our costume designer bailed. We have nothing, and the show is in a few weeks. Mallory tried to get Agnes to step in, but she's retiring. She won't do anything. So now we have a tight deadline and . . . a small budget."

"How small?" Max said.

"We can work that part out," Mallory said quickly. "The most important thing is that we need an amazing, creative designer who can work fast. We thought you might know of someone. Maybe even someone you have on staff here."

Max looked at the two women. Nadia did not meet his gaze, but instead seemed fascinated by the floor.

"I only have one designer here," he said after a minute. "And she's gearing up for our first performance of the fall season. I just spent two hours in a meeting with her. She's busy with what she has to deliver for us."

"Okay, thanks anyway. . . ." Nadia said, standing to leave.

"Wait a minute," Mallory said, grabbing her arm. "Do you think she might have old costumes somewhere that she could alter to fit the three of us? We just need them to be unified thematically. We had even been planning to do something from Ballet Russes."

"*Apollo*," Nadia added.

"You were going to do a burlesque *Apollo*? You guys are crazy."

"But we'll change the theme if your woman has costumes we can roll with. What did you do last year?"

"We did *Jewels*, and an original production that Pauline and I choreographed called *Imperial*." He saw the excitement in their faces and couldn't say no. "Okay, let me call Devla in here—she's my costumer. But I'm not making any promises. I really don't know if she will have anything that works or if she even has the time to alter the costumes for you."

He walked back to his phone and dialed. Out of the corner of his eye, he saw Mallory and Nadia smile at each other. And he wanted to make Nadia smile—even if it was just in this small way.

Devla appeared, as summoned, in the doorway. Her body language was timid, as if she expected to be yelled at. This was not because of him; she'd held herself that way ever since he'd met her.

"Devla, come in. I want you to meet my friends, Nadia Grant and Mallory Dale."

He was sure Devla had heard of Nadia—gossip about Max's personal life was rampant in the company. She might even have seen her around the studio.

Devla told Nadia and Mallory it was nice to meet them, and then she looked back at Max questioningly.

"Mallory runs a burlesque club in Nolita called The Painted Lady."

"I love burlesque," said Devla. This was news to Max, but it had to be true. Devla was nothing if not genuine and direct.

"We're in a bit of bind, and we are hoping maybe you can help us out," Mallory said.

"They have a show coming up, and they don't have costumes," Max explained. "The costume designer left before finishing the job."

"It's not just a show—it's a competition. It's a big deal in burlesque. You have to be invited to participate, and there's a lot of money at stake. The Painted Lady is a new club, and winning this would really put us on the map. Plus, we need the money to help keep things going."

Max glanced at Nadia. She'd never mentioned the club was in financial jeopardy. Maybe she had not known.

"We were wondering if you had any old costumes that we could borrow for the show."

"How many costumes would you need?"

"Just three—but we need them to be the same theme. Ironically, we were going to do a ballet theme... *Apollo.* I know you haven't done *Apollo,* but that's just an example of the high concept we need."

"One of the things we're judged on is costumes," said Nadia.

"Hmm. Did Max tell you about *Imperial*?" Devla asked.

"He mentioned it."

Devla looked at Max, as if for permission. He nodded.

"Come with me," she said.

Mallory's phone rang. She looked at the incoming number and said, "I'm so sorry. I have to take this. Excuse me for one minute."

She stepped out of the office, leaving Max, Nadia, and Devla to stand around awkwardly.

"Maybe I can find some photos on my computer of the *Imperial* performance," Max said to fill the silence.

"Why don't I bring Nadia upstairs, and you can meet us when Mallory is off the phone," Devla said.

"Great idea."

Just as Nadia was following Devla out, Mallory returned.

"I'm so sorry—I have to go," she said. Then, to Nadia, she explained, "Martha wants to see me."

Max was torn—he both hoped Nadia would leave with Mallory and at the same time wanted her to stay.

"But you stay," Mallory said.

"We can come back another time...." Nadia protested.

"We don't have time to waste. I trust you. Check out the costumes. Try one on—imagine if it will work onstage for us. Call me."

She kissed Nadia on the cheek and was out the door.

"Um, I guess I'll take a quick look," she said.

"Let's go," said Devla.

Max knew he could just let Devla and Nadia look at the costumes themselves. But the weaker part of him could not resist joining them. He told himself that it could be the last bit of time he spent with Nadia, and it was harmless to indulge. And really, he was just doing her a favor. It was selfless even.

They took the elevator to the third floor.

"After you," Max said, following behind them.

Devla unlocked the costume studio and turned on the lights. Nadia wandered to the far side of the room, examining sketches for the upcoming show. He couldn't take his eyes off her; even in her simple gray T-shirt, her hair pulled back, her legs hidden by faded jeans and her feet in worn, white espadrilles, she was the most elegant, alluring creature he'd ever met. He wanted to stand beside her, to breathe in her smell. But then he would be tempted to tell her she was right—he was being ridiculous. Forget it—they should just be together and work the rest out. But he knew that was a recipe for disaster. He'd grown up on the wrong end of that disaster.

"Here we go," Devla said, holding a deep blue, embroidered dress with a mandarin top that tapered into a tight bodice; underneath was a skirt with a short layer of tulle. The satin-stitch embroidery showed a pattern of dragons, lotus flowers, and butterflies. In the back, a Peking knot gathered at the base of the bodice. "I know you mentioned Ballet Russes as inspiration, and while they did do some Asian-themed costumes, this is an entirely modern take. I was inspired by reading the Lisa See novel *Snow Flower and the Secret Fan.*"

Devla hung the dress on a hook and retrieved a shoe box.

"Look at these," she said with unabashed pride. Nadia gasped. Max knew they were undoubtedly the most exquisite toe shoes she'd ever seen. Devla was a genius: The deep red satin was embroidered with intricately detailed flowers and butterflies. The ribbons of the shoes were purple, picking up the small purple accents in the flowers.

"These are stunning. Just... stunning," Nadia said. "They remind me of the most beautiful pair of Christian Louboutins I've ever seen: They were red satin, with black passementerie details. Four-inch heels."

"I know exactly what you're talking about," Devla said. "I think it was from his 2008 collection. They were open-toed?"

"Yes!" Nadia said.

"I'm going to leave you two." Max opened the door, then paused. "Nadia, good to see you. Good luck with the event. Devla, if you need to rearrange your schedule to accommodate fittings for Mallory, don't stress about it."

"You're leaving?" Nadia said.

He met her eyes across the room, and he realized what a mistake it was to have let her come up to see him in the first place.

He left without another word.

* * *

Mallory sat on the couch in Martha's living room. It felt strange to be in the empty apartment. Without all the people around, it felt smaller, not larger. She knew that was the opposite of how it was supposed to feel. She said so out loud, for lack of anything else to say to break the uncomfortable silence.

"My whole world feels smaller right now," Martha said.

"Oh, Martha! I'm sorry. I really don't even know what to say," said Mallory.

"Well, forget about it. I didn't bring you here to talk about my divorce. At least, not in that way. I do, however, want to apologize for how it's affecting you and Alec professionally. I want you to know it's not personal. I just need to terminate any and all intermingled business ventures with my soon-to-be ex-husband. And that includes The Painted Lady."

"I understand," Mallory said. And she did. When she and Alec used to have those horrendous fights, and when they had all of their jealousy issues, she wouldn't have been able to be in business with him or work with him on a daily basis.

She took a sip of the tea brought to her by Martha's assistant. "You know, Alec and I had a lot of ups and downs. Of course, we weren't married, but I just wonder if maybe you guys could find some way to talk through this stuff. And I'm not saying that because of the club—please, you have to know that. I just always thought you two were a unique couple. But every couple has ups and downs."

Martha shifted in her seat, leaning on her cane. "Mallory, I appreciate what you're saying. And I know you're not speaking out of self-interest. But the time has come to admit to myself that the marriage was a folly—a failed experiment."

"Weren't you in love?"

Martha made an odd noise—sort of a *garumph*. "To quote Prince Charles—'whatever that means.' "

"What do you mean, to quote Prince Charles?"

"Don't you know that famous quote? When he got engaged to Princess Diana, a reporter asked, 'Are you in love?' And he said, 'Whatever that means.' "

"Really?"

"Yes. At the time, what was I, ten years old? It seemed weird to me. Everyone knew what love was. Now, I think I understand better. Did I love Justin? Probably not. But I sure as hell loved looking at him. And I loved the way it felt to have him in bed with me. I'm sure people have based marriages on far less. I don't mean you and Alec, of course. You two are different."

Mallory looked away. Martha had married Justin just for the hell of it—maybe to see what would happen. But Mallory was really and truly in love, yet she could not even let herself think of setting a date out of some undoubtedly ridiculous fear.

"Can I ask you a question?"

"Sure," said Martha.

"If you don't love him, then why is it so bad that he slept with someone else?"

"I don't mind that he's married to me and not in love with me. But I sure as hell don't want him married to me when he's in love with someone else."

Mallory nodded. "I can't argue with that logic. Will you at least come to Vegas to see us compete? It would really mean a lot to me—and the rest of the girls—to have you there."

"I'll think about it," she said. "But I'll tell you what I will do: I'll go see Agnes now and settle up the Painted Lady tab. At least you won't have to worry about that."

"Thanks so much, Martha. Really. And please come to the show in Vegas. It will be fun. And you know, it will be a great place to market your products. The sponsors are putting together gift bags—you should get some of your stuff in there."

"Brilliant idea. I'm going to do it—and I'll go."

Mallory's phone buzzed with a text from Nadia.

The costumes are amazing. Devla wants to know if you and

Poppy and Bette can come in tonight for alterations. Let her know ASAP. "Martha, thank you so much for having me over to talk about the club in person. I am upset, I'm disappointed, but of course I don't blame you."

Martha stood up with a grunt. "Mallory," she huffed. "You are a good girl. You will succeed. I have no doubt."

Mallory glanced back at the text message. *The costumes are amazing*.

"I hope you're right," she said.

28

Nadia closed the door to her apartment and leaned against it. And she let loose the sob she'd been holding ever since leaving the studio.

The day had been a setback.

She should have told Mallory no, that she couldn't see Max no matter how badly Mallory needed the costumes. She should have told Mallory to go on her own. Seeing Max had hurt her in a way she hadn't anticipated: It had confirmed that she was in love with him.

She'd braced herself during the entire cab ride to the studio: Of course she'd anticipated that she'd feel attracted to him, feel awkward, feel sad. But what she hadn't expected to feel was the agonizing *empathy*. She could see him looking at her with the same longing and sadness that she herself felt. And she wanted to walk across that office, put her arms around him, and tell him she understood how he felt. She wanted to ease the look of discomfort and sadness on his face. She felt an urge to take care of him in a way she'd never felt for a man before, not even Jackson. She'd probably never felt it for Jackson because she'd never seen him look at her with the longing Max had shown today.

"This is crazy," she said. Twiggy paced at her ankles, pausing to rub her face against her feet. "I'll feed you, don't worry," she said.

Nadia poured the cat food into a bowl, her mind racing.

This was crazy. She was miserable without him; he was miserable without her. And what was keeping them apart? A disagreement over her dancing burlesque! It didn't make sense. Was it that she was dancing burlesque, or the fact that she had, as he perceived it, turned her back on ballet? Had every woman he'd ever dated been a ballet dancer? Did he have some sort of pathological snobbery?

Nadia poured herself a bourbon and logged onto her laptop. She Googled "Max Jasper girlfriends." A few images came up of Max with statuesque women at various events, but it was impossible to tell whether they were actually girlfriends. She tried the search "Max Jasper, relationship." And yes, she felt like a stalker. But when a dozen images of the same woman filled the screen, she realized she'd hit pay dirt. And she immediately wished she had not: The woman was distressingly beautiful. She had enormous, almond-shaped dark eyes, shiny dark hair that tumbled down her back, and a body that made Nadia blush.

One thing was for certain: With those breasts and hips, she was not a ballet dancer. And then she saw the link to a Wikipedia entry: Janine Jasper.

Max had been married? Nearly shaking, she clicked on the name.

Janine Jasper (born Janine Piña on August 6, 1954) is a Spanish-Canadian model and actress. Jasper was chosen as Playboy's *Playmate of the Month in January, 1975. She became Playmate of the Year in 1976. She dropped out of her career during the early part of her marriage to financier Thomas Jasper in which she gave birth to her only child, a son Max Jasper (born September 22, 1981). In 1984, she reemerged in the erotic thriller* Run, Emily, Run. *She divorced Jasper in 1984.*

His mother.

Nadia sat back in her chair. She tried to remember the things Max had said about his mother. He had said he never understood why his parents got married in the first place—that much she did remember. Had he said his mother was a dancer? She thought, for some reason, that he had. But no—he had said she was an artist. Or that she was artistic.

She stood up and paced the living room. It was crazy, but she knew this was the piece of the puzzle she had been looking for.

The night Max had come back to her apartment after the Painted Lady show, he'd had a pained look on his face when he'd spoken about his mother. He'd been telling her that she was Canadian, that she liked hockey.

He obviously thought about her a lot. And she was the one who'd encouraged him to be a dancer. But Max clearly wasn't proud of his mother's risqué career. Or was it that he blamed his parents' divorce on her nude modeling? Nadia read the Wikipedia entry again, paying attention to the timeline. Janine Jasper had stopped modeling during her marriage, and started up again either when the marriage was over, or at a point in her marriage when the nude modeling would be the last straw in a difficult relationship.

She had chosen the nude modeling over her marriage.

Now it made sense: his seemingly irrational feelings about burlesque; the way he took it so personally that she refused to quit; his willingness to leave the relationship before it even got started.

She reached for the phone.

* * *

"This better be good because I'm going to be late for an appointment," Violet said, walking past Gemma into the 'borrowed" Park Avenue apartment, 22B. She carried an oversized black leather bag.

"This will only take a minute. Just want to make sure I'm on the right track."

That morning, she had realized that the costumes would not, for the most part, be pieces she had to create from scratch, but would rather be built around key odds and ends she collected at vintage shops, the Village army navy store, and Paragon Sports. And so she spent five hours scouring the city and found most of what she needed. Now she was wearing it all under a bathrobe.

Violet sat on the couch, crossing and uncrossing her legs with impatience. Gemma stood on the zebra-skin rug in front of her and dropped her robe to reveal a black bustier left over from an old costume, frayed denim short-shorts, a wide, army green canvas belt, black fishnet stockings with holes in them, black knee pads, and combat boots. On her face she wore large yellow goggles. Around one thigh, over the black fishnets, she wore a red garter.

"You look badass."

"I'm glad you approve," Gemma said.

"I more than approve. I want to fuck the shit out of you."

"That won't be necessary," said Gemma, although the words made her stomach flip.

"It might not be necessary, but it's going to happen," said Violet. "Oh, but that's right: You don't like to be fucked. You like to do the fucking. Okay, I can roll with that."

Violet moved quickly from the couch to close the heavy living room drapes. She then got busy looking through her black bag.

"You'd better leave," Gemma said, nervously. "I don't want you to be late for your... appointment."

Violet glanced up at her, but ignored the comment.

"Catch," she said, tossing her a rope.

"Violet, I really don't think..."

But Violet was already taking off her T-shirt and leggings. She walked to Gemma slowly, wearing only a purple G-string and her four-inch Louboutins. Gemma could not take her eyes off Violet's full, round but taut breasts, her tapered waist, and her muscled thighs. She felt like a cow next to Violet. She felt unworthy.

Violet stood before her, her green eyes amused, almost daring.

"Do it," Violet said.

Gemma wanted to touch her, but she couldn't.

"I'm not going to fuck you, so if you want to get off, you'd better get up the nerve to do what I know you're dying to do."

Gemma hesitated for only a minute, then said, "Lie down."

Violet stretched out on the zebra rug. Gemma picked up the rope.

"Put your hands over your head," she said. Violet did, and Gemma tied her wrists together. Then she pulled down Violet's G-string. She couldn't believe the urges she felt: She wanted to touch Violet's shaved pussy. She wanted to stick her tongue inside of her. Gingerly, she stroked Violet's outer lips. Violet spread her legs. Gemma stared at her glistening pinkness. "You didn't give me enough rope," she said.

"You're making me wet," Violet purred. "You can go into my bag."

Gemma crossed the room, happy to be wearing the Tank Girl costume. She was able to pretend she was someone else, someone who had every reason to be doing what she was about to do.

She found another rope and a blindfold. She also found a collection of dildos, from which she selected the one that was the least alarming in size. She probably wouldn't use it, but just in case.

Violet watched her silently from the rug. She didn't seem to have moved from the position in which Gemma had left her.

Before she lost her nerve, Gemma set to work.

"Spread your legs wider," she said in barely a whisper.

"I can't hear you," Violet taunted.

"Spread your legs," Gemma said, a bark. A command.

Violet did as she was told.

Gemma used one rope to tie Violet's right ankle to the edge of the couch, and the other to tie her left ankle to a chair. She surveyed her work: Violet was naked except for her shoes and spread-eagle. Gemma would have felt totally in control if it weren't for Violet's unnerving gaze. But there was a solution to that.

Gemma knelt by Violet's head and tied the blindfold over her eyes. Of course, all Violet had to do was speak, and Gemma would lose the illusion of authority. She wondered if there was a gag somewhere in the black satchel. But she knew enough about the game to try a simpler solution.

"Don't speak," she commanded.

She felt she could relax for a minute, and she let her eyes wander over the perfect form splayed out before her. She thought of the intense pleasure she'd experienced at the fetish club—a feeling she'd never had before in her life. A feeling she wanted again—badly.

She thought of the way it had felt to do things to that redheaded woman, regardless of what that woman wanted. Maybe even doing things the woman didn't want.

Gemma had no idea what would bring Violet physical pleasure. She realized it was better that way, because it gave her room for trial and error. And maybe the errors would be the most fun.

She knelt in between Violet's legs and circled her finger along the outside of Violet's pussy. Then she did something she'd never done before: She flicked her tongue against Violet's clit, then pressed it down lower and deeper, tasting her sweet and pungent wetness.

"Yeah," Violet said.

"I said, don't speak," Gemma warned. Then she knew it was the perfect opportunity to get what she really wanted. She moved her face from Violet's pussy and stood up. She walked up to Violet's shoulders, then put a foot on either side of her head. She got down on her knees, her own pussy inches from Violet's lips. "This should keep your mouth occupied," Gemma said. Just saying the words thrilled her. She lowered her pussy onto Violet's face, and sure enough, Violet's darting tongue licked her. Violet's experienced mouth sucked on her clit, and Gemma felt a shock of pleasure that made her lose her balance. She needed Violet to fuck her—she needed her to do things to her that she could barely imagine. Quickly, she untied Violet's hands and then her feet.

"Take off your blindfold," Gemma said. Violet sat up, and Gemma stood in front of her. "I need you to fuck me," she told her, peeling of her denim shorts and fishnet stockings.

"Lie down," Violet said, without hesitation. Gemma did, spreading her legs. Her need was so great, she pressed her own fingers inside of herself. Violet smacked her hand away and pressed the head of the dildo against her, rubbing it slowly against her clit.

Gemma moaned, pressing her pelvis up toward Violet. She couldn't believe the heat in her cunt, the throbbing need she'd never felt before in her life. She didn't know why no man had ever been able to bring her to this edge, but they hadn't.

Violet pressed the dildo inside of her, sliding it in and out.

"Harder," Gemma said, and this elicited a wicked smile from Violet. She stopped for a minute and went to her black bag. She returned with a dildo of intimidating girth.

"This will be better," Violet said. Gemma felt nervous, but there was no turning back. Violet eased the massive object inside of her slowly, filling Gemma with a satisfying pain. With only a few strokes, she came with a violent shudder and an animalistic scream.

"Yes, baby," said Violet. When Gemma was finally still, Violet slid the dildo out and ran her tongue gently along Gemma's pussy.

"Just for the record," Violet said. "You can't expect this with clients."

"I don't intend to do this professionally," Gemma said.

"I'm not taking no for an answer," Violet said. "I can't let this talent go to waste."

29

Nadia's doorman, Francisco, announced that Max was in the lobby to see her.

"Thanks—I'll be right down," she said into the intercom.

She was relieved that he'd actually shown up. When she'd called to tell him they needed to talk, he'd balked. And then even after he'd agreed to meet her, it had taken him so long to arrive, she thought maybe he'd changed his mind. But apparently she would get the chance to have her say after all.

She took one quick look in the mirror. Just the promise of seeing him had made her face come alive, her cheeks slightly flushed and her eyes bright. Yes, this was love, and the realization both terrified and thrilled her.

He was waiting outside the building—a clear indication that he had no intention of going up to her apartment. She hadn't planned to invite him up, and yet the not-so-subtle message stung.

"Hey," she said. He was wearing a white button-down shirt and madras plaid shorts. The casual clothes emphasized his deep tan, and he'd never looked more beautiful to her. She had to fight the urge to just throw her arms around him and tell him he was being crazy—that she loved him and they would work the other stuff out. "Thanks for meeting me."

"No problem," he said. "But I don't have a lot of time."

"Okay. We can just... do you want to walk over to Fifth Avenue and sit on a bench near the park?"

"Whatever," he said. Okay, not exactly making things easy on her.

They crossed Park and walked silently to Madison, and then Fifth. The benches lining the cobbled promenade in front of Central Park were empty. Nadia sat in the first one they passed.

Max sat on the bench, leaving such distance between them that anyone passing by would not have realized they were together.

"First, I, um, wanted to thank you for helping out with the costumes. It means a lot to me—and Mallory, too."

"I appreciate the thanks, Nadia. But it's not a big deal, and we could have, you know, had this conversation over the phone."

"That's not why I called you," she said, avoiding eye contact. She suddenly felt stupid for initiating this meeting. He said nothing, just waited for her to continue. How could she say what she wanted to say with the most sensitivity? "I know about your mother," she blurted. Okay, that probably was not the most delicate approach.

"What do you mean?" he said.

"I was thinking about you when I got home tonight, and I Googled you, and I found the name Janine Jasper. I was thinking maybe you'd been married or something so I followed the links, and I read about your mom. She's beautiful, by the way."

He shook his head. "Nadia, I don't know what this has to do with..."

"I couldn't understand why you were being so judgmental

about the burlesque thing, or why you were making it into a deal breaker for us. And now I get it."

"Oh really? What do you 'get'?" he said, seeming more irritated than impressed by her cyber-sleuthing.

"I'm guessing that your mom's nude modeling upset your father, and maybe she stopped for a while but then resented having to give up her career and she went back to it, and then your dad left because they couldn't agree on it. But I have to think, Max, that it wasn't just her career that made him leave. There had to be other things that didn't work between them. And so you're thinking that because we don't agree on the burlesque issue, our relationship will never work out. But I think that's just an oversimplification—and now I understand *why* you think that way, but it doesn't make it any more valid."

He shook his head, but less angry now, more wistful. "Nadia, I'm glad you were thinking about me and care enough about our relationship to try to understand why I believe it won't work. And maybe there is some truth to what you are saying. But that doesn't change the way I feel. If people are too different, the relationship won't work. If every decision is a compromise, the constant negotiating will take its toll. And what we have between us is a major philosophical disagreement. I admit, I have no right to tell you how to live your life. But you can't tell me that I'm crazy to not want my girlfriend getting naked onstage every week. Neither one of us is wrong, but that doesn't solve the problem."

"I know. I get that. What I'm trying to say is that now I understand more of why you feel that way, and it makes me realize you're not trying to control me or judge me—that this is something that really bothers you, and you don't want to spend the next five years of your life fighting about it only to see us break up anyway. And what I'm realizing is that I'm still so angry about the way things went down with my ex-fiancé, I'm not willing to give an inch for a relationship. And it's stupid, because I'm more upset at the thought of losing you than I am at the thought of not performing burlesque."

"So what are you saying?"

"I'd rather stop burlesque than lose the chance to see if this relationship can work."

"Nadia, now I feel like a total jerk."

"I'm not trying to make you feel like a jerk. I just want to fix this. I want you to know that if burlesque is the only thing standing between us and our having a good relationship, I put the relationship first. And, honestly, if the relationship isn't working, I can always go back to burlesque. But I want to give us a chance."

"Are you going to resent me for making you compromise like this?"

She shook her head. "No. Now that I understand things better, I'm relieved to be able to compromise."

He pulled her to him, an embrace so fierce that she knew he had been as distraught about the impasse as she had been.

"I can't believe you would do that for me," he said, still holding her.

"I want to give it a try," she said.

"So do I." He sat back and looked at her. She could see the happiness on his face, and she knew she'd made the right decision.

"Will you do one thing for me?" she said.

"Yes."

"You don't even know what I'm going to ask you!"

"The answer is still yes."

"Okay—good. Because I want you to come with me to Vegas in three weeks. I'm going to go with Mallory and the girls for moral support. And I want you there with me."

"I think I can manage that," he said. He stood up from the bench and held his hand out to help her up.

"You have to go?" she asked, trying to hide her disappointment.

"How's your lower back feeling?"

"What? It's . . . okay."

"Just okay? That sounds like you need a massage." He smiled.

"You're coming over?"

"I can't let my girlfriend walk around with a backache," he said, pulling her to him.

"I love you," she said. She surprised herself by saying it aloud, but she didn't regret it.

"I love you, too," he said. "And I promise, even though you were the first to sacrifice and compromise for this relationship, I won't let you be the only one."

"I barely feel like I sacrificed anything," she said. And it was true.

30

Mallory stood in the center of a terrace suite at the Cosmopolitan Hotel in Las Vegas.

They'd booked the rooms long before Martha had pulled the plug on the cash. Now it was an extravagance that unnerved her, but at the same time one she couldn't help enjoying.

"Vegas is like LA on crack," she said to Alec, sprawling out on the bed. The room had to be one thousand square feet, with sliding glass doors that opened to a private terrace with amazing views of the city skyline—including the faux Eiffel Tower.

"That's why they call it Disneyland for adults," he said.

"Is that what they call it?" she said. "Hmm. I wonder if what happens here really stays here."

"I can think of one thing I wouldn't mind leaving with," he said, climbing onto the bed next to her.

They had an hour until it was time to register for the conference, and she had just one idea of how to spend it. She curled up against him, running her hand down his chest to the bulge in his shorts.

"Oh, yeah? What's that?" she said.

"A wife."

She pulled her hand away from his pants.

"Very funny," she said.

"I'm serious. I know it stresses you out to think about planning a wedding. And I know you've been busy. But look—here we are... Vegas! Quickie wedding capital of the world. Problem solved."

He kissed her.

"You're serious?" she said slowly.

"Yeah. Sort of."

"Alec, listen: I love you. And I'm sorry I've put all this other planning ahead of our wedding. I've been meaning to tell you that I'm going to focus on setting a date and making some plans as soon as this competition is over and we know we have The Painted Lady on track. I'm really sorry—I want to marry you so much. But I do not want to go to some cheesy Vegas wedding chapel. I want to get married in a way we'll always remember, surrounded by friends."

"You want a big, traditional wedding? Because I've been getting the distinct feeling you're avoiding that. Or maybe you're just trying to avoid marriage altogether."

"I'm not! As soon as this competition is over, it's my top priority."

"Aren't you at all curious what kind of wedding I want?" he asked, putting her hand back on his hard cock.

"Does talking about marriage get you this excited?" she said.

"Clearly, it does."

She knelt by his side and unbuttoned his jeans, sliding them down over his hips. She stroked his cock through his boxers for a moment, then pulled them off, too.

"Okay, tell me what kind of wedding you want," she said, untying the single strap of her sundress. With one motion, the yellow cotton fell from her shoulders, exposing her breasts.

"You are going to be the hottest geisha ever."

"I'm not dressing as a geisha, silly. That's Japanese. Our costumes are Chinese."

"I knew that," he said, stroking her breasts. "But I don't know a Chinese word for a sex maniac like you. What did they have in China if they didn't have geishas?"

"They had concubines," Mallory said, taking off her underwear.

"Concubines! Of course. Were the concubines, like, in sexual servitude?"

"Basically," Mallory said.

"Men had it so easy back then," he said. "They should only know what we put up with today."

"Shut up!" She smacked his hand playfully.

"Hey—you're my concubine. No back talk. Sit on my cock."

She smiled, more than willing to play along. With a knee on either side of him, she straddled his waist. He reached forward and stroked her clit with his thumb, then pressed his index finger deep inside her. She ground against his hand until she was slick with her own juice, then pulled his hand away and lowered herself onto his stiff cock.

When he was fully inside her, he gripped her ass, holding her against him as the thrusts of his pelvis set the rhythm. He didn't often come when she was on top, and she suspected it had something to do with her being dominant in that position. But even with her on top, he was clearly the one fucking her, each stroke deep and hard.

"Oh, my God," she gasped.

"Turn around," he said, smacking her ass. She climbed off him and got on all fours.

Her cell phone rang.

"Ignore it," he said, fingering her pussy from behind. He replaced his finger with his cock, entering her roughly. His hands gripped her hips, and he slid his cock in and out with agonizing slowness.

"You feel so good," she said, and his movements became faster. She felt the swell of pleasure building, and then a sense that his cock was almost vibrating inside of her. His thrusting became more intense and rhythmic, and she came just as he cried out.

When he finished, he pulled out slowly, and she collapsed onto her stomach. She rolled over into the crook of his arm, his chest damp with perspiration.

"That felt unbelievable," she said. And then her phone rang again. She reached for it.

"Let it go to voice mail," he said.

"I can't. All evidence to the contrary, this is a work trip, remember?" She kissed him and pressed the button to answer it. "Hello?" she said, still a little breathless.

"Is this a bad time?" Bette said.

"Sort of," Mallory said.

"Perfect—because I have bad news."

"Don't joke around."

"I'm not joking, babe: I can't make it to Vegas."

"What? You have to be here. You have to! The show is in two days. If you can't make the rehearsals tomorrow, fine. But you have to be here by Saturday. We need three girls to qualify."

"I can't leave the set—the schedule is all fucked up, and Saturday is a shooting day."

"Bette, if you don't get your ass to Vegas, I am going to shoot *you!*"

"No can do, babe. It's killing me—seriously. But there is nothing I can do."

"I can't fucking believe this," Mallory said. Alec reached for her hand.

"Chill out," Bette said. "This is show business, baby. Sometimes you have to improvise. Remember when I had to bail on that show for Justin because I had to be in Vegas?"

"You didn't have to be in Vegas—you were choosing to run off with your superstar lover...."

"The point is, I didn't panic. What did I do?"

"You had me step in."

"That's right—I trained your sorry ass. And Mallory, need I remind you, you didn't know a tassel from your own tit...."

"Yeah, okay, I get it. Bette, you can't even compare the two events. There was nothing at stake that night."

"That's your whole problem with this thing, Mal. You're putting too much weight on it. It's just a show. Take a deep breath and tell yourself that over and over again until you get it through your head."

"I still need three performers to qualify, even if it is 'just' a show."

"Babe, I have to run. I wasn't even supposed to leave the set for this call. You'll figure something out. I have faith in you, Moxie."

Mallory hung up the phone.

"Bette's not coming," she said. Even as she said the words, she could barely believe it.

"Why the hell not?"

"They rearranged the shooting schedule. She has to be in Toronto."

Alec pulled on his boxers and started pacing the room. Mallory sat still on the bed. She was furious at Bette, even though she knew it wasn't really Bette's fault. But she felt terribly let down.

"I'm so mad at Bette! She never should have committed to doing this show. Or I should have known better. Either way, we're just fucked."

"Calm down. Getting hysterical does not help."

She looked at him and tried to do as he said: She took a deep breath and then another. He sat next to her and took her hand.

"Obviously, we need a replacement dancer."

"Who is going to fly out here in time to learn the routines, rehearse, and then perform the day after tomorrow? We don't have one girl capable of that."

"We have someone here who knows Bette's routine... who has watched it a dozen times and who stood in for a costume fitting when Bette didn't have time."

Mallory realized where he was going.

"You can't be serious," she said.

"Do we have any other choice?"

Nadia and Max stopped in front of the nine-foot tall, red, high-heeled shoe.

"Something tells me that's not just here for the burlesque convention," she said.

"I feel like the burlesque convention is just background to all this other art," said Max.

Everywhere they looked, there was art: on video screens, projected on walls, in the middle of the lobby. Even in vending machines: They had old cigarette machines converted into "Art-o-mats"—you put coins in and got an original sketch or painting.

"I have to admit, this place is better than I thought it would be," Max said, his arm around her.

Everything was better than she'd thought it could be—and not just the hotel. The last three weeks with Max had been the purest joy she'd ever experienced off the stage. Without the burlesque issue between them, they were like two giddy lovers on a honeymoon. She felt him giving more of himself to her, not holding back. And she was able to be more herself with him; she spoke about the loss of ballet, and didn't feel she had to act like she had it all figured out and replaced with burlesque. She felt, for the first time in a long time, a complete absence of pressure. She felt like herself, but an older, wiser, calmer version of herself.

"What did you expect?"

"I was here for a convention a few years ago, and it was just awful. The place we stayed was like a facsimile of someone's idea of glamour. I don't remember the name of it—I think I blocked it out for my own sanity. I never wanted to come back to Vegas. But I like this place. I read that we have to see the Chandelier bar."

"We'll see it Saturday night—that's where Alec and Mallory are having the party. Right now, I have to go upstairs and change into more comfortable shoes. Then I'm going to see if Mallory needs help arranging a practice space for tomorrow."

"Don't they give you practice space?"

"They gave all the troupes an assigned time to use the actual stage—it's in one of the clubs downstairs. I think it's the Bond room or something. But the thing is, there's no privacy. Mallory and the girls can use the stage, but the other competitors could sit and watch them."

"Got it," Max said. "So tomorrow is just practice day?"

"Yes—Friday rehearsal, Saturday is the show and they announce the winner at the end, and Sunday is the awards ceremony."

"You know what?" Max said. "I'm really happy to share the show with you as spectators. Are you okay with this?"

"Yes. Absolutely. I never intended to perform here. Even before I officially quit." She put her arms around him, and he held her close.

They took the elevator up to the suite Mallory and Alec had booked for her. She had been thrilled when she'd first walked in that morning. Everything charmed her, especially the soft curves of the furniture—rounded, azure-colored couch, round coffee table, even rounded terrace furniture overlooking the fountains and the faux Eiffel Tower in the distance. There were square glass vases of fresh-cut white flowers in every room. Every corner seemed to hold a charming design detail—like the quirky wallpaper lining the inside of her closet.

Nadia retrieved a more comfortable pair of flats from her closet. She wondered if she'd ever feel comfortable in heels again. The doctor had assured her that in time, if she took care of her foot, it would feel normal eventually. The thought of someday being back in her favorite shoes helped ease the pain of never again being in *pointe* shoes. At least she would be able to dress up and feel like a lady, if not a dancer.

"Those red embroidered toe shoes that Devla made are really something," Nadia said.

"I agree," said Max, and she could tell he was watching her face with particular interest.

"What?" she said.

"Nothing. I just remember the way you looked at those shoes."

"They inspired me."

"Devla is as much an artist as the dancers."

"Yeah. I could see that. So I was thinking, maybe I could find some satisfaction in working with costumes." She felt nervous admitting it—it was as if she was quitting ballet all over again. But the look on Max's face was worth it.

"Are you serious?"

She nodded.

"Babe, nothing would make me happier. And Devla is the perfect person to learn from. Oh, Nadia—I'm just so happy," he repeated, kissing her and looking into her eyes. Her stomach did a little flip, the way it always did when he kissed her. "I love you," he said.

"I love you, too."

Her cell phone rang.

"Let it go to voice mail," he said, kissing her neck. She was about to turn her phone off when she saw that the caller was Mallory.

"It's Mallory. I'll be quick. Hello?" she said.

"Hey—where are you?" Mallory said.

"In my room."

"I need to talk to you—don't go anywhere," Mallory said.

"Can we make it a half hour or maybe..."

"It can't wait. Just stay there. I'll see you in five minutes."

Nadia looked at her phone, then tossed it onto the blue couch.

"What's that about?" Max said.

"I don't know. But she's on her way over here, so we'll find out soon enough."

The knock on the door came with remarkable speed.

"Were you standing outside my room when you called?" Nadia said as she opened the door.

"No," Mallory said. "Max—good to see you. Devla did a phenomenal job altering the costumes for us. She's amazing."

"Yes, she is," Max said.

Nadia was slightly unnerved by the stiff formality underneath Mallory's light conversation. Max would never notice it, but Nadia knew Mallory well enough by now to understand that she was upset.

They sat on the couch. Nadia offered Mallory a drink—they'd already stocked the fridge with wine. Mallory said just water was fine for her.

"So, I'm here because there's a slight... glitch in the weekend," Mallory said.

"What is it?" said Nadia.

"Bette can't make it. She's held up on the set. And as you know, we need three performers to qualify—no more, no less."

"Oh, no! Mallory, I'm so sorry. Are you sure Bette can't make it even by Saturday afternoon?"

"I'm certain."

"I'm sorry to hear that, Mallory, but I don't see what Nadia and I can do. Are you pulling out of the show?" said Max. Nadia looked at him, realizing that he'd figured out before she had why Mallory was sitting in their hotel room.

"No. That's not an option. I'll get someone off the street if it comes to it. But I'm hoping it won't." She looked at Nadia. "Could you step in for Bette?"

Even though she'd guessed the request was coming, Nadia almost gasped. She didn't dare look at Max.

"Mallory, I'm flattered that you think I could help you with this. But you know I've never even completed a performance at The Painted Lady, never mind in an intense situation like this."

"Yes. I know that. But I also know that you're a professional dancer. You know how to perform under stress. I'm sure you've pushed through lots of performances when the circumstances were not ideal. I believe you can do this, and I'm asking you—begging you, really—to try."

"You're asking too much of her," said Max.

"Both of you—stop. Just give me a minute to think."

Nadia walked over to the sliding glass doors of the terrace. She stepped outside, looking out over all of Las Vegas. She weighed her promise to Max against the debt of gratitude she felt she owed Mallory. And then, of course, there were her own fears and issues about her short-lived, almost-burlesque career.

Maybe this was a sign. Maybe here, in this place of fake Eiffel Towers and an endless strip of buildings designed for spending money, making money, and experiencing pleasure, she was meant to dance her first and last burlesque performance. Deep down, she suspected it was something she needed to do, or she might always wonder what it would be like.

She returned to the living room, where Max and Mallory were locked in adversarial silence.

"Mallory, I need to talk to Max alone for a minute."

Nadia could tell Mallory had to fight not to smile. She knew Nadia was leaning toward helping her.

"I'll wait on the terrace," Mallory said.

Alone with Max, Nadia had to think of how to explain her reasoning. She couldn't find the words.

"You don't have to do this, you know," he said.

"I want to do it," she said.

He took a deep breath. "Does that mean you're rethinking what you said to me that night at Central Park?"

"No. I meant what I said that night. This would be a one-time thing. I wasn't looking for the opening, but now I have one last chance to just see if I can do it. And I'd be giving something back to Mallory, who helped me pick myself up off the ground last year. And whether I pull it off on that stage Saturday or I don't, I will at least know I saw this experience through. And I won't ever look back."

Max stood up and paced for a minute. And then he turned to her and said, "You made a big compromise for this relationship when you offered to give up burlesque. I guess the least I can do is compromise over this one show."

Nadia jumped up and threw her arms around him.

"Thanks for understanding," she said. "It means so much to me."

"You mean so much to me," he said. "I'll do whatever I can to make this work."

31

Violet loved Vegas.

Her biggest decision of the day was which of the three Cosmopolitan pools she should go to. Now this was the way to live.

She decided on the pool they called the Marquee Dayclub. It was "adults only"—the party pool, she felt certain.

"We can leave our bags here to hold the chairs while we swim," Violet said to Gemma, whose skin was porcelain white against her black bikini. "And seriously, you have *got* to get some sun."

"I don't tan, I just burn. And I don't swim," she said in that clipped accent of hers.

"Wow, you're quite the party. I don't know why you didn't just stay in New York," Violet said. She untied her white Alice + Olivia cover-up, revealing her tight body in the tiniest of red bikinis. Of all the poolside hotties, Violet knew she stood out.

She kept her black platform heels on as she strutted to the side of the pool, removing them only when she got to the edge and sat down to dip her feet in the water. In less than a minute, a man appeared next to her. He was middle-aged, deeply tanned, and had the sheen of wealth.

"That's a dynamite set of tattoos you've got there," he said.

"Yes, it is," she said coolly. The tattoos were her pride and joy: On her front, just above her bikini line, it read in gothic letters, *Merci.* On her backside, just above her ass, in the same lettering, it read *No Mercy.*

"Are you, by any chance, here for the burlesque festival?" he asked.

She sized him up. Maybe she could pick up a quick dom gig while she was out here.

"I'm here for work," she said.

"So am I," he said with a smile. He held out his hand, "Marty Bandinow."

For a minute, the name didn't register. Then she carefully recalibrated her expression. She was talking to the sponsor of the entire festival.

"I know who you are," she said.

"So I take it your work is burlesque?" he said.

She nodded and finally shook his hand. "I'm Violet. I own Violet's Blue Angel."

"Ah, the elusive Blue Angel. I'm happy to finally have your club joining in all the fun. The previous owner was not a fan of our little competition."

The smile they shared was suddenly one of coconspirators.

"Yes, well, I'm happy to bring the Blue Angel into the twenty-first century," Violet said.

"So what attracted you to our competition? The prestige or the prize money?"

"The money, of course," she said.

He laughed. "A girl after my own heart. And what would you do with the winnings?"

"I don't know—" She shrugged. "Maybe bring Blue Angel to Vegas."

He smiled and clapped his hands. "Violet, I look forward to seeing your performance on Saturday. In the meantime, enjoy. I know you New Yorkers love your city, but I have to say we've got a lot to offer in this town."

A cocktail waitress stopped by and asked them if they'd like a drink. Violet ordered a margarita.

"Marty, I think you're right. And it was great to meet you." She pulled her legs from the water and stood up, giving him another view of her ass. "Do me a favor? If you see the waitress, send my drink over there?" She pointed to the shaded lounge chairs where Gemma was hidden under a wide-brimmed hat.

"Will do," Marty said.

She got a thrill having people do tasks for her, even a small one like that. She was sure Marty was used to being the one to tell people how to direct his beverages—and everything else he wanted served up on a silver platter. She bet that her telling him what to do got him hard.

Violet walked slowly back to the lounge chair, holding her heels in her hand, letting Marty get a nice long look at her from behind.

"It's a hundred degrees out here," said Gemma.

"We're in the desert," said Violet. "So guess who I was talking to over there."

Gemma shaded her eyes and looked in the vague direction of the pool.

"I dunno. An actor?"

"No. I would never waste my time talking to an actor. I met the guy who sponsors the whole competition. And, frankly, I think we had a little moment."

"A . . . moment?"

"Yes. A connection."

"You mean he wants to sleep with you."

"Exactly."

"No offense, Violet, but this is a burlesque convention. It's not like he's hosting a hotdog-eating contest. He must want to sleep with everyone. Maybe he is."

Violet shot her a dirty look. "Maybe he is; maybe he isn't. All I know is that I did a little strategic networking out there. It got me thinking maybe he'd step up and bankroll the opening of a Blue Angel Las Vegas. I could really rock this town. But first, on Saturday, Spider, Cookies and I are going to tear up that stage. Let's just hope your costumes aren't the weak link."

Gemma pulled her hat down farther over her face, but not before taking a good long look at Marty Bandinow.

32

Mallory paced in the dressing room behind the stage at Bond, the performance space in the Cosmopolitan Hotel.

They were an hour into the competition, and she had not yet ventured onto the floor to watch any of the acts. But the next performer was from Violet's troupe, a woman with the singular name "Spider."

Poppy and Nadia had both told her they didn't want to watch anyone else—they needed to keep their heads in the game and focused. Mallory knew that watching other performers could go either way: Sometimes they were unimpressive, and it gave her all the more confidence to rock it when she took the stage. Occasionally, the other women were so good it left her feeling rattled. She knew she shouldn't risk the latter outcome, but her curiosity was too intense to ignore. She wanted to see who Violet had in her arsenal, and she wanted to see the costumes designed by Gemma, that traitor.

"She's the biggest British turncoat since Benedict Arnold," Alec said.

"Benedict Arnold wasn't British—he was American and went to the British side."

"Even worse!"

"Come out with me—I need to see what's going on," Mallory said.

They made their way through the crowd to the designated Painted Lady table. Each troupe had its own table, but most performers, like Mallory, were not sitting in the audience. The only people at the Painted Lady table were Martha, Poppy's girlfriend, Patricia, and Billy Barton.

Speaking of traitors—what was he doing there?

"How's it going backstage?" Martha said.

"Um, fine," Mallory said, distracted by the enemy in their camp.

"Hi, Mallory! You look stunning. I can't wait to see you up there," Billy said. His thick brown hair was slicked back, and he wore a lightweight plaid sports jacket, crisp white shirt, and black tie.

"No offense, but what are you doing here?" she said. She was in no mood for this—not when she had to be onstage in less than an hour.

"It's a long story," Alec said, pulling out a seat for her. "Let's just say Billy is back where he belongs—with us. And really, always has been." He clapped Billy on the shoulder.

"Okay, whatever—I can't deal with this right now."

"Want a drink?" Martha asked. She was wearing a floral muumuu and fanning herself with a Chinese folding fan Mallory had given her out of their prop collection. The air-conditioning was straining against the triple digit heat. This was hot—even by desert standards.

"No, thanks. I shouldn't drink until I'm done performing," said Mallory.

Martha consulted her program. "There're two acts after Violet and then you, right?"

Mallory nodded. "How has it been so far? I haven't watched anything."

"It's been solid. But nothing that's blown me away. You can take 'em," Alec said.

"Are you ready for more?" asked the MC from center stage, a question that elicited a roar from the crowd. She was a well-known cross-dressing lesbian from New York named Chelsea Corners, and from what Mallory could tell, was doing a terrific job running the show with her trademark ribald humor.

"Lord knows I don't know what to do with a pole between my legs, but this next lady sure does. Give it up for the most twisted lady in burlesque, Spider!"

The curtain pulled back to reveal a floor-to-ceiling stripper pole, a trademark prop that had gotten Violet fired from the Blue Angel back in the days when Agnes was running it "old school." Mallory was not surprised to see the controversial pole make an appearance on the Vegas stage. If anything, it seemed to belong in that town. And Spider seemed equally suited to the vast stage and flashy venue.

Mallory looked at Alec, and he shrugged.

Spider's hair was shaved in the shortest of buzz cuts, and the crown of her head was tattooed with a snake. Both ears were pierced and ringed from lobe to the highest point around the top. Mallory could also see rings in her nose and her upper lip. It was obvious to Mallory these were not a part of her costume. However, the goggles, knee pads, and combat boots clearly were. And with the cranking punk music, the roar of the crowd, and Spider's long limbs already clambering to the top of the pole, the overall effect was electrifying.

Mallory felt her stomach drop. The performer's steampunk hotness was undeniable. Somehow, the woman got her bustier and shorts off while still in the air, either her arms or legs wrapped around the pole at all times. The crowd was going wild, clapping and screaming with delight. By the time she made her way down the pole, Spider was wearing only the requisite G-string. Her body was tight and hard as a rock, and when she flashed her ass at the audience, she did a little trick where she shimmied her buttocks. And then she turned her body, slid to the floor, and folded herself like a pretzel.

"Is this burlesque?" said Patricia.

"Let's put it this way: If Agnes were dead, she'd be rolling over in her grave," said Alec. They laughed, but Mallory knew there was really nothing funny about this. Agnes wasn't a judge. This wasn't the Blue Angel. It wasn't even New York: It was Vegas; it was the Cosmopolitan—the place that had heralded its arrival on the Strip with the tagline, "Just the right amount of wrong."

By the time the song ended, the audience was giving a standing ovation.

Mallory wished she had not seen the performance. By comparison, her choreography and costumes could only be called quaint. And that was on top of the question of whether or not Nadia would actually make it through her performance.

She didn't have the stomach to sit through Violet's performance.

"Okay, well—that was interesting. I'd better go back and get ready to show them how it's really done," she said with a bravado she in no way felt.

"Do you need anything back there?" Alec said.

"No, you stay. Watch everything. You're my eyes and ear out here," she said, kissing him again.

Martha, Patricia and Billy wished her luck, and she took a deep bracing breath and walked quickly back to the dressing room.

She found Nadia tucked in a corner, head down, listening to her iPod. Her slim body was elegant in the crimson bodice embroidered with lotus flowers. Her long black wig lent an edge to her usually benign prettiness.

"Hey—how are you doing?" Mallory said. Nadia looked up and removed her ear buds.

"Okay. Fine. Did you watch any of the show out there?"

"Yes. I saw one act."

"How was it?"

"Not bad," she said.

"But not great?"

"No," Mallory lied.

"Is Max out there?"

"Not yet—but I'm sure he'll be here any minute. I just wanted to tell you to go out there and do your best. You look absolutely gorgeous. I hope you can almost feel like someone else in that costume—you're not Nadia when you're onstage, okay? There are only a handful of people in that audience who even know you as Nadia. That audience will be seeing Naughty Natasha. Make her come alive for them?"

Nadia nodded. "I won't let you down, Mallory."

"You're doing me proud just by stepping out there. I know you didn't plan to do this show. Just try to have fun with it."

She hugged Nadia, taking care not to mess up her wig or makeup. Nadia's arms were tight around her shoulders, and Mallory felt her tension. "You're going to be great," she whispered.

"Yes," Nadia said. "I will be."

Max needed an usher to help him find the designated Painted Lady table. By the time he got to the venue, the room was dark, crowded with hundreds of people, and virtually throbbing with music. On the stage, a woman was dancing around wearing only a hot pink thong and waving a pink feathered boa.

Alec and a few other people were at the table. He was happy to see Alec. He liked the guy and wondered if, despite his own involvement with burlesque, he shared any of Max's discomfort with seeing his girlfriend on that stage.

"Hey, man—glad you made it," Alec said. He had the woman next to him move over so Max could take the seat. "Are you ready?"

"I don't know if I'm ready, exactly. But I couldn't very well miss this."

"No, you couldn't," said Alec. "Don't stress about it. It's been a great show so far."

Max looked at his program. "How much longer before they go on?"

"Are you serious? You're just in time. Five more minutes you might have missed her."

On some level, Max knew that. He had been tempted to "accidentally" miss it. The way he figured, he was screwed either way. If Nadia froze, he'd feel somehow responsible because he'd denied her the chance to have performed successfully at the Baxter party. And the way they had argued over her performing couldn't have helped her confidence. If she didn't succeed today, he would be as much to blame as she was. But if she did perform, he would have to watch her take off her clothes in front of this crowd, a crowd four times the size of a packed house at The Painted Lady. But because he loved her, he wanted her to succeed. If he had to share the sight of her naked body with hundreds of people for one night, so be it. She deserved to hear applause, to feel in command of a crowd. She deserved to feel like the star that he knew she was.

The pink dancer finished up her act amid a shower of pink rose petals. The curtain closed, and a slender young man dressed in a shiny silver tuxedo took the stage.

"Wow. I haven't seen that much pink since the Wakowski triplets invited me to join them for a four-way," said the MC, whom Max realized was a woman in drag. The crowd erupted in laughter that lasted so long it prevented her from continuing.

She started laughing, too. Finally, the room settled down. "I am excited to introduce the ladies of New York City's newest burlesque club, The Painted Lady. Let me just say, I saw one of these gals backstage, and while you'll never get me to shut my mouth, I would actually consider a little footbinding to get in on this action. You'll know what I mean in a minute: People, give a shout to welcome Naughty Natasha."

Max leaned forward in his seat. As the curtain lifted, the opening of David Bowie's "China Girl" filled the room. The back of the stage was decorated with a giant canvas scroll covered in Chinese calligraphy. The only other props on the stage were a transparent Asian folding screen, through which the audience could see Nadia's silhouette, and an ornate rosewood bench, which was technically a Japanese altar bench and not, in fact, Chinese at all.

Nadia extended one long leg outside the screen, and the crowd applauded. Slowly, she moved into full view. The vivid red costume was breathtaking even from the distance of the table, the mandarin collar now shining with red sequins, and Swarovski crystals sewn into the tulle skirt. As skeptical as he'd been that first day, Max realized what a smart move Mallory and Nadia had made in going to Devla—and Devla had told him she'd loved "burlesque-ifying" the costumes. On her feet, Nadia wore demure red slippers—an unusual sight on a burlesque stage. Around her ankles she'd wrapped embroidered bandages to convey the notion of a bound foot. It was brilliant, really: To accommodate Nadia's delicate feet, Mallory and Nadia had decided to improvise on Bette's original choreography: Instead of wearing the four-inch red heels throughout the performance, the last thing Nadia would take off would be the bindings and the slippers, and she would don the red heels only at the very end—her liberation.

Despite his ambivalence about this performance, he wanted desperately for Nadia to make it through.

And he had to admit, that long black wig was hot.

Nadia carried oversized Chinese folding fans in each hand, which she used to obscure her face as she approached the front of the stage. She slowly extended her right arm to the side, then brought the fan back in. She repeated the motion with the left hand, then simultaneously moved both fans away from her face, shimmied her shoulders, and tossed the fans to the floor. Her pale face makeup and heavily kohl-rimmed eyes were dramatic and lovely, and he felt a rush of pride.

She moved into a series of turns, then, with her back to the audience, removed the tulle skirt, leaving her clad in only the high-necked red bodysuit. She turned back to the audience, her impossibly long legs moving into a wide stance as she did a bump and grind. The audience clapped, but more important, he could tell she was having fun with it. Then she reached behind her back, and he knew she was unzipping the bodysuit. Her movements were painstakingly slow, and he didn't know if this was hesitation or a calculated part of the performance. He found he was holding his breath.

Finally, with a snap of her hand, Nadia pulled away the bodysuit, revealing her body in just a red G-string, breasts bare except for red sequined pasties with tassels covering her nipples.

She was naked.

The crowd shouted its excitement, and Nadia turned to the wooden bench. She bent in an exaggerated motion, her ass to the audience, as she pulled the red stilettos from underneath the bench. Then, sitting down, she extended one leg and began unwinding the bandage slowly and methodically. Max could honestly say that the removal of a shoe had never seemed more erotic to him.

When both feet were freed from the bandages and the slippers, she pulled on the heels. The crowd, to its credit, went wild with applause, clearly understanding the subtext of the gesture. And finally, she returned to the edge of the stage, shimmied her shoulders and arched her back, her breasts bouncing to make the tassels twirl as she continued to bend backwards at an angle that only a ballerina could pull off.

The curtain closed.

33

The room buzzed with the post-performance energy of all the dancers, who were now making their way to the tables. Any minute now, the judges would announce the winner of the grand prize.

Mallory was proud of their performances. And in the end, Bette's absence was a blessing in disguise: Seeing Nadia rise to the occasion had pushed Mallory and Poppy to their own personal bests. She knew the three of them had accomplished something special on that stage. She just hoped it was enough to overcome the pure spectacle displayed by some of the other troupes.

She watched some of the girls table-hop, greeting old friends or making new ones. She herself was in no mood for small talk; She was rooted to her seat, clutching Alec's hand, the suspense almost unbearable. She noticed, too, that Violet was similarly anti-social: Mallory saw her sitting three tables away, her short-cropped, platinum hair a standout even in this crowd of peacocks. Her back was rigid, and she was watching the stage. Mallory could only imagine the intensity in those cat-like green eyes of hers. She knew what it was like to be the object of Violet's focus, and the memory made her almost shudder. It was hard to believe they had hung out together, performed at the same club, and almost become friends.

Finally, Chelsea Corners took the stage. "All right, sexy beasts—settle down. There'll be plenty of time to hit on each other tonight at the after-parties. But right now, we still have some business to attend to: Three of you hot bitches are going to walk out of here twenty grand richer."

The crowd erupted in applause and catcalls.

"That's right! Now, keep it going for the puppet master behind all these gorgeous dolls, Mr. Marty Bandinow."

Marty strolled onto the stage, waving to the crowd like Miss America. He wore an expensive-looking dark suit, and his thick silver hair was perfectly coiffed. Mallory had had only the briefest interaction with him the day before when she was checking out the dressing room. She found him a bit on the smarmy side, but he was, in the end, supporting burlesque in a very big way.

"Ladies, let me start by saying that in the ten years I've been doing this competition, I have never seen a show like the one you put on for us today. Give yourselves a round of applause." The room became very loud. Someone threw a garter onstage. "And you made the judges' decision extremely difficult. If there was ever a year when we would have liked to be able to have more than one winner, this was that year." Alec squeezed Mallory's hand. "But unfortunately, we could only pick one troupe. And this year, the prize goes to a newcomer to the competition..." He opened an envelope as if he were announcing the Academy Award. "Violet's Blue Angel."

Tina Turner's song "Simply the Best" filled the room. Marty called Violet onto the stage.

"Bullshit!" yelled Billy Barton.

"I'm going to get some air," Mallory told Alec.

"No—stay. It's okay, Mallory. And we have to set a good example for Poppy and Nadia and everyone else. . . ."

Mallory couldn't stay. She couldn't endure the awkward glances of condolence that Martha and Max were already sending in her direction.

"I'll be right back," she said. She maneuvered her way through the tightly packed tables. No one paid any attention to her; mercifully, all eyes were on Violet, who was making her way to the stage.

Mallory pushed through the double doors and didn't stop walking until she found the elevator bank that would take her to her room.

"Mallory!" Alec called from behind her.

"I'm fine," she said. "I just can't be in that club right now."

"I understand," he said. "But I don't want you to be so upset. You were incredible today—and so were Nadia and Poppy. And if Agnes had been here, she wouldn't have traded your performances for anyone else's in that room. If Bette were here, she'd tell you the same thing."

"That's all well and good, Alec, but the only thing that matters right now is that we didn't win the money. No money, no club. And this whole year has been for nothing."

"It hasn't been for nothing. We created a great club, and in building it I fell in love with you even more." He hugged her.

"I just want to be alone for a while. Can you give this little pep talk to Nadia and Poppy? I don't want them to feel bad, but I don't have it in me to take care of them right now."

Alec nodded. "Yes—but you have to promise me you'll show up for the party tonight."

"Oh, my God. The party. I forgot." Alec had planned a celebration and rented out the Chandelier bar for the night. Another extravagance from the days before money was an issue.

"Yeah, we have a lot of people coming. So you can indulge

in all of these negative feelings for a few hours, but you have to pull it together by tonight."

She nodded. "Will you call Bette and tell her what happened?"

"Yes," he said, kissing her forehead. "I'll take care of everything. I'll come get you in time for the party."

Violet squinted under the stage light, trying to make out individual faces in the crowd applauding her, but they were just a blur.

Marty Bandinow was saying something as he handed her the twenty thousand-dollar check, but she had no idea what words were coming out of his mouth. He held both of her hands in his, presenting her to the audience like a father giving away the bride. She wondered, fleetingly, if their poolside encounter had had anything to do with her win, and then decided she didn't care either way: She would get her money, and she would keep the club going until she found a new sucker to throw some cash in her direction. Maybe even that clown Marty. He was obviously way into her shit. She'd tell him she'd bring Violet's Blue Angel to Vegas if he also subsidized the club in New York. Forget running a dinky little contest once a year—he'd be a burlesque mogul on both coasts.

He presented her with the microphone, and she mumbled a few words of thanks. She had no interest in being in that room one second longer than she had to be. No need to mingle among the riffraff.

Chelsea Corners guided her offstage.

"Congratulations!" she said. "I've seen a lot of burlesque, but your performance had an edge that really electrified the room."

"Thanks," Violet said. She looked around the dressing room. Someone had already sent her flowers. She looked at the folded white card. "For Violet and Gemma—congratulations—Marty."

Gemma? What the hell was her name doing on the card?

"How's my star?" Marty said in the doorway.

"I'm thinking Vegas is my lucky charm," said Violet.

"I realized the same thing when I first came out here," Marty said. "And I don't even want to tell you how long ago that was."

I can imagine, Violet thought.

"You know," Marty said, "I think you should consider opening a Blue Angel out here."

Violet flashed him her best smile. "That's a brilliant idea, Marty. If I did, I could really use the help of an insider like you. We should talk."

"At some point, maybe. But I've just committed to a new business venture that will be taking a lot of time and capital next year."

"No rush," Violet said coolly. "I'm busy running the hottest club in New York. But I am going to seriously consider Vegas."

"And your costume designer will already be out here."

Violet felt as if the wind had been knocked out of her. He could not have shocked her more if he'd slapped her across the face.

"What are you talking about?" she said slowly.

"Gemma and I got to talking the other night, and I was really taken with her talent and business goals. I'm going to set her up with her own burlesque fashion line."

Violet, heart pounding, said, "Excuse me for a minute, would you, Marty?"

The lights were now on in the club, but it was still difficult to find Gemma. People had abandoned the tables and were mingling, laughing, and making plans for the night now that the pressure was off. Other dancers tried to pull Violet aside to talk to her, but she shrugged them off. She finally spotted Gemma talking amidst a small group. Violet grabbed her arm. Hard.

"Ouch!" Gemma said. "What are you doing?"

"I need to speak with you. Alone."

Violet pulled her to the nearest exit. It was dramatically colder in the lobby, and she shivered—though she wasn't sure if it was from the change in climate or her rage.

"What did you do with Marty Bandinow?"

Gemma's pale face flooded with color. "Nothing, really."

"Are you moving here to Vegas? Is he bankrolling your clothing line?"

"Yes."

"Did you fuck him?" Violet said, so loudly a passing hotel guest turned to look at her.

"No—I let him fuck me. The only one I ever fucked is you."

"You did fuck me, you dumb British cunt. He probably would have helped me open a club out here if you hadn't distracted him with your stupid clothing idea."

"Marty doesn't seem to think it's stupid," Gemma said.

Violet had to work very hard not to slap her smug face.

"He will once he wakes up from this pussy fog," Violet said.

"That won't be for a very long time. And I have you to thank for urging me not to let my talents go to waste. God bless America," said Gemma.

34

Nadia felt like she was floating.

She pressed her keycard into the door to her room, Max's hand on her lower back. He had been telling her over and over again how proud he was of her, and each time felt like a kiss.

And she had to admit, she could scarcely remember a time when she'd felt more proud of herself. Yes, she had accomplished a lot in ballet, but it had been a gradual ascent, years of grueling work. The work in burlesque—emotional and physical—had evolved in such a relatively short amount of time, the overall sense of accomplishment was more intense.

She had felt such a rush out on that stage. She had thought she would feel vulnerable and exposed once she took off her clothes, but it was just the opposite: She felt completely empowered. And the applause felt much more personal than the applause she had experienced as a member of the corps de ballet; today's applause had been just for her.

"What time do we have to be downstairs for the party?" she said when Max closed the door behind her.

"We have plenty of time. You could even nap if you want."

"I'm not going to sleep. But I am going to take a long shower."

Max kissed her cheek and hugged her. "Whatever you want, babe. I'm just going to check my e-mail and make sure that everything is under control back in New York."

Nadia walked into the bedroom, humming "China Girl." And then she noticed the large, gift-wrapped box on the bed.

She approached it gingerly, as if someone or something were going to jump out at her.

"Max?" she called.

"Yeah?"

"Come here for a sec."

He appeared in the doorway.

"What is this?"

He grinned. "A performance gift. I was going to get you roses, but flowers are for ballerinas. I needed something for a burlesque dancer, and this seemed to fit the bill."

She shook her head.

"You didn't have to do that."

"Open it," he said.

She slowly untied the wide black ribbon and lifted the lid. Whatever was inside was covered with tissue paper. She pulled the paper aside and gasped.

"You didn't...." She pulled out one shoe, then the other. They looked like the red passementerie Louboutins. But that couldn't be.

"I'm so proud of you, Nadia."

She ran over to him, and he pulled her into his arms.

"How did you find them?"

"I can't share my trade secrets," he said.

"No, seriously Max—how did you get a pair of these?"

"Let's just say I employ a very resourceful costumer. And I

know you're not comfortable in heels yet, but you'll get there. I don't intend for these to just sit on a shelf."

The gesture so overwhelmed her, she started to cry. He kissed her eyelashes and wiped away her tears.

"Don't shower yet," he said softly. "I'm just going to make you dirty again."

Max lifted Nadia's dress up and off over her shoulders. She got busy unbuttoning his shirt and pants.

He cupped her breasts, slowly stroking her nipples to hard points.

"Put on the shoes," he whispered.

"Really?" she said.

"Yeah—I want to see them on you."

"Now?" she said.

He nodded. She stood, wearing only her white cotton underwear, and carefully stepped into the Louboutins. As magnificent as they were in the box, they were meant to be worn.

He pulled off his pants and underwear. His cock was erect. She stood in front of him and stroked him.

"Don't stand in the shoes," he whispered. She could sense he was already breathing more quickly. "I don't want to stress your feet. Just lie down."

She complied, lying across the bed on her back. Max looked at her as if she was a piece of art in a museum, then he slowly pulled off her underwear, but left her shoes on.

He stretched out beside her, stroking her breasts, then her pussy, while his tongue played with her nipples. His fingers moved over her so lightly she could close her eyes and almost wonder if she was really feeling it. Then he grazed her clit, and finally rubbed it more firmly. She squirmed.

"More," she said. But he didn't touch her inside, even though after a minute or so she had spread her legs, and it took all of her willpower not to just grab his hand and press his fingers where she wanted them.

Sensing her impatience, he moved on top of her, and she eagerly guided him inside. He had to work his way slowly into her, even though she felt totally ready for him.

"Oh, my God," she said.

"Are you okay?"

"Yes—you feel so good."

He pulled back slightly and pulled her right leg over his shoulder, then the left. The angle gave him deeper penetration—and it gave her a view of the shoes as he fucked her.

The pleasure between her legs was so intense, it almost felt like pain. She didn't know if it was the post-performance high, the position, or the sight of the shoes, but a tremor rippled through her pelvis, to her breasts, and higher, until it felt like her mouth was vibrating. By the time she cried out, Max was bucking against her with an intensity she had never experienced. Their hands were clasped together over her head, and the noise they both made was enough to worry her about someone calling security.

Nadia slowly pulled her legs down, and Max collapsed on top of her.

"What *was* that?" she said, stroking his head. His hair was soaked with sweat.

"We came together," he said. "I'm so glad we finally did."

"I'm so glad I finally did," she said.

"Wait a minute." He rolled off of her and propped himself up on one elbow, looking at her. "You've never had that before?"

"No," she said. "I thought that was something people just made up for books and movies."

He hugged her, and she tasted the saltiness of his chest. "Oh, Nadia. Ballet dancing might be in your past, but there is a whole future full of physical experiences ahead of you. I will be your personal choreographer," he said.

"And exclusive?" she said. She couldn't believe she'd had the nerve to say it. She thought of the adage that a guy isn't thinking clearly before sex, and a woman isn't thinking clearly after.

"Yes. Exclusively," he said, kissing her. "Let me ask you something," he went on, stroking her hair. She ran her hand over his chest and felt his heart still beating fast. "Do you want to keep doing burlesque? I mean, the way you danced today... I don't want to be the one responsible for holding you back."

She tilted her head up to look at him. "My God, I love you for asking me that. But the truth is, no—I don't. I'm glad I did it, but no burlesque performance could ever top the experience I had today. I'm ready to let it go."

"You're really going to work with me at Ballet Arts?" he said.

"Yes. I want to work with you."

"I've spent my whole career looking for my muse. I think I've finally found her," he said.

"That's my job, head muse?"

"Well, I'd say that's your unofficial title."

"What will be my official one?"

"We'll figure it out. We have plenty of time."

"Oh, we do?"

"I'm hoping the rest of our lives."

She pulled him close and slid her shoes off gently. She would wear them soon. She wasn't sure when, but she wasn't worried about it. The bones and muscles would strengthen and mend.

As for now, the most painfully broken part of her was finally healed.

Mallory woke up disoriented. Where was she? Was it day or night? And why was Alec shaking her?

"Come on, Mal—time to get up."

She groaned. "What time is it?"

"Almost five. The party starts in an hour."

The party. Everything came back to her in a rush: Vegas, the competition, Billy Barton, the loss. And now she had to get dressed as if she had something to celebrate.

She sat up and propped an extra pillow behind her head.

"Can you explain to me now what Billy was doing at our table?"

"Really, it's the craziest story: The only reason he backed Violet and the club was because she was blackmailing him."

"That's ridiculous. I don't believe it."

"It's true. Apparently, she had some very explicit photos of him and Tyler, and he couldn't risk outing Tyler just as his career was taking off with Burberry. But once he and Tyler felt ready to go public with their relationship, Billy pulled the plug on her and the club."

She rolled over. But now Violet had the prize money.

Her head was spinning. Taking that Tylenol PM in the late afternoon had probably not been the best idea.

"I need coffee," she said.

"I'll make you coffee. Just get in the shower."

She sat up as Alec opened the curtains. Sunlight flooded the room. "I'm not in the mood for a party. I wish you hadn't planned this."

"Everyone who came out here to support us should have a nice way to end the weekend," he said to her. "And we should, too. Come on, Mal. It's not the end of the world. Maybe another investor will come along."

"This is our livelihood, Alec," she said. "We can't live on some fantasy."

"Mallory, you have to relax. Martha will pay us our salaries through the end of the year. And by that time we'll know if the club is viable or not."

"Winning the contest would have gotten us through the spring."

"But we didn't win. And now we have to move on." He kissed her. "I'm going to get your coffee. Shower and you'll feel better."

Mallory watched him leave in search of the coffeemaker. Then she buried herself under the covers.

The place they called "The Chandelier" was spectacular: It was a three-story bar wrapped around a spiral staircase, with the top two tiers enclosed by ropes of millions of beaded crystals.

Mallory held Alec's hand. She was glad she'd made the effort to blow out her hair and do a decent job with her makeup. She wore a black Morgane Le Fay cocktail dress; it was a little on the austere side, but it suited her mood.

As they approached the bar, she had a view of the back of the curved, red banquettes. She thought she recognized the messy, auburn ponytail on one of the women seated, but knew that wasn't possible.

"That looks like Allison from behind," said Mallory.

"You are right—it absolutely looks like Allison," Alec said. And something about the playfulness in his voice made her walk more quickly so she could get a better look.

Before she could even circle to the front of the banquette, she knew that, sure enough, her friend had made the trip from New York.

"Oh, my God, what are you *doing* here?" Mallory said. Allison jumped up and threw her arms around her.

"Mallie! It was Alec's idea. I missed your opening night a

few months ago, and I didn't want to miss this, too. Julie wanted to come, but she couldn't get off from work."

"I can't believe this. You saw the show?"

Allison nodded. "And for the record, you were robbed!"

"Where were you sitting?"

"In the balcony. I made some new friends, and they're here to party tonight." She waved at three very hot guys seated next to the spot she'd just vacated.

Mallory laughed. "I'm not sure Andrew would be excited about this development."

"It's Vegas, baby. I'm allowed to look."

Mallory called Alec over. "I can't believe you got Allison to come out here."

Alec smiled and gestured at the scene all around them. "I didn't really have to twist her arm."

Mallory looked around the room and spotted Martha. Instead of her usual baggy dress, she was wearing an unusually pretty gown that was almost fitted. "Wow. Martha went all-out for this party. Vegas must be having some sort of effect on her."

In fact, everyone looked particularly polished and festive. She felt bad for being the only scrooge in the mix.

"I'm sorry for being in a bad mood earlier," she said to Alec.

"Forget about it," he said. "But come with me for a second."

He took her hand and led her up the staircase to the second level.

"Unbelievable," she said. She felt as if they were standing inside a sixty-five-foot chandelier.

Only one other person was in the room, a good-looking guy in his mid-forties wearing a dark suit and drinking a blood orange-colored cocktail out of a martini glass. Mallory couldn't imagine why Alec was bringing her to see this guy, unless he thought maybe it would take a throwback to their kinky past to get her out of her funk.

The man crossed the room, extending his hand to Mallory.

"You must be Mallory," he said.

She looked at Alec.

"Um, yeah. And you are?"

"Randy Kelly," he said. She wasn't sure if Randy was his first name or an adjective.

A cocktail waitress strolled by holding a tray filled with the brightly colored drink that "Randy" was drinking.

"Fire-Breathing Dragon?" said the waitress.

"Um. No. Thanks—maybe later." Mallory looked to Alec to tell her what the hell was going on. But Alec didn't say anything—he just stood there with a nervous smile on his face. "Do you... work for the hotel, Randy?" she said.

"No. I do a lot of work for their guests, but I work all over the strip."

She could not believe Alec had hired a male prostitute. Had he lost his mind?

"Alec told me you might be a little reluctant," Randy said with a grin.

"Yeah, that's putting it mildly. Would you—can you excuse us for a minute?"

"Absolutely. I'll just go upstairs with the paperwork. Whenever you're ready."

Paperwork? Very officious for a gigolo. He must cost a fortune.

"Have you lost your mind?" she hissed to Alec when Randy was out of earshot.

"I didn't get a chance to explain...."

"Are you trying to cheer me up? Is this some sort of wacky consolation prize? Because Alec, seriously, we're *engaged* now...."

"I'm tired of being engaged."

"You *are*?" She looked around for the cocktail waitress. She was going to need that drink after all.

"Yes. I'm ready to be married."

"Okay... so what does that have to do with gigolo Bob over there?"

"Who? You mean Randy?"

She nodded, and he laughed. "He's not a gigolo. He's a marriage officiate."

"A what?"

"Like a justice of the peace. He's here to perform our wedding. If that's okay with you."

Mallory looked down through the labyrinth of beads to the crowd of their friends below. She started to laugh. "I can't believe this," she said.

"Is that a yes?"

She looked at him, her heart pounding. Maybe she was crazy, but she felt no more hesitation than she had that night onstage when he'd proposed to her. Once she'd said yes to getting married, the how, when, and where of it made little difference to her. Maybe that was why the planning had felt like a burden to her—she knew it wasn't because she felt any hesitation to actually go through with the wedding. "Yes—let's do it."

He grabbed her and kissed her. She breathed in his smell, closed her eyes, and in his arms, everything else fell away—the competition, Violet, even the crowd below. Only when she opened her eyes, the twinkling crystals surprising her all over again, did she get her bearings in the moment: She was wrapped in a giant chandelier, and moments away from getting married.

"I'll get started on the paperwork. Go to our room and change," Alec said.

"Change into what?"

"Look inside the black garment bag in my closet. Agnes sent it for you."

"My wedding dress?" Mallory gasped.

He nodded. "Martha brought it along and put it in our room while you were at rehearsal yesterday."

"Why would she do that?"

"It was Agnes's idea."

Mallory tried to absorb everything, but it was almost too much to get her mind around.

One of her favorite Rihanna songs reached them from down below.

"Go get dressed," Alec said.

He didn't have to ask her again.

35

Mallory stood at the top of The Chandelier with Nadia and Martha by her side. The papers were signed, and the guests were being herded into some semblance of order below on the second floor by Allison, the consummate PR professional.

"I live for this shit," Allison said, when Mallory asked if she was sure she didn't mind getting things organized. Allison was tasked with moving the hundred or so partiers from the bottom-level bar to the second floor, so Alec and Mallory could say their vows in the most dramatic space in the club. Her only regret was that Bette would not be there to share in the celebration. As she'd told Bette that day that now felt very long ago, none of this would be happening without her. She also wished Agnes could see the perfection of the dress—made all the more striking by the majestic curtain of crystal surrounding it.

Nadia refastened one final hook on Mallory's corset and then arranged the tulle billowing around her body. They stood at the top of the stairs, waiting for their cue. And then the song began playing: Lady Gaga's "Bad Romance." Martha and Nadia walked down the stairs first as makeshift bridesmaids. Then

Mallory descended the stairs slowly, her hands shaking as she held a bouquet of white calla lilies.

Some of her friends and the other partiers were sitting on banquettes and a few folding chairs, while many just stood on either side of the makeshift aisle. Mallory didn't look at anyone except for Alec, who stood waiting for her at the other side of the room. Allison stood near the front as her maid of honor. And behind Alec stood Billy Barton, who, even in that room, was a standout in his purple velvet Paul Smith blazer.

Mallory took her place next to Alec and handed her flowers to Allison.

Randy smiled at them, and said, "Everyone, we are delighted to have you with us to witness the union of this beautiful couple, Alec and Mallory." The crowd clapped and hooted as if they were at a burlesque show. Randy looked slightly startled, but patiently waited for the noise to quiet down. "Alec, do you take Mallory to be your wife, to whom you will be true in good times and in bad, in sickness and in health, to love and honor all the days of your life?"

"I do."

Billy handed Alec a platinum band, which Alec slipped on her finger. It was simple, and Mallory wondered how, when she'd been consumed with the competition, he'd had the foresight to take care of all of this. She bit her lip to hold back her tears. Randy turned to her, and she tried to keep it together, knowing she would have to speak in another moment. "And Mallory, do you take Alec to be your husband, to whom you will be true in good times and in bad, in sickness and in health, to love and honor all the days of your life?"

"I do."

Allison handed her a matching platinum band, triggering Mallory's realization that her friend had not flown across the country to watch a burlesque show. Mallory smiled at her gratefully and took the ring, thankful for the years of movies and TV shows that had indoctrinated her into the wedding ritual so that she could function without thinking. She felt so clueless—as if she was in the middle of a dream.

"With the power vested in me..."

"Wait!" Mallory said.

Alec and Randy looked at her. The room got very still. "Alec and I promised each other we would include something in our vows. Remember, Alec? The night we got engaged?"

He looked at her in bewilderment. She raised her dress and flashed him her garters.

"Oh! Yes. Now I remember: I, Alec, promise to always sexually objectify you," he said.

Everyone laughed.

Randy looked at Mallory. "May I proceed?"

"Yes—we're good," Mallory said.

"With the power vested in me by the good state of Nevada, and our fabulous town of Las Vegas, I now pronounce you husband and wife. You may kiss the bride."

The room erupted into the most magical applause she'd ever experienced: Nothing she'd received while onstage could compare.

By midnight, a new DJ had started his shift. Even the guests who had started to fade got back on the dance floor once his masterful playlist kicked in.

"My nickname is Graveyard," he told Mallory. "I will keep this crowd going 'til daybreak."

Martha overheard this and was quick to tell Mallory, "He couldn't keep me up another hour even if he was fucking me."

"Come on—your parties are notorious for going into the next morning. They say the only thing better than the drinks at your events is the breakfast."

Martha looked wistful. "My soon-to-be ex-husband is a night owl. But it was always a stretch for me. Now I have no one to please but myself, and I'm sorry to tell you, my dear, I am going to bed."

Mallory kissed her on the cheek. "Thanks for being here, Martha. It meant a lot to us."

"I'll see you at the awards ceremony tomorrow."

Mallory rolled her eyes. "I'm a bad sport. I wish I could skip it."

"Are you kidding? I know you'll pick up something. Oh, that reminds me." She reached into her clutch and pulled out an envelope. She handed it to Mallory.

"What's this?"

"Your wedding gift," said Martha.

"Oh, Martha! You didn't have to do that."

"Open it," Martha said.

Reluctantly, Mallory looked into the envelope. Inside was a check. She opened it to find that it was for twenty thousand dollars.

She gasped. "Martha... are you serious?"

"What? You think I'm going to let that schmuck Marty Bandinow have final say in picking the best burlesque troupe?"

Mallory's eyes teared up for the umpteenth time that night. She threw her arms around Martha and hugged her so fiercely that they both toppled over. They hit the floor laughing.

"What's all the commotion over here?" Alec said, helping them up.

"We're back in business!" Mallory said, waving the check at him. He took it from her, and after a quick glance, his face registered the same surprise and delight that Mallory felt.

"Martha. I don't know what to say... except that now I have no chance of making a respectable woman out of my wife. You have just ensured that she will be taking off her clothes in public for at least another year." He hugged Martha.

"Well, my mother always had a saying: Don't throw out the baby with the bathwater. My marriage might be down the drain, but I'll be damned if I lose the best burlesque club New

York has ever seen." She looked around the room. "I'm thinking we might have to talk about a Painted Lady, Vegas."

Mallory and Alec looked at one another and smiled.

"But for now, I'm going to bed. Party on, kids."

Martha shuffled away, leaving Mallory and Alec to stare after her in wonderment.

"I think Martha has the right idea," Alec said, kissing her. "I say we retire to the bedroom ourselves."

"We can't leave our own party," Mallory said, running her hand down his back and squeezing his ass.

"We'll be back down in time to join them all for breakfast," Alec said. "It will be the perfect way to start our life as husband and wife."

"Husband and wife...I like the way that sounds." She kissed him. "So no more surprises for me tonight?"

"You always tell me you don't like surprises."

"And you never listen to me! It's funny—I guess I didn't know myself as well as I thought I did. And somehow, you've always pointed me in the right direction."

"That's right," Alec said. "And now I'm directing your hot ass to the elevator."

Mallory let him lead her by the hand.

As soon as the elevator doors closed, he pulled her against him and kissed her neck and then her lips.

"I can't wait to fuck my wife," he said.

"I hope you're not disappointed," she said.

"What's that supposed to mean?"

"I've heard married sex can be pretty dull," Mallory said, rubbing his hardness through his pants.

Alec pressed one of the elevator buttons.

"That's not our floor," she said.

"I know. That's the roof." He kissed her again, his hands sneaking under the bottom of her corset.

"I thought you were going to fuck your wife?" she said.

"I am."

"On the roof?"

"That's right, baby. Our sex life will keep reaching new heights."

"What if someone sees us?"

"I'm hoping someone sees us."

"You are bad," she said. "You don't want me getting naked onstage, but you don't mind a stranger seeing us having sex?"

"I want all of our naked adventures to be together, Mallory."

"They will," she said, as the elevator stopped on the top floor.

"So let's start now. The first of our married adventures."

The door slid open. She walked outside, and he followed behind her.

If you enjoyed Mallory and Alec's sensual adventure, go back to where it all started, in BLUE ANGEL....

"Dancing begets warmth, which
is the parent of wantonness.
It is, Sir, the great-grandfather of cuckoldom."

—Henry Fielding

"I'm a free bitch, baby."

—Lady Gaga

1

During the entire cab ride he kept telling her, it's a surprise.

"I don't like surprises," Mallory said, following him into the dark, barely marked building off of Bowery.

"It's your birthday! What's a birthday without a surprise?" He winked at her, and she couldn't resist smiling back. That was the thing about Alec: no matter how much he aggravated her, she loved him too much to stay angry.

And why should she be in a bad mood? They'd finally moved in together after three years of dating long distance while she finished law school. She had a good job at a midsize firm. And yes, it was her birthday—the big twenty-five—and Alec was taking her out for a night on the town, in her new city, just the two of them.

Except...the dark location did not seem to be a romantic restaurant.

A woman with a clipboard greeted them inside the door. She had a butterfly tattoo on her neck and a perfect face. Behind her, a blue velvet curtain prevented Mallory from seeing into the room.

"Alec Martin and Mallory Dale. We're on the list," Alec said, taking Mallory's hand.

Once inside, Mallory saw that the venue was a bar of some sort, with a seating area and a stage and... dwarves. Two that she counted. And a topless woman wearing a garter belt, black-seamed stockings, and red patent leather stilettos. And a man dressed for a rodeo carrying a bullwhip.

"What the hell is this?" Mallory asked.

"It's the Blue Angel. A burlesque club," Alec said, smiling like he'd just presented her with a diamond.

Burlesque—the topic of the article Alec was writing for *Gruff*, the pop culture magazine he worked for. And his latest excuse for constantly ogling other women.

"We're spending my birthday doing research for your article?"

He steered her to the table closest to the stage. The room was packed, but the table had a reserved card on it. Now she *knew* the evening was a *Gruff* magazine gig. The owner of *Gruff* was a rich kid named Billy Barton. Alec had met Billy thanks to the long tentacles of the Penn alumni network. And unlike Alec and most of their friends, who had only been in New York a few years, Billy could open any door, pull any string, and reserve any table.

"No," Alec said. "We're doing something fun and interesting on your birthday that I happen to be writing about but that I know you will enjoy. Wait here—I'm going to get our drinks."

And he was off to the bar before she could protest.

She wished she had worn something different. Her long, houndstooth Ann Taylor skirt suddenly seemed overly prim. There was a lot of leg showing in the room—bare legs, garter-belted legs, legs in fishnets and heels. At least she was wearing a simple black turtleneck, so the overall effect wasn't too dressed.

In the corner at the far end of the room, two women were laughing and talking to the guy in the Western getup. The one in the faux leopard coat was the first person Mallory had noticed in the room. How could she not? Aside from being model gorgeous, she had an ultra-stylized look, with dramatically pale skin, full red lips, and straight black hair cut in a fabulous, razor-sharp bob. As if sensing Mallory's stare, the woman turned and looked at her with sharp blue eyes. Startled, Mallory quickly looked away. But when she glanced back, the woman was still watching her, as if expecting that her gaze would return. Their eyes locked, and Mallory's stomach did the oddest little flip.

"Hey," Alec said, sitting next to her and sliding over a bottle of Stella Artois. "You're not mad, are you?"

Mallory accepted the beer, trying to resist the urge to look back at the beautiful dark-haired woman. "What? Oh, I don't know. A little. Come on, Alec. Admit it—you're just killing two birds with one stone: you want to do research, but it's my birthday and we're going out so this is what you chose to do. It has nothing to do with how I'd actually want to celebrate."

She hated the way she sounded, but she was worried. It wasn't just about her birthday—it was about *them*. She didn't want to admit it, but their relationship hadn't felt right since she'd moved to Manhattan six months ago. Alec was consumed with the cutthroat world of New York media. She was working crazy hours at the law firm and studying to retake the bar exam. And lately, he kept bringing up the idea of their hooking up with another girl—of having a three-way. At first when he brought it up, she had thought he was just being provocative. But she finally realized he was completely serious. She didn't quite know what to make of this, so she mentally filed it under Things I Can't Deal With Right Now.

And it wasn't that she was appalled at the thought of being with a woman; she'd had minor girl crushes when she was younger. There was that one girl at overnight camp, Carly Klein. She wore tube socks pulled up to her knees even in ninety-degree heat, and she spiked a volleyball like she was going for the gold medal. She'd even had a sex dream about that girl and felt guilty about it for weeks. But this wasn't overnight camp, and she didn't have girl crushes anymore. She was an adult, and she was allegedly in an adult relationship.

Alec put his hand over hers, but before he could tell her how wrong she was or whatever he was going to say, Lady Gaga's "Beautiful, Dirty, Rich" pulsed through the room, the lights dimmed, and the thick, blue curtain on the stage slowly parted.

Rodeo Guy stepped into the spotlight, and the crowd erupted in hoots and applause.

"Ladies... and those annoying creatures you felt compelled to bring with you tonight," said Rodeo Guy, "welcome to the Blue Angel!"

He cracked his whip, and Mallory jumped in her seat.

More hollering. Despite herself, Mallory felt a slight rush. The energy in the room reminded her of being at a rock concert. She didn't want to give Alec the satisfaction of smiling—because no matter what he said, this night was just about his story—but for the first time since stepping inside the club, she was just a little excited to see what would happen.

But her history with these types of places made her less than optimistic. She had gone to a strip club in Philadelphia sophomore year of college and again, reluctantly, when she first moved to New York. She'd hated both experiences. The girls seemed miserable, and she felt like a perv for looking at them, even though there was little else to do. And giving them money had made *her* feel exposed. Both times, her friends had just had a laugh and told her to lighten up. But she'd minored in women's studies, for God's sake. She couldn't just walk in the club and check her mind at the door.

She dreaded that feeling of not knowing where to look or what to do with her hands, of feeling both sorry for the girl and embarrassed for just being in the room.

And so when the first girl came on stage, Mallory was nervous. But the crowd was raucous and exuberant, and she was aware of being the only one in the club not making some sort of noise. Alec, especially, was yelling, clapping. He looked over at her only briefly, and winked.

Mallory turned back to the stage. The song "Diamonds Are a Girl's Best Friend" played, and the stage lights bathed the dancer in fuchsia. She was blond, and she wore a surprising amount of clothes: thigh-high, pink patent leather boots with a platform heel, a white corset, long white gloves, and in both hands, gigantic fans made out of pink and white feathers. She waved the fans around so that sometimes they concealed her face and most of her body. Other times, she just covered her body and looked at the audience with a sly smile. When the hooting and hollering reached a peak, she tossed the fans aside, stood with her feet squarely apart, and slowly tugged off one glove. The crowd roared as if she'd just flashed her bare breasts. Did women get completely naked in these shows? Mallory didn't know what to expect.

Little by little, the blonde pealed away her costume—first the gloves, then the boots, and then she turned her back to the audience and eased down the zipper of her corset so slowly, Mallory was shocked to realize she could not wait for the woman to get it off. And when she finally shook herself free and turned to face the audience with her hands over her breasts, Mallory found she was holding her breath.

The blonde moved her hands away, striking a pose like Madonna in her "Vogue" video. Her breasts were small, pert, and perfectly shaped, the nipples covered in red sequined flowers. When she danced around in her pasties and red thong, Mallory was simultaneously relieved and disappointed—the performer was probably not going to get totally nude, after all.

The crowd was in a frenzy, and Mallory joined in, whistling and clapping. The woman responded to the crowd, seeming to feed off of the excitement, gyrating close to the edge of the stage, where she slowly bent over, flashing her ass to the crowd, playfully squeezing both cheeks.

Once again, the cheers escalated, though Mallory did not think a higher decibel level was humanly possible.

The rodeo guy returned to the stage.

"One more round, everyone, for Poppy LaRue," he said, though he didn't have to ask. The room was still wild.

"What do you think?" Alec asked, squeezing her leg.

"It's . . . I like it," Mallory said.

"I knew you would." He leaned over and kissed her cheek.

As the rodeo guy launched into a brief monologue, surprisingly clever, full of sly political commentary and pop culture references, Billy Barton slipped into the seat next to Alec. He wore a lavender shirt and purple suspenders. He was handsome and rich, so he could get away with dressing like Scott Disick on *Keeping Up with the Kardashians*.

"Did I miss anything?" he asked, a little too loudly.

"I don't know. What do you think, Mal? Did he miss anything?"

She rolled her eyes.

"Ladies and gentlemen, please give it up for the gorgeous, the glamorous, the *dangerous* . . . Bette Noir."

The regulars in the crowd chanted the dancer's first name. The curtain remained down, but Marilyn Manson's "I Put a Spell on You" began to play. As the low, pounding, eerie first beats filled the room, the curtain slid back to reveal two wooden chairs and a small table with a crystal ball. In one chair, a woman was crouched, a towering black witch hat obscuring her face.

She rose slowly, her figure shrouded in a long, black dress. She swayed and looked directly at the audience, moody and defiant; Mallory saw that it was *her*—the stunning, leopard-coat woman.

Mallory knew the song well—had heard it long ago in a David Lynch film and loved it. It had been years since she'd heard it, but it had an unforgettable early crescendo and when it reached that initial peak, the dancer pulled off her black dress to reveal her perfect body in only a bullet bra, black lace panties, black seamed stockings, garter belt, and six-inch patent leather stilettos. In one hand, she held a shiny black wand. This time, when she looked at the audience, she focused on Mallory.

And then—and at first Mallory thought she was imagining this—she pointed her wand at Mallory and gestured for her to come on stage.

Mallory looked away, pretended not to see. But the crowd was cheering her on, and Mr. Rodeo appeared to assist her. Damn Billy Barton and his front row seats! She looked back at Alec, but he was laughing and waving her on.

The exact mechanics of how she got on stage were details she would never quite grasp. But somehow she found herself seated in one of the wooden chairs, in front of the crystal ball, with Bette Noir dancing around her. And then Bette sat in the chair opposite her, back to Mallory, and gestured for her to undo her bra.

Hands shaking, Mallory somehow managed the metal clasp. Her fingertips brushed the woman's pale skin, as remarkably soft as it was fair. And when Bette turned to face her, bare breasted, Mallory felt she was an audience of one. She did not hear the crowd or the music. She did not know if she even heard Bette speaking to her—but it felt like she was. And Bette was telling her to remove her sweater. The only reason she did it was because she couldn't be responsible for ruining this gorgeous spectacle. She hesitated for maybe twenty seconds, and then, with a rush of adrenaline, Mallory slowly pulled off her sweater.

Bette did not smile, did not even bat her fake eyelashes. She calmly took the turtleneck from Mallory, walked to the edge of the stage, and tossed it to the seat Mallory had vacated. The crowd was roaring—yes, she heard it now, like a television set that had become unmuted. Mallory, now wearing only her Anne Taylor skirt and white Victoria's Secret bra, felt her heart pounding. She wondered how much longer she would have to be on stage, but at the same time didn't want to leave. It was like she was hyper-alive—everything felt louder, brighter, and bigger than life off the stage. It was dizzying, and to ground herself she looked out at the audience to find Alec. She could see that his gaze was riveted on her, only her. She took a deep breath and kept still as Bette worked the stage around her, wearing only a bejeweled thong and impossibly high heels and still holding the wand and dancing—all the while dancing, moving in the most deliberate and perfectly choreographed way.

And then the curtain came down.